BLOODLINES

BLOODLINES

Marian Veevers

VICTOR GOLLANCZ

LONDON

First published in Great Britain 1996
by Victor Gollancz
An imprint of the Cassell Group
Wellington House, 125 Strand, London WC2R 0BB

A catalogue record for this book is
available from the British Library.

ISBN 0 575 06196 0

Typeset by CentraCet Ltd, Cambridge
Printed in Great Britain by
St Edmundsbury Press Ltd, Bury St Edmunds, Suffolk

Toad that under cold stone
Days and nights has thirty-one
Sweltered venom sleeping got,
Boil thou first i' th' charmèd pot.

Double, double, toil and trouble,
Fire burn, and cauldron bubble.

Fillet of a fenny snake,
In the cauldron boil and bake.
Eye of newt and toe of frog,
Wool of bat and tongue of dog,
Adder's fork and blind-worm's sting,
Lizard's leg and owlet's wing,
For a charm of powerful trouble,
Like a hell-broth boil and bubble.

Double, double, toil and trouble,
Fire burn, and cauldron bubble.

Scale of dragon, tooth of wolf,
Witches' mummy, maw and gulf,
Of the ravined salt-sea shark,
Root of hemlock digged i' th' dark,
Liver of blaspheming Jew,
Gall of goat, and slips of yew,
Slivered in the moon's eclipse,
Nose of Turk, and Tartar's lips
Finger of birth-strangled babe
Ditch-delivered by a drab,
Make the gruel thick and slab.

(The witches' spell, *Macbeth* Act IV, Scene 1)

1057

Tomorrow the traitor Macduff will come with the army he has bought and as surely as man is born of woman, the raw new walls of Dunsinane will fall. We can expect no mercy from one who has been shown none.

At dawn the carrion birds will begin to gather . . .

Don't weep, girl. I'll see you're gone to safety before they close the gates – and what happens to me no longer matters. The worst has already happened. Let Macduff come on, let him traipse through blood and take the crown of Scots for himself or else sell it to the child Canmore if he wishes.

But you and I must be about other business. There's treasure here that must not fall to the traitors tonight and it's to you, girl, that I must entrust it. You're very young and I can see that the priests have made you scared of the old ways. But I've read your future and I know you'll be the first of a long line of women that'll keep my words safe. For there are words and memories I'd have live on when I, Gruoch, wife of Macbeth MacFindlay, am no more than the dust of charred bones blowing across the hill of Dunsinane . . .

Nay, just listen. Don't try to quiet me. I know they've told you I'm mad, or possessed. Old Morag came yesterday to take away my knife and the pins from my hair, the way they do from mad folk. 'For your own safety, my lady,' she whined in that little frightened voice she talks in now. So I let her take the knife just to be rid of her, but when she bent over me to take the pins, I saw a greasy leather thong with a wooden cross strung on it hanging round her cracked old neck.

'Is it the priests that have got your loyalty now, Morag?'
I asked.

As if she needed the power of the priests to protect her!
To protect her from me I don't doubt, for even Morag can't
be fool enough to think two bits of stick can save her from
Macduff's murderers.

It angered me, which was strange, for I don't often feel
anger now, mostly I just feel an emptiness inside. I almost
liked being angry. I felt warm and alive for a moment. I
pulled the foolish little charm off her neck and threw it in
the fire . . .

Aye, girl, I know her neck was hurt. The cord cut her
flesh before it broke. I was sorry for that after. I told her to
get herself another one from the priest if she wanted it.
Poor Morag, she may be the priest's creature now, but she
has been a good friend to me in the past and if she can take
comfort from a bit of wood on a string, then I'll not stop
her.

There's little enough comfort to be had in Dunsinane.

Look here below our window: it's a scene like the hell
that Christian priests describe to scare us into virtue. The
men are struggling almost waist-deep in the mud, desperately trying to raise the new outer walls in the blood red
light of the torches. Even up here, in this room right under
the fighting platforms, I can hear the whips cutting at the
straining oxen. But they beat the wretched beasts in vain;
Macduff will be here before they can be ready for him.
Macbeth knows that as well as I do, but he works on. He's
somewhere down there now amid the muck and the fear
and the rope-bound stone, straining under the loads himself probably – or else wielding the whip on beasts and men
alike. He doesn't come near me any longer . . . even after
these long, bitter years I ache for him.

Macbeth, it was all done for you. For you I faced the
worst horror any woman could know. It would have been
better if I'd driven the knife into your own heart.

Better for us both.

Look, girl. Come here and look. Do you see him there
below? He doesn't once raise his eyes to my window.
We're both alone in our misery; but he has a comfort that I
lack. He thinks death will end our suffering. I know it
won't.

I have done the unthinkable and there is no peace for
my spirit. The curse must live on. I have known that for
years. And for years I have sought for a way of escape.

Now it is done.

The charm is wound up and the three sisters are joined
across time. Two other women will share my fate, my
weakness. And through them I have got the power I need.

May the Christ God, if he cares at all what women do,
forgive me this last desperate sorcery. It is the only thing
that can save me now.

1606

The devil is a handsome gentleman on a fine grey horse. I
know, I've seen him. He has a gold ring on his finger and a
blue coat. I met him in the harvest field two years back and
he gave me a blind-worm to be my familiar . . .

Listen to me. Listen and I'll tell you everything you want
to hear. And may you both be damned to hell when you've
heard it. You with your fat, blubber face and slack greedy
lips; you who look at me all fascinated and sickened, as if I
was a snake you'd found in your ale. And you with your
saintly eyes and skinny body, who look as if you eat your
Bible instead of good wholesome bread. I'll tell you both all
about it and then, maybe, you'll let me sleep there in the
sweet, dirty straw, till you take me out to hang me. Let me
sleep and may the devil take you.

I don't care what happens any longer.

I never chose to be evil. Do you hear me? I never wanted

to be damned. I didn't want to have dealings with the devil
or to let that spirit of the past possess me. But it's written
in the Bible, isn't it? I've heard it read in church. Not in the
old priests' Latin either, but in words I understand, like
Saintly Eyes says it should be. I understood very well. I
understood that I was damned. A weed sown among God's
wheat that must be burned come Judgement Day. Well,
there's no way a tare can become an ear of corn, is there?
I've sown and weeded and harvested these many years and
I know that for a certainty. So if I'm damned, I'm damned
and it's none of my doing. And if I'm to burn in hell
anyway, then why should I not use all the power I can get?
All the power that the fine gentleman in the harvest field
and the old spirit could give me? What care I for your
church and your common priests that don't even know the
Latin or the words of the Mass any more?

Damn you all!

Listen to me. I tried to be a good woman in spite of all.
And when they took my mother and burned her for a
witch I got right away. Away from all those folk that
expected me to be the same. And I tried to forget the words
she taught me. And I worked right hard to feed myself and
kept myself as virtuous as a lone woman can. I tried to be
good. For sixteen years I tried. Till the devil came in the
harvest field and he changed me. He lay with me and told
me I was a lady and a great many other fine things. Things
that made me discontent. They say that women who've
been loved by Satan will never be satisfied by a mortal
lover. And will want no dealings with ordinary men. And
maybe it's true . . .

Nay, Blubber Face, I'll not tell you what his love was
like. I'll let your own foul brain make up that. But I'll tell
you this: in one night the devil could give a woman more
pleasure than you could in a lifetime . . .

Please! Leave me be, masters. Don't beat me. Leave me
be and I'll tell you all. I'm nothing but a weak woman,

masters, that's been led astray by the devil and an evil spirit. Listen and I'll tell you how the devil works. He sent a spirit, an old spirit from the past, to possess me.

I have heard since what folk say about the devil and the evil sabats where his witches dance. And very like it's true, for learned men believe it. But then I didn't know about such things and I didn't understand what was happening to me. It seemed like nothing more than a dream, though a very bad dream. A dream that came again and again. After I had lain with the devil, I was never free of it.

Listen. It happened first one night two years back at my cottage down at Eldridge's Hollow. My soul was ravished clean out of my body and borne away through the walls of the cottage, while my body lay by the fire as if dead . . .

Aye, you have read in books of such things, have you? Well then, they're wise men who write those books, for it's all true. I've seen it.

Listen, masters, I'll tell you all.

It was dark in that other place and there were three of us there, dancing round and round. Spirits of the present, the future and the past. 'The charm's wound up,' said a voice, and round we danced, round and round. And all I could see was their faces, white as skulls.

Round and round, faster and faster.

Then all was darkness and one voice talking to me, forcing me to do its bidding. Till I woke, all muddle-headed by the fire. Cold and frightened.

Afterwards?

After that, nothing was the same: for I woke from that trance possessed. The evil spirit haunted me. I was never really free of it. Time and time again when I was alone I'd have this feeling of something – or someone – close to me: watching everything I did. And often in my sleep I'd be taken back to that dark, evil place. Twice the spirit put words into my mouth that I never meant to say.

And once, masters, it drove me to kill.

1996

I don't usually give interviews. I can't see why anybody should be interested in my life or my ideas. Why on earth should anyone want to know what my favourite room looks like or how I spend my day? Most of my life is pretty boring – except for my work. And if people want to know about my work they can watch my performances – they'll learn more about it that way than reading trite little articles in magazines.

But there's been a lot of nonsense written about what happened here at the Maypole Theatre and I want to set the record straight.

I wanted to talk to you here because there are things you'll understand better if you see the place where they happened . . .

Yes, I know most actresses wouldn't talk about *Macbeth* in a theatre; it's supposed to invite bad luck, to bring on the curse that haunts the play. But I don't care about that. Not now. You see, I believe the curse has worked itself out – that the worst has already happened . . .

Oh, it's not that I'm not superstitious. Far from it. By the time you've finished recording this interview, you'll probably think I'm a good deal too superstitious. I've always had what you might call an open mind about the supernatural. Like all actresses, I have my own little rituals and my lucky pendant that I wear every time I set foot on stage. And when John offered me the part of Lady Macbeth, my first thought was of the play's sinister reputation; the curse that's supposed to haunt it. I thought of all those stories of accidents, broken limbs and sudden illnesses. As you know, most theatre people are a bit afraid of it. If it hadn't been for Greg, I would never have accepted the part.

Greg was thrilled by the idea of us acting 'as a team'.

'Darling, it's years since we worked together!'

In actual fact Greg and I had never acted together since

we met. He was probably getting confused: he and his first wife used to work together a lot. Anyway, I didn't argue about it. It's not possible to argue with Greg at times like that. Not when he's all big brown eyes and enthusiasm. He sort of sweeps you along with him: makes you want what he wants. It's hard to explain, but he made me feel that refusing to work with him would be a kind of adultery.

I did try suggesting tentatively that I might not be up to the part. As you probably know, I'd not worked since my last illness. I was supposed to be convalescing; in fact the offer of the part had come up while I was away on a short trip that Greg and my grandmother had talked me into taking. Greg met me at the door with the news when I got home.

'It's wonderful, isn't it?' I remember him standing in the hall with my suitcase in his hand, willing me to be pleased about it.

It didn't really sound that wonderful to me, but it wasn't a good moment. I'd just driven down from Scotland with my grandmother, who had seemed determined to try the coffee in every service station from Gretna to Watford just for the sake of complaining about it. 'I don't know, love,' I said wearily. 'I'll have to think about it.'

'But you said you were going to start working again after you'd had a bit of a break.'

Only Greg could talk about a week spent driving Gran around Scottish glens in the rain (and stopping to look for a lavatory every twenty miles) as if it were a rest cure.

I played for time. 'Give me a few days to think about it.'

'People will love to see us working together.'

'Oh yes! *Greg Mortimer and Abby West: the theatre's ideal couple.* I saw that article too.'

'Well, it's true, isn't it?'

I ignored that. 'What about the bad luck?' I said warily.

'Abby, you're not going to turn it down because of that "curse" nonsense?'

'I don't know.' I was just too tired to argue.

'Darling, it means so much to me.'

'You can play Macbeth, whether I play Lady Macbeth or not.'

'But for my first big Shakespearean part I need the best Lady Macbeth I can get. I need *you*, Abby.'

I gave in to that, of course. And the decision seemed to please everyone.

My father was pleased because it was the only Shakespeare play he knew. 'We did it in school, love. It's a good story – not any of that awful lovey-dovey stuff.'

And Gran was delighted. Safely ensconced back in her home, where she could complain about the coffee at her leisure, she would ring me at regular intervals to practise the terrible Scottish accent she'd developed on our travels. She's Canadian, is Gran, but very proud of her Scottish origins. She'd insisted that I took her up north to look for the place from where her ancestors originated. And now she seemed to think that by playing the part of a Scottish queen, I would somehow be rediscovering my roots.

'It's in your blood, lass.'

'Don't be ridiculous, Gran. Our ancestors were destitute crofters, not royalty.'

Anyway, blood or no blood, I didn't make a very good job of the part at first. I certainly wasn't as good as I wanted to be. And, in a strange way, it was my determination to do better that brought the curse on us.

Here, come and look at the stage. There's still stuff left on it from the production and it's one of the things I wanted to show you.

There, at the back, that great gilded pole, that's what they hung the king's banner on for the battle scenes, and lying by it is the king's ceremonial sword. In this dull, flat light the fake jewels look like half-eaten fruit gums, don't they? But when Greg flexed his muscles and swung it around, the spotlights caught the jewels and made them look pretty impressive – a memorable sight. And down here at the front of the stage is the witches' cauldron with all its grisly paraphernalia of bones and stuff. But here, look, if you step past the cauldron this way ... Don't worry about that heap of entrails, it's just red paint and plastic tubes: looks nasty but it's as false as the jewels in the sword. Over here, between the cauldron and the banner, in the middle of the stage, is the really sinister bit. There. Those big brown stains there are real blood.

So much blood! Who would have thought there could be so much blood?

Spread out like that in the middle of the stage it looks like the curse itself – something dark and sinister at the heart of the play. Describe the stage in your article. I think it sort of captures the essence of my story.

Of course, everyone blames me for what happened. The newspapers have judged me and found me guilty. And I don't deny that I was guilty – up to a point. I admit that I was angry and jealous. It couldn't have happened otherwise. But I had good reason to be angry, and besides, something else happened to me. Something that I've not explained to the other reporters. I'm sure it was the 'Curse of Macbeth'.

I'll tell you what I think happened: I believe that somehow the spirit of Lady Macbeth took me over. There's no way I could have done what I did myself. No way.

You smile at that and you're probably remembering everything you've been told about my mental illness. But is it really so strange? Doesn't every actress want to get into the part she's playing? To actually become that character? Well, I think that's just what I did. I did it too well.

All right, I can see you're still not convinced; but that is what it felt like. It's not easy to explain what happened to me. You may not believe me, your readers may not believe me, but I've got to try to make people understand.

Almost as soon as we started rehearsing I knew something was wrong: that something was happening to me.
But I tried to ignore it. The only person I talked to about it
was Alan. Most of the company knew nothing about it at
all.

John, always the optimist, was sure our production was
going to disprove all the stories of bad luck. Ironic, really. I
thought of him when all those CURSE OF MACBETH HITS
MAYPOLE THEATRE headlines were in the papers. Poor
John.

When the first night came and a capacity audience filled
his nice new theatre, John thought the worst thing he'd
got to worry about was a Lady Macbeth that the preview
critics had damned with the faint praise of 'adequate and
intelligent'. Set against that, of course, he'd got, 'One of the
most powerful, thought-provoking Macbeths that the
London stage has seen this decade.' 'Gregory Mortimer, a
sensual, attractive, heroic Macbeth dragged inevitably
down to murder by the evil of the witches and his wife.'

Incidentally, has it ever struck you what a strange play
Macbeth is?

It's a simple enough story. At the beginning of the play,
Macbeth is a heroic warrior; he meets three witches and
they prophesy that he'll become king. After quite a lot of
dithering he decides to kill King Duncan so he can get the
crown. Consequently, he gets to be king but he's never
happy; he doesn't trust anyone and he keeps murdering
more and more people.

In a way it's a very realistic account of the rise of a tyrant.
Except that it's not realistic because of the witches.

Have you read the first couple of scenes? They're full of
accounts of how Macbeth has been slaughtering people on
the battlefield, slicing them down the middle and all sorts
of things. But remember, this is the beginning of the play –
he's not a tyrant yet. He's a hero. Well, this bloodthirsty
killer meets up with three little old ladies and – here's my

point – we're supposed to believe that it's the old ladies who're evil!

Odd, don't you think?

Seems to me that anyone who enjoys slicing people up with his sword is well on the way to murdering without any help from fortune-tellers . . .

Ah yes, you're right: Lady Macbeth does push him towards murder. But why?

That's what I just couldn't understand. Why does she do it? At first I couldn't understand the character. When rehearsals began I struggled with the role; it was really hard to make her come alive. It's like that sometimes. It's one of the most terrifying things about acting and it was what I'd been afraid would happen.

The fact is that for several years – since my marriage really – I'd just not been feeling very confident about my own abilities. I mean, I'd had some marvellous opportunities in that time and the critics had liked a lot of my work, but . . . but for years I seemed to have had this terrible fear of failure. Then I'd been ill and I hadn't worked since.

It was nearly two years since I'd set foot on stage and here I was planning to come back and play one of the hardest female roles in the English language.

The role of Lady Macbeth just puzzled me.

John said she was ambitious. 'A power-hungry woman, getting power the only way she can – through her husband.'

But I couldn't see it myself. She doesn't seem to think about herself, just her husband. She never talks about being Queen – she just talks about Macbeth being King. And she only seems to want that because he wants it.

So to begin with I struggled through rehearsals – a drag on everyone. And I felt that they were all just putting up with me because I was Gregory Mortimer's wife. I felt as phoney as the fruit-gum jewels in that sword there . . .

Yes. How did you know that? Did John tell you? It's true, there were moments even at the beginning when I did seem to be getting into the part properly: moments when the role seemed to be taking over. But they never lasted . . .

Why? Because I was frightened, I think. At first I wouldn't let her take over. And it wasn't till the first night that I gave in to her completely. By then I was too angry to resist her.

By the time the play opened I was confused and very scared.

God, it was awful! First night. Roses in the dressing room, jangling nerves and John's little talk that was a cross between a headmaster's chat in school assembly and a military chaplain's address to the troops! Sweat and adrenalin.

And there was Greg, all heroic in leather and tartan, with his body oiled to look sweaty for the opening battle scenes, staring at me as if he didn't trust me. 'Abby, for God's sake don't let me down.'

His success depended on me.

You know, of course – thanks to the press, everyone knows – that my personal life was in chaos by then. But it was a matter of pride with me that I was going to do well in spite of everything. I just had to give a performance that everyone would remember. My first entrance was over there, centre back, near where the banner's standing now. And I came downstage to – let me see – to about here. I remember it so clearly! In my hand I'd got the letter from Macbeth that tells of his meeting with the witches. Isolated in the light, I moved through the well-rehearsed pattern of the words. Everything was familiar: the heat of a light on the back of my neck, cool smooth wood under my bare feet. And my struggle with the words was familiar too.

'Hie thee hither,
That I may pour my spirits in thine ear

And chastise with the valour of my tongue
All that impedes thee from the golden round . . .'

I was struggling, wishing the words would come alive in my mouth. But it wasn't working – not until I came to the part where Lady Macbeth invokes the help of evil spirits in the murder of King Duncan.

It's hard to explain what happened to me when I started on that bit of the speech. I hardly know myself. It was terrifying – but exciting too. I stood here: the lights in my eyes, the letter in my hand – aware of the unseen audience out there. And something seemed to take over.

'Come, you spirits . . .
. . . Come to my woman's breasts,
And take my milk for gall, you murd'ring ministers.'

And suddenly I understood.

I knew that she wanted Macbeth to be King so much she was prepared to do anything to get him what he wanted. I could feel her longing: I understood what it was to want something so badly, and to want it not for yourself, but simply because it was what the man you loved wanted. I understood how she could do the terrible things she did.

At last I was Lady Macbeth.

1606

How did the spirit come to possess me? Through love, masters, through love of a handsome man. I loved him so much I couldn't help but do what he wanted. And he was no mortal man, but the devil in human shape.

It wasn't till he came and tempted me I fell. As a young lass I'd learned things from my mother, but I'd never used them. Mark that. Tare of Satan I may be, but for sixteen years I tried hard to be a good woman. I tried to forget the old things she taught me.

Ah, masters, they were old and wicked things she told me of; older than anyone knows.

'As old as Eve herself,' my mother called them. 'Aye, and maybe they were what she used to get her way with Adam,' she said, and laughed. She'd a way, had Mother, of laughing at things I didn't understand. Things I still don't understand. I reckon she was a clever woman despite being wicked – or called so.

But I swear, I didn't want to learn her witchcraft. Bairn though I was, it frightened me, as if I knew it was evil. I remember once, when she tried to teach me the bad thing about the toad and the bats and the blind-worm, I was too frightened to repeat the words. Then she sat me on her lap in the chimney corner and gave me bits of sugar out of the old man's store cupboard. And she said, 'Jennet, my dear, you must learn it. For I learned it all from my mother and she of hers and so on for a long, long time.'

'Since Eve?' I asked, for I was still very young.

'Well, maybe not so long. But for a very long time. Since a woman of our line was first taught these things by a Queen of Scotland.'

Aye, that's what she told me, masters, I promise. Though maybe it was no more than a pretty tale to make a child remember her lesson.

So I learned the wicked things.

We were living then in North Berwick; in just such a stout-walled house within sound of the sea as the one where I was born. Though now we lived in the kitchen and slept on a sort of shelf among the hams and onions, my mother being only the keeper of the house, for a gouty old merchant. I could just remember the old times before my father died. I remembered lying on good linen at my mother's breast as she lulled me to sleep, my fingers clutching at the golden brooch she wore and tracing the engraving on it; three little round faces that were so familiar they wove themselves into my dreams. I remembered too the house we lived in then and its good chamber with a high settle and a big table that smelled of bees' wax. But that was when I was very young; most of my childhood was spent there in that old man's kitchen, or on the streets of Berwick where even the bairns playing in the gutters would mock me, saying that my mother did more than keep house for that ugly old man . . .

Nay, they were lies, Blubber Face! My mother was no whore! She was a fine woman. And she was a gentlewoman. As I would be too, if pirates hadn't drowned my father on a voyage to the Low Countries. Aye, then you would be speaking differently to me and I warrant I'd not be here, under accusation of witchcraft with no way out of this filthy hole but to the Assizes and the gallows.

My mother was a gentlewoman. She baked the bread and cleaned the house of that grudging old fellow to keep a roof over our heads. But she did him no other services . . .

Very well, very well, masters. There's no need to be angry. I'll talk more calmly. And I don't know why I should be so anxious about her virtue. The last time I saw her she was squirming in the smoke and flames. And those same urchins that'd mocked her were crowding around with black, oily smuts settling on their grinning faces. Her good name was the last thing I worried about then, for it'd been a wet night and the faggots burned ill. By noon she was still alive and I was screaming at the men standing by, begging them to pour pitch on the wood.

Such a death!

Do you think I wanted the same for myself? Do you think that having seen what was done to her – or rather, masters, do you think that having seen the just fate of the wicked – I'd not have chosen goodness if I could?

I thought that by running away, I could escape from being wicked. But there was no escape for me; the evil was in my blood. I came down south to England, masters and I'd been more than ten years settled in the cottage down in Eldridge's Hollow before the devil found me and put on the form of a comely man to tempt me. He won my love and sent an evil spirit to possess me.

And that spirit made me take a life. Though in my senses, I swear I'd never have the heart to harm a living creature.

1996

The public have judged me and found me guilty already, I know. They have decided that what happened here at the Maypole on the first night – that terribly public scene of bloodshed – was all my fault. That's not true. But I admit I made some mistakes. Bad mistakes. And the first mistake I made was to let myself get involved in a play that everyone knows is unlucky.

I was stupid about the whole business. Looking back now, I can see that I was an idiot then. I was so weak!

It was Lady Macbeth who taught me that, you know. She taught me that you've got to know what you want and go all out to get it. It's no good trying to please other people all the time. I can see now that I should never have let Greg talk me into taking the part.

I think we all – or most of us, anyway – believed in the curse a bit. But we believed in different ways. Meg (our First Witch) took it personally: if anyone was going to have bad luck, it would be her, while Joanne (she's the Second Witch) tackled it head on with garlic, crucifix and the practical approach of a professional vampire hunter in a horror film. John, our director, seemed to fear not so much the curse as our fear of it. He believed that believing in bad luck was dangerous: which is a kind of superstition in itself. And Chrissie, our young and giggling Lady Macduff, talked primly about 'a sense of evil in the play', like a virginal Sunday School teacher.

But to begin with, all I felt was a kind of vague uneasiness: a feeling that something was wrong but I didn't know exactly what it was.

'It's like just glimpsing something strange out of the very corner of your eye.' That's how I tried to explain it to Greg. 'But when you turn to look, there's nothing there.'. . .

What did Greg say? Something like 'Don't be ridiculous', or 'Don't start imagining things, for God's sake, Abby. You'll make yourself ill again.'

Greg was probably the only member of the cast who didn't believe in the curse at all. To him it was just a nuisance – something that made other people behave stupidly. Superstition is a closed book to Greg. It's something he doesn't understand because his mind just doesn't work that way. It's as if superstition exists in a dimension he knows nothing about and he can't understand it any more than a person born blind can understand colour. Macbeth's a great part, but all this business irritated him. The truth is, I think he'd have been better pleased if he could have got, say, Hamlet for his first big Shakespearean role. As it was, he had to make the best of the chance he'd got and he wanted a Lady Macbeth he could rely on.

So I did my best to ignore the uneasiness I felt, to pretend it didn't exist or else that it was just caused by the play's reputation: anything to stop him thinking I was being neurotic and ridiculous.

And then the dreams started. Dreams in which a voice would speak, forcing me against my will to follow its commands. That really frightened me.

The first time it happened was early on in the rehearsal period. Greg and I had taken Luke down to the cottage for a good family weekend of muddy wellingtons and burnt sausages on the barbecue.

We have two houses, by the way: the place in north

London, which Greg calls home, and a Tudor cottage set in a wooded hollow in the depths of Oxfordshire. My father bought it and renovated it thirty years ago and it's been home to me ever since. Greg's not too keen on it; he doesn't like the bats in the roof or the spiders in the bath. But I love it dearly. There are low beams with mysterious hooks and holes; you can look at them for hours and wonder what they were all used for. A twisting staircase leads up from the living room to the bedrooms and there's a big open fireplace with one huge black beam very low across it. It's a great fire for making love by.

A stack of logs, a bottle of wine and Greg. That was my idea of the perfect evening! Though that evening he was perhaps a bit too inclined to talk about work.

'The relationship between Macbeth and his wife is a crucial part of the play.' He was sitting at my feet, I remember, and the fire reflected tiny orange flames in the darkness of his eyes.

'They are very close,' I said half-heartedly.

'And she has tremendous power over him.'

'Power?' I brushed the hair from his brow. 'What kind of power?'

'Isn't that obvious?' He pressed his thin cheek against my thigh and smiled.

'Is it?' I mused. To begin with I remember I really was thinking about the play. But then I looked back down at those fire-lit eyes, so strikingly dark under the thick fall of fair hair – and work didn't seem to matter so much. I'd been about to say that wasn't quite how I saw her. But I knew he'd not like me to disagree with him. So I kissed him instead; that seemed like a better way to use the time than arguing.

After that I was oblivious for a while to everything except Greg – and trying to stop my bare bits scorching. (Always a bit of a problem, that, but I think it's part of the fun.) In fact the fire must have been particularly hot that evening because I managed to go to sleep afterwards; usually I get shivery and uncomfortable.

As soon as I was asleep, the dream started. It seemed as if I stood up from the fireside and immediately I was on the stage at the Maypole. But you know what it's like in dreams, nothing's ever exactly right. In some way the stage was still the living room in the cottage. And I wasn't playing the part of Lady Macbeth, I seemed to be one of the witches. It was dark and we were dancing round and round, and all the time we were circling faster and faster. You know how your movement seems to build up a kind of momentum in dreams. Until you just can't stop.

I could feel the hands of the other two in mine. Very cold, they were. But it was getting harder and harder to hold on because we were going so fast – and because our hands seemed wet as well as cold. Suddenly their hands slipped out of mine and when I looked down I saw my hands were covered in blood – slimy wet and dripping with the stuff. 'Peace,' said a voice. 'The charm's wound up.'

Then the dream changed and I was alone, but still on the stage – or in the living room, whichever it was. My hands were still all bloody and ahead of me I could see a steep, narrow flight of stairs leading up to a big wooden door.

'Go on,' said a voice. 'Climb the stairs. You must climb the stairs.'

It was crazy. Even as I dreamed it, I knew it was crazy. I knew I didn't want to climb those stairs. For some reason I was terrified of what lay beyond the door; but I knew I'd got to do what the voice said. The words were filling my head, pressing my body forward with that stifling, nightmare feeling. Up and up the stairs. I was sweating in terror but all the time my feet were climbing the stairs. I could feel cold stone beneath my bare toes, feel the smoothness of the hollow worn in the middle of each step. But I couldn't stop. I opened my mouth to scream but the sound trickled out, tiny and distorted. Ahead of me the door was nearer now. It was not quite closed; there was a slice of pale light down its side. And now I could see that it was black across the bottom, as if it had been burned.

It was a terrible door. I really didn't want to see what lay beyond it. I tried to scream again and this time the sound broke through, clumsy and surprising, dragging me back to shivering reality. I woke to find that the firelight had become a dull red glow below me. I was standing naked at the top of the twisting stairs outside the door to Luke's bedroom. Shakily I gripped the banister and peered down into the fire-lit room. Greg was still sprawled asleep on the floor in a clutter of discarded clothes. The embers' glow was ruddy on his tanned limbs, his white shirt loosely embraced his shoulder with a trailing sleeve and a half-full glass stood perilously close to his toes. I was relieved to see he'd not woken; I didn't want him to know I'd started walking in my sleep again. But the terror of the dream clung to me, its hold not much weakened by the pull of normality which can usually dislodge a nightmare . . .

Yes, I did tell him about the dream, but not till the next morning when Luke and Alan were both there too.

Alan arrived while I was getting breakfast the next day, looming suddenly and rather incongruously through the back door. I remembered we'd given him a vague invitation to come down and join us if he had time but, to be honest, I'd not expected him to accept. He had always seemed a bit of a loner.

Alan Stewart is a Scot and an old acquaintance of John's. He'd joined the Maypole to play Seyton, Macbeth's servant. That's a small part, but he's a kind of historian as well as an actor and I know he was giving the props department a lot of advice on historical detail. He'd written a series of books on Scottish history and now he was, apparently, working on a new one about Scotland in the nineteenth century. An unlikely friendship had formed between him and Greg. I could only assume that Greg had heard none of the theatre gossip that credited Alan with being 'a bit of a head-case'. Greg has a horror of illness of any kind and treats mental illness with utter disgust.

Looking back now, I think Greg probably took to Alan because no one else seemed to like him. It's Greg's way often to be rather cool towards most of the people he's working with, but to honour someone fairly insignificant with his friendship. Makes him feel important, I suppose. Anyway, I said nothing to Greg about Alan's reputation because I felt rather sorry for the man.

Much to my surprise, it was Alan who was most sympathetic about my dream that morning.

Greg's response was predictable. 'You're OK, aren't you, Abby? You're not getting depressed again?' He sounded more disgusted than sympathetic. The truth is my illness – you know I was badly depressed a couple of years ago? – well, it had frightened him – because he couldn't understand it, I suppose.

Meanwhile Luke was shovelling away at bloated bits of sugary cereal. He showed a ten-year-old's blissful preoccupation with his own affairs.

'Can I go up to the farm to see if they've got any chestnuts, Mum?'

It was Alan, brooding over black coffee, who said abruptly, 'Do you often have nightmares, Abigail?'

I was surprised by the sudden question. It seemed rather personal considering we'd not known each other long. But as I looked at him crouching awkwardly on the narrow kitchen chair, I realized he was glad to have something to talk about. He was the kind of man who found it almost impossible to make small talk.

'No,' I said, 'as far as I can remember, I've not had a nightmare for years.'

'You're worrying about the play?'

'Yes, maybe I am, Alan.'

I certainly started to worry more about it in the weeks

that followed. The dream kept coming back and it made me fear the play more than ever. And being frightened stopped me from getting to grips with the part.

I remember telling Alan a week or so later, 'When I read the lines on my own I feel as if there's something – or someone – there with me. Listening. Watching.'

Instead of accusing me of being sick, Alan looked as if he understood and said, 'It's certainly a strange, powerful play. A lot of people have found it frightening.'

'I wish I'd not got involved. I didn't mean to start working again so soon.'

'Have you talked to Gregory about this?'

'I can't,' I admitted. 'This production means too much to him.'

Greg really was desperate for the Maypole *Macbeth* to be a success. As you know, he's made himself a name in television, films and modern stuff, but this was his first chance in Shakespeare. His chance to prove he'd got real talent, not just rampant sex-appeal.

I just couldn't let him down now. I owed him too much.

You know the story of my career, I suppose?

I think most people still see me as Gregory Mortimer's protegée. It's common knowledge that he rescued me from obscurity and got me my first good parts. I owe Greg a lot, I admit. If it wasn't for him, I'd not have had the opportunities I've had.

In the end it was hard to tell whether I loved him or hated him. But at the time we started rehearsing *Macbeth*, it was definitely love I felt. I would have done anything for him. That's what you've got to understand. I only agreed to take the part because he wanted me to. And the trouble started not because I was angry with him, but simply because I loved him.

1057

Long ago, child, before the holy, unwashed culdees came with their books and their bells to subdue our hearts, before the horned men came from the sea to slaughter our children and ravish our bodies, long ago, before even the legions marched from Rome, there was a power in this land of Alba.

Her name is lost now. Perhaps she never had one. Perhaps she belonged to a time before there were names. But the memory of her lives on – the memory of one goddess who bears three faces. She lives in my very earliest memories. For don't I wear on my breast the gold brooch with the three round faces of the goddess; haven't I worn it ever since I was old enough to be trusted not to hurt myself on the pin? It was all I had left of my mother except for a dim memory of a voice singing over my cradle in a strange, wild tongue.

And in womanhood didn't I take the power that the goddess offered? When I was helpless, I took the only power I could get. That's what men hate me for. Hate me and fear me. I've seen the fear of me often in men's faces: in the face of the man I love as well as the men I have hated. They say there is a look comes on me sometimes when I'm touched with the old power; a look so strange and wild it can unman them. But men will often fear the things they don't understand.

Aye, and most women will too. The fat white-faced women crowded into the hall for protection – the wives of the few thanes that remain loyal to us – they're wetting their skirts in terror. They fear the evil woman in the room above their heads as much as they fear Macduff.

'Keep away from the stairs,' I heard one of them tell her straying brat yesterday. 'Keep well away or the witch will catch you.'

Well, maybe I am evil, maybe I am a witch. I did what I

must to get what I wanted; to get what Macbeth wanted. But the power I got was that born of helplessness.

Come here, girl. Stop wringing your hands and come away from the window. There's nothing to see yet. It'll be hours before Macduff comes. There, that's right, sit here by the brazier and listen. What I tell you tonight you must remember all your life. You must listen now, and when I've done you must get away from Dunsinane. Get right away and take my memories with you. Go back to the Highlands, but not to Moray, our enemies will hunt you there. Go instead to Glenlagan; there's a man there who'll see you're safe.

Listen now.

I was saying that I have known helplessness. I was helpless, weak and silent when Macbeth MacFindlay first shot like a comet into my life, changing despair into hope.

'Look at her!' Gillacomgain, my husband, would roar. 'She sits brooding there like a toad brewing poison. It's enough to curdle a man's blood. What goes on in that ugly little black head of hers?' And he'd heave his great belly up and down in a laugh or turn to fondle some fair-haired, fat bosomed slut. And I'd keep my head bent down over the table, hoping to be spared any blows and to suffer nothing worse than cruel words.

How long had it lasted? For how many nights had I sat at that board, frozen into misery, before the night that MacFindlay's voice broke into the dark cell of my thoughts? It seems as if it must have been a lifetime, but in truth it was not so very long, for Lulach was barely weaned when Macbeth and his men came to Moray, and the child must have been gotten nearly on my wedding night.

In fact the bitter, brooding woman who sat in Gillacomgain's hall was scarcely three years older than the wench who was playing behind the pig sties the day the men first came to talk marriage with my father.

Beatrice and I were barefoot in the mud, our hair

unbraided. We were playing *The Thane of Fife* and Beatrice was supposed to be running away to hide while I skidded round and round in the slime by the midden chanting the old rhyme.

> 'The Thane of Fife had a wife,
> An ox, a sheep and big fat sow.
> The Thane of Fife had a wife,
> Where, oh where, oh where is she now?'

But when I opened dizzy eyes and cried 'Coming to find you!' I saw the yard spinning round me with the fly-swarming heap of refuse, the gutter choked with yesterday's pig-killing – and Beatrice, not hiding at all, but bent over to peer through a gap in the rotten wood of the palisade.

'What's wrong with you?' I demanded, giving her out-thrust behind a shove. 'Why aren't you hiding?'

'Look,' she said, breathless and self-important. 'There're two men riding down the track. I'm sure they're coming to the gates.'

When wenches are a certain age they have a way of saying the word 'men' that fills it with excitement and meaning. Beatrice and I were about that age and strange men were rare within our walls. We exchanged one wide-eyed look and darted across the yard, sending the hens clattering round us. We scrambled, giggling, up the ladder that led to the rickety platform by the gate, bare toes curling round the rough rungs. From there we could see across the moorland, steaming after midsummer rain, and along the peat track where two men in leather jerkins were riding gracelessly, like sacks of meal perched on good horses.

'Let's go back to the game,' I said. These two fellows were not worth wasting time on. One was gross-bellied with blotchy purple skin and the other, though he was younger, thinner and cleaner-looking, had a dour priestish look to him; his face was all pulled down in sneering lines.

Strangers though they were, there was nothing to hold our interest here. Better go back to the game – or to the house to play with little Kenneth, my brother's new bairn. Or, better still, to the stables to tease big, tow-haired, hot-handed Ban into kissing us.

'But I was right, they are coming here,' said Beatrice smugly, though I can't think where else they'd have been going since such well-mounted men were unlikely to be bound for the clansmen's tumbled huts. 'Maybe they're from the King. I wonder what their business is with my uncle.'

'Come on,' I said, 'Let's go to the stables.' I never could understand her interest in the business and all the boring comings and goings of the household.

Anyway, we found out soon enough that what these two men wanted was us.

It wasn't long before Morag came, in a great hurry, flapping like a hen to fetch us from the stables and Ban's hot dirty hands and clumsy kisses. In the space of an hour she had forced our hair into braids of eye-smarting tightness, our feet into unfamiliar shoes and the notion of husbands into our unwilling minds.

'Great men they are,' she muttered, though her eyes were red as if she'd been crying. 'You're both lucky wenches.'

It seemed that the fat blotchy one, Gillacomgain Lord of Moray, was for me, and the priestish one, Constantine MacGirrick, my father's brother's son, was for Beatrice.

The marriage vows were made that day, though my father bargained with them to keep us both with him six months longer, 'Till they're more of an age to be bedded.' I understand now why, young as we were, he was so eager to secure us husbands. Already the tyrant king Malcolm was bleeding his lands like a leech and he reckoned that, at best, he'd won himself strong allies and, at worst, he'd got us two away into safer places.

So that night Gillacomgain's fat, greasy hand was put into mine and the priest said the words. We made as good a show at a feast as we could with the pig that'd been killed and the men on their bride-quest probably had no notion of how hard times were with us. Gillacomgain's heavy jowls were grinning wetly when Morag herded the pair of us into the hall. But his look changed when my father, bleary-eyed and ale-fuddled as usual, claimed me as his child and named Beatrice as 'my cousin's bairn that I've raised as my own.'

I saw disappointment in the black pits of his eyes and I watched his gaze move coldly from Beatrice's burgeoning breasts and hips to my hard, flat little figure. The whole hall: the filthy rushes on the floor that'd not been changed since Mother died; the cold stones of the hearth, clammy damp with the heavy weather; the stained board, the hacked meat, the ale cups, a straying hen pecking for fleas in the dirt just inside the door, all blurred into the greyness of tears.

I could have borne his ugliness, I thought under my straining scalp, I could have borne even the brown stumps of teeth in swollen gums and the way that, close to, he stank like a privy, if only he had smiled and seemed to like me. Marriage was my fate, just like chilblains in winter and head-lice in summer, and a stinking ugly husband was no worse than I'd expected. But I'd always thought he'd like me.

'She's got her mother's looks,' muttered my father dotingly, his hand on one of my hard braids, quite blind to the Lord of Moray's scorn. 'The dark beauty of the Picts.'

Gillacomgain turned away from me, emptied his cup down his gullet and belched. 'It's her father's inheritance that interests me, Bodhe, not her mother's looks.'

Aye, well, by the time they sent Beatrice off to Mac-Girrick's house in Fife and took me to that great stone tower in Moray, there was little to hope for from my father's line and Gillacomgain was sure he had made a bad bargain.

That terrible arrival, at the beginning of a hard winter, passed before me in a haze of weariness. My body, aching with cold and chaffed sore from long days on horseback, moved like a sleepwalker through the thick grey arch of stone into the dungeon stillness within the walls. Here a wooden hall and kitchens were built against the dank, moss-crusted walls; a fire of green wood was burning smokily in the open, ringed by half a dozen great hounds with gauntly curving bodies and tails.

'Where is my Lord of Moray?' demanded Morag hoarsely of a grinning lad. He jerked a grimy thumb towards the far side of the tower and, to my exhausted mind, it seemed as if a woman suddenly appeared – a woman in decent grey with a linen neckcloth that was at least half-way clean.

'I'm Bethoc, keeper of the house,' she said. 'Follow me, please.'

She led us through the smoky muddle to a door and a flight of stairs built within the tower wall. I'd never known anything like it before and it seemed clammy and smothering. The dark shallow stairs twisted round and led into a room: a small room with a wooden floor and stone walls that sloped inwards and a fire that burned in an opening in the stone so that most of the smoke – and much of the heat too – was carried off through the wall. A strange room that seemed half-full with the vast bulk of Gillacomgain – my husband.

He looked once at me and his lip lifted to show his rotten teeth. Then he turned away to the messenger my father had sent. 'Is it true what I hear of Bodhe MacKenneth?' he demanded. 'Is he really a bigger fool than I took him for?'

'He has been unfortunate.'

'Unfortunate! He's been behaving like a foolish woman, practically giving his lands away to the High King. He's cheated me!'

There wasn't so much as a stool in the suffocating little room and we'd been offered no rest or refreshment. My aching head was spinning and my sore legs sagging; the men's words came and went in my mind: the quiet steady voice of my father's man of business and the growing roar of my husband. The last things I knew were a rushing noise as the rough planks of the floor rose up to meet me and a sharp jab of pain as my head hit the corner of the strange hearth.

When light came back to me, I was lying in a bulky bed in another clammy, stone-walled room, and Morag was sitting beside me.

'Rest now,' she croaked. She'd caught cold on the journey and she'd not got much voice left. 'They've gone to the hall.'

'To argue?'

'And drink and eat.'

'Morag,' I whispered, 'the Lord of Moray doesn't like me.'

'Ah,' she said. A noise that was meant to have no meaning.

My mind was busy with what I knew should follow the marriage negotiations and the priest's words. My ideas of the business were simple and vague, based on stories Beatrice and I had made up for each other, and the funny hot embraces we'd teased Ban into in the empty stall at the end of the stables. It was all pretty much a muddle in my head, of handsome men in battle gear being very gentle and the smell of horse-muck and hay.

'Maybe,' I said hopefully, 'if he doesn't like me, he won't come to me tonight.'

'Ah,' said Morag again and coughed painfully.

In my innocence and weakness, I thought that the thing must be an act of liking. That night I learned that it could be an act of hate and revenge.

I've done my best to bar the memories of that night from

my waking thoughts. But in my nightmares still some things come back: his footsteps slow and drunken on the stair; his bloated shadow looming over me; my own hateful body, flat-chested, childish and shockingly white except for the red chaffed sores on my thighs from the journey. And after that, pain and self-hatred, the whole of which I've never been able to tell, even to Macbeth.

Morag found me in the morning, shivering like a dog on the floor, because in the end he had even denied me the bed.

1996

I first met Greg in a church hall. I was wearing fishnet stockings and a rubber miniskirt at the time. Greg was bright and cheerful; handsomely dishevelled and haggard from the hands of make-up and wardrobe. They'd just started making the third series of *Maynard* and he was enjoying being 'television's most charismatic detective'. I was a tart with one line somewhere in the script and I'd been waiting all morning in the cold to say it. The way things were looking I'd probably not get my scene done till the next day.

It was dismal just hanging around. I knew no one to talk to; my feet were strapped into shoes with crippling heels and the rain was seeping down my cleavage. I was feeling pretty miserable, but in those days – before I got married – I was tough and I had boundless confidence in my own talents. Hunched over my hundredth cup of tea in the hall where they were serving refreshments, I was feeling strong enough to write a letter to my father.

It's funny, but that day is so important in my memory I can even remember what I was writing. *It's not a big part,* I'd confessed. No good pretending otherwise; he'd see it. *But it's a great opportunity and . . .* I remember staring round the draughty hall – tea urns, miscellaneous costumes, bored, unfriendly faces – and trying to find something else positive to say . . . *and I'm enjoying it.*

I had to pretend; in fact I only wrote home when I'd got proper work. I didn't want him to know about the in-between times: waiting at tables and typing. That just wasn't what he wanted for his university educated daughter. I hated having to deceive him and it seemed unfair that I had to. I knew I was talented; all I needed was a decent chance to prove it.

'I hate waiting around like this, don't you?' said a voice beside me.

I looked up to see Greg: the great Gregory Mortimer, who had been annoying everyone all day with his offhand manner, impatience and arrogance. Now he was clutching a mug that smoked in the draught from an open door and smiling at me. He sat down and focused his attention on me.

That's the only way I can describe it. It's a knack he has. He makes you feel interesting by giving you the impression that you have his undivided attention. I'd never come across anything quite like it before and it had an immediate effect. Suddenly I wasn't an insignificant bit-part who no one could be bothered with. Instead I was a professional, sharing the minor irritations of the job with a fellow professional.

Gregory Mortimer.

The very name was a kind of charm to ward off trouble. And it wasn't long before I used it.

The next time I visited home I made a bad mistake. Hurrying to catch the train on a gloomy autumn evening, I remembered to change the clothes I'd worn for an after-noon's waitressing, but forgot to wash my hair. I got home smelling like a greasy kitchen.

'A waitress!' stormed Dad, when I confessed. 'A waitress! For the love of God, Ab, you've got a degree.' I remember him rooted to the lounge carpet with the shock of it, the patio doors behind him reflecting his disgust on to the night.

'It's only temporary, Dad. Just a stopgap. Everybody does it.'

'No, not everybody. People with proper jobs, proper careers, don't need stopgaps.'

'I've got a proper career.'

'A career! A few days' work here and there. And serving dinners to every Tom, Dick and Harry in between. That's not a career.'

I just stared down at the red swirls of the carpet's pattern and kept my mouth shut. We'd been through all this so many times before.

'You could do anything. You've got opportunities I never dreamed of when I was your age.'

'I want to act, Dad.'

There was a baffled silence from him.

'But you've got a degree, Ab.'

Poor Dad, to him that was the key that should unlock all the doors that were closed to him. Dad's a builder with his own business: self-made and successful, with a BMW and plans for a swimming pool. But his lack of education really bothers him. It always irritates me to see the way he'll sort of shrink in the company of fellow Rotarians who have professions and letters after their names.

After a while his anger seeped away. The colour began to fade from his puffed cheeks. He hitched his trousers over his stomach and shook his head.

'I just want the best for you, love.'

'I know, Dad. But can't you see, I'm doing what I want to do. I'm happy.'

'Maybe you are now, love. But what about the future?'

This was always the worst part; when he stopped being angry and let me see his hurt and bewilderment. I was on the point of tears. I hated hurting him; I hated him for being hurt.

It was then, my eyes full of red carpet swirls, desperate to stop the misery, I used the magic of Greg's name.

I can't remember exactly what I said, but I let the name drop into the stuffy tension of the lounge. And the effect was immediate. Dad's voice lifted as he repeated the well-known name. 'Gregory Mortimer? Do you know him?' There was just a hint, just the slightest trace, of respect in the words.

'I've been . . .' I hesitated, still intent on the red swirls. 'I've been seeing him. He's introduced me to some useful people.'

I raised my eyes from the carpet and saw Dad's face suddenly pale and bright, lips twitching slightly. It was like the face that used to beam from the front row of parents as I walked across the stage to get prizes on school speech days.

It was just the name that meant so much to him, I think. Before I'd even started building success on the few – the very few – opportunities those useful people gave me, Dad was telling his Rotary Club cronies about my talents and my connections with famous people.

My grandmother reacted rather differently when she heard about the business.

'Are you sleeping with him, Abigail?' she demanded.

I laughed. 'Not yet, Gran. He's not given me the chance.'

I seem to remember I got the chance soon after. And I took it, of course.

I adored him. He'd changed my whole life, turned the hurt into triumph and hope.

1057

Macbeth used to say he didn't know how I had the courage to face those early days in Moray. But I don't think I was brave, just weak. I endured because there was nothing else for me to do. It's true that the first morning, as I lay curled like a fist in the bed to which Morag lifted me – the bed which still stank of him – I did want to die. But I was little more than a child and I had no notion how to get my own death. And, as the nightmare wore on in the months that followed, I found comfort and relief in what I could.

First there was Morag, lifting me and tending me with stringy strength that morning and coming in the evening when the light was fading and my heart was beating fast in terror of the night. She had been out; thick mud clogged her shoes and hemmed her skirts and her cheeks were red raw with cold.

'There's a wise woman on the hill,' she croaked. 'See, she gave me what might help.'

There were two things: one was a salve for the sore place between my legs and the other was a bitter syrup that Morag made me drink. 'It's the best I can do for you, child,' she muttered. 'If your poor mother was alive there's plenty more she could do, I swear. But that's foolish, if she was alive you'd not be here.' She turned away and added, more to herself than me, 'She had sense enough for both of them. Bodhe's naught without her.'

I blessed the wise woman for that syrup.

It didn't exactly make me sleep. I saw everything that happened to the woman in Gillacomgain's bed; saw the blows fall, saw her hanging like a doll in his hands and lying unmoving under his thrashing body. I seemed to hang high up in a corner of the room and watch it all, pitying her and hating her for her weakness and waiting for the torture to end.

Night after night.

And then there was a second comfort. Soon after Yule, I knew that I was with child.

Gillacomgain wanted his son born safely and that spared me some blows, and somehow the knowledge that I carried a new life made me despise myself a little less. During the dark winter days, sitting by the fire in my room or in the hall spinning with Morag and Bethoc, my hand would stray to my belly and though my bowed head didn't lift, I'd feel a strange, warm surge of pleasure. A baby, sweet-smelling and soft-skinned with dear little smiles like little Kenneth whom I'd loved dearly and grieved over leaving. A child of my own. He would make me less ugly, less worthless.

Then, after he was born strong and healthy and dearer even than I had dreamed, there was the pleasure of nursing him and better still, relief from Gillacomgain. Brute though he was, he wanted his child to thrive and kept away from my bed for fear of souring my milk. It was almost like freedom. I remember at that time Bethoc telling me of how the Norse and Angle women think it no shame to have their bairns nursed by another and how the ladies among them give up their babies to wet nurses. I nearly laughed aloud as I said how glad I was to be a Scot.

All the time, though, I knew the days of freedom were slipping one by one through my fingers. By the time Lammastide of my second year at Moray came, my body was bruised again and my head was thick and muddled with the brew I swallowed whenever I heard those stumbling footsteps on the stairs.

But at Lammastide, Macbeth MacFindlay came and changed everything.

I didn't take much notice of what went on in Gillacomgain's household; there was little enough in the place to interest me. Apart from Bethoc, all the women in the house seemed to be his whores and the men were single, fighting men. The better sort lived on the lands they tenanted for him, kept their wives out of his way and came only to pay their dues and air their grievances. He wasn't a man whose company anyone sought for pleasure and he'd plenty of enemies. So he lived with his fighting men within strong walls.

'The wretch has good reason to be scared,' Morag told me. 'For he and his brother killed their uncle Findlay to get Moray and now Findlay's son is of an age to take back what's his.'

She was talking, as she often did, in an effort to interest me in anything beyond my own wretchedness. I was sore, I was aching and my head was heavy. Lulach's small weight dragged at my arms as we walked outside the walls in scorching heat.

'Then why does this son of Findlay come here as his guest?' I asked, trying to sound as if it mattered, as if anything mattered except the minutes trickling by, wearing the day mercilessly into night.

'He comes unasked and Gillacomgain needs must make a guest of him. MacFindlay has power now – and the favour of the High King, for what that's worth up here in Moray.'

'I pray God they don't talk about King Malcolm; nothing makes him more angry with me.'

But they did.

The hall was crowded almost to overflowing with Macbeth's men that night. It was stiflingly hot with the heat of the torches and bodies packed close on the benches. The air smelled of hot flesh and meat tainted by the sultry weather. And for long hours I must sit wretchedly at Gillacomgain's side, head bowed over my food and avoiding the eyes of the strangers, while he railed against the King – and against me.

'Look at her brooding there like a toad,' he spluttered, getting louder and slacker-lipped every minute with liquor. 'Daughter of the High King's Tannaisse! I wed her in good faith, cousin, but I've been cheated. He might be called the

King's heir, but Bodhe will never succeed. Malcolm's too clever for him. He's already stripped away half his lands and the crown will pass to the King's daughter's boy, Duncan, you mark my words.'

'Times are changing, it's true,' said a low voice. 'And men are turning their backs on the old ways of succession. Now men look to keep titles in their own line instead of letting them pass from branch to branch of a clan as they used to. But cousin, this is hardly the Lady Gruoch's fault and see, we confuse her by speaking harshly of her father.'

I couldn't help looking up furtively at this stranger, but was shocked to find his dark eyes fixed on me. He was a straight, lean, long-legged man with muscle knotted on bare arms. His beard was shaven clean away and he'd have looked like a Norman if it hadn't been for the black hair that curled thickly to his shoulders. But it was his smile that sent a shock through me.

With his brown eyes lingering on me and his lips just brushing the edge of his ale cup, he was smiling as if he saw in me something worth attending to.

Gillacomgain sneered. 'Ach, Macbeth, your tongue's as smooth as a Romish priest's. You need more ale, man.' He pushed the jug towards his guest with the chop bone he was holding, slopping the stuff on to the board. But I noticed that Macbeth made no move to refill his cup and a quick glance down the hall told me that all his men were drinking less than their hosts. The strangers were sitting straight among the slouching bodies of our household. Gillacomgain saw none of this; his mind was too full of his own grievances.

'Look at her,' he said. 'Her body's as meagre as what the old King's left me of her marriage portion.' He jabbed a thumb into my breasts, shrunk back smaller than ever now after nursing my baby.

The blow was slight compared to many I had known, but it brought the blood scalding to my cheeks. I didn't want to be shamed in front of this man. 'I must go,' I stammered and made an effort to get to my feet. 'The child will need me.'

'Sit down!' Gillacomgain seized my wrist, his hot greasy fingers pressing painfully. 'You can't go to your bairn now. Sit down and get some food inside you. You certainly need it.' His belly bounced with senseless laughter and a few other men within earshot joined him.

Macbeth MacFindlay was silent.

'Though the truth is,' Gillacomgain slurred, leaning across the table, 'it makes no difference what she eats. Nothing seems to put any flesh on her sharp bones. Do you know what I think?' he demanded, striking MacFindlay on the chest.

'No cousin, I have no idea.'

'I don't think she's a mortal woman at all, but a changeling from the fairy mounds!'

He pushed back his bench to let his belly bounce freely as he laughed. It was one of his favourite taunts and it struck my bowed head like a bullying hand. I looked to see how Macbeth took the joke. He was still watching me, his eyes wide and thoughtful. Slowly he uncurled his long brown fingers from his cup and turned to his host.

'Perhaps you're right, cousin,' he said and the hot blood swept back to my cheeks. Tears smarted behind my eyes: tears that it had long been beyond Gillacomgain's worst cruelty to start. 'For all the stories say that men who stray into the fairy mounds never return. And indeed,' he went on, 'what man would want to leave a place where all the women were like the Lady Gruoch? No man would wish to return from such an enchanted place to coarse, mortal women.'

He'd spoken quietly but very clearly and along the board men paused in their eating and drinking. Our folk cast wondering looks from Gillacomgain to the stranger, half expecting my husband to make some protest. The big, scowling, one-handed servant who stood behind Macbeth shifted uneasily, as if he thought his master might have started a fight with his compliments.

And I sat, unable to drag my eyes away from his smile. A tear that had sprung in shame now found its way coldly down my cheek. As it ran I saw one long brown hand stir from the table and reach half towards me as if he'd wipe it away. But he checked himself in time and the hand fell back. Gillacomgain meanwhile had remembered that he mustn't anger his cousin. Not now, anyway. So he fell back on laughter, stupid, belly-bouncing, jowl-wobbling laughter.

But later, in my chamber, he let his anger show.

'So you like MacFindlay, do you? You like his smiles and his sweet words,' he sneered. 'Maybe you'd like to kiss him, hey? Well so you shall, my girl. For one day soon – as soon as I've raised my men – I'll be bringing his head home to hang on our walls. And then you can kiss him. I'll see that you do it in front of all the company. Do you hear? You'll kiss his dead lips!'

I cowered against the wall, crouching on the bed with my knees near my chin and my arms raised protectively around my head. The room, lit only by a handful of sticks burning on the hearth, seemed full of his voice and the stink of drunken breath.

'You think you can smile at other men and make me look a fool in my own hall! I'll show you what I think of that.'

'No!'

I surprised myself by crying out and scrambling along the bed. Never before had I resisted. What was the point? But, tonight I felt different. Tonight I met his anger with fury of my own. To my astonishment I found myself sliding off the bed's end and stumbling across the floor.

And then I was wrenching at the wooden bar that held the door closed, my fingers slippery with sweat. There was

a bellow like an enraged bull behind me and just as I'd got
the bar lifted clear, his great hot hand seized me from
behind, spinning me round dizzily in the firelight. With a
grunt he threw me across the room and I fell on my back
on the bed, the breath forced out of me. He roared, purple-
faced, as he stood over me and raised his hands.

I closed my eyes and waited for the blows to fall, cringing
behind the blackness of my lids, braced ready for the pain.

The blows never fell.

The roar changed to a grunt and there was a kind of
muffled crash as something heavy hit the floor. I opened
my eyes, blackness merging into the red fire glow. There
was the figure looming over me still, but it had changed:
no longer bloated and slouching, but straight and lean and
bare-armed.

Macbeth MacFindlay.

In his hand he held a knife; blood was dripping from it
on to the bed's linen coverlet in thick, dark gouts. At his
feet, writhing hideously, was Gillacomgain's fat body, with
more blood spreading from the back of his tunic across the
splintery floor. Behind Macbeth the door was open, letting
in the light and the reek of a torch from a bracket on the
stairs. It threw his shadow, very long, across the bed. He
must have crept in unheard while Gillacomgain was
making so much noise himself.

'Lady Gruoch,' he said, as calmly as when he'd spoken
compliments at table, 'I mean you no harm. This,' he
nudged the convulsing body with his boot, 'is an old feud.
His death in return for my father's. I've no quarrel with the
house of Bodhe MacKenneth. If you'll accept my protection, I'll get you and your bairn out of the house before my
men fire the hall.'

Your protection, Macbeth! My heart was already in your
keeping and my life was yours to do with as you pleased.

Gillacomgain was still struggling horribly for life; one
hand groped through the pool of blood to clutch stickily at

the bed. I watched Macbeth kick away the grasping fingers, and smiled.

1996

Talking about that first meeting has reminded me. What it used to feel like when I knew I had Greg's whole, undivided attention. It was like a drug I used to crave. I never got enough of it and the doses he allowed me got smaller as our marriage went on.

However, I remember that two, maybe three, weeks after rehearsals for *Macbeth* began, we went for another of those blissful weekends at the cottage. Greg all to myself for two days!

I'd not seen much of him for the week before – his rehearsal schedule was much fuller than mine and he'd spent several evenings with an accountant friend who was investing money for him – or maybe he'd been seeing his agent. I can't remember; but he'd been out a lot. Anyway he came home on Friday evening with a vast armful of red roses – and Luke.

'We're going up to Oxfordshire for a rest,' he announced. In an hour I'd packed and we were on the motorway.

We had fun in front of the fire that night and the next day we walked under the big yellow hands of the chestnut trees that seemed to trap and magnify the sunlight with their brilliance. Luke was greedily stuffing his pockets with the glossy brown fruit.

I remember the smell of leaf mould and the shadow patterns that the dying leaves made across Greg's face. I remember how he asked, 'Are you happy, darling?' as we leaned against the massive trunk of a tree.

He pushed the hair back from my face, tucking it neatly behind my ears as if I was a child and I knew that what he was really saying was, 'Are you well?'

'I'm fine, Greg.'

'Really?'

I stared down at the mud and the golden fingers of the fallen chestnut leaves – and at his light-coloured, unsuitable shoes. 'Yes.'

'It's just that you seem to be struggling in rehearsals. You've not rushed back into work too soon?' Typically he seemed to have forgotten that he'd rushed me back into work. 'I don't want to see you fail, darling.'

'I'm not failing, Greg. It always takes me a little while to really get into a part.'

He smiled with relief. 'I do love you, Abby.'

Looking back now I get the feeling that was said more to convince himself than to please me. But I didn't think that at the time.

'Mum! Look what I've found!' Luke's voice rang through the trees, jagged with excitement and he came running towards us, chestnuts dropping from his pockets, sunshine dancing on his cropped brown hair. With a proud grin he held out his hands.

'Put that down, for God's sake!' barked Greg, but Luke just laughed.

I looked at what the hot, dirty little hands were holding and laughed too. 'Don't be silly, Greg. It's quite safe.'

'Put it down. You can't be too sure with snakes.'

'It's not a snake!' chorused Luke and I; we laughed again at Greg's ignorance.

'It's a blind-worm,' said Luke taking pride in using the slow-worm's old local name. 'It's not a snake, it's a lizard without legs. Look, you can tell by the colour – and there's no "v" on its head – you can tell it's not an adder. Go on, Dad, hold it.' Luke thrust the writhing strip of silver towards him. 'It won't hurt you.'

Greg flinched and I took it to save him from having to admit that he daren't touch it. I enjoyed the dry, silky feeling of it as it reared up through my fingers. I used to

find slow-worms for myself on the edge of the wood when
I was a little girl and I'd always liked them.

'Can I take it home?' said Luke.

'No, you know that's not fair,' I said. Luke and I have an
agreement about wildlife: look at it, enjoy it, then leave it
alone. 'Put it back where you found it, love.'

Reluctantly he took the silver coils from my fingers and
turned back to the sunny bank where the fields began
beyond the trees.

'Coward!' I teased Greg as Luke walked away.

He scowled with disgust. 'It's a horrible thing, whatever
you say.'

'It's harmless.'

'Is it?'

'Of course it is.' I leaned against his chest happily,
enjoying the sun's warmth and his closeness.

'What about the "blind-worm's sting" then?' he said
suddenly.

'What?'

'In the play.' He put his arm round me and whispered
against my ear:

> 'Eye of newt and toe of frog,
> Wool of bat and tongue of dog,
> Adder's fork and blind-worm's sting . . .'

'Greg!' I jumped away from him, crossing my fingers and
shivering in the sunshine. 'Don't quote from the play!'

'Now who's a coward?' He laughed, happy to be in
control again.

'I'm not a coward. But you know it's bad luck to quote
it.'

'That's a load of rubbish. How can a play be unlucky?'

'I don't know. But . . .'

'But what, Abby?' He took my arm, made me face him
and tidied up my hair again.

'But there's no point in tempting fate, is there?' I tried to smile.

'You've not been dreaming again, have you?'

'No,' I lied. The dreams had been coming fairly regularly in fact, but after that first time I didn't even try to talk to him about them.

'Good.' He grinned. 'Shall we make a truce then? You promise not to pick up any more snakes and I'll promise not to quote from – "The Scottish Play".' He used the euphemistic name with heavy sarcasm.

'Okay.'

We walked back to the cottage hand in hand through the patterns of sun and shadow. And it was that night that I first became aware of something – a kind of presence – haunting me when I said the words of the play.

I had stayed downstairs alone in the living room after Greg and Luke had gone to bed. I was working on my part. I remember how, stung by Greg's suggestion that I was failing, I was struggling to understand Lady Macbeth and the things she does. I 'd gone through the play quite calmly, reading by a desk light over the drift of slightly glowing ash that was all that remained of our fire. The room was still and the sound of the grandfather clock which had meas-ured out childhood evenings was comforting. Then I came to Lady Macbeth's final scene. You know, the famous sleepwalking scene. Lady Macbeth rambling wildly and guiltily about the murder of King Duncan: snatches of memory all confused:

'Out, damned spot, out, I say! One; two, – why, then 'tis time to do't. Hell is murky. Fie, my Lord, fie, a soldier, and afeard? . . . Yet who would have thought the old man to have had so much blood in him? . . . The Thane of Fife had a wife. Where is she now?'

I put the book down on the hearth and picked up my coffee mug, cradling it in my hands. Why is she rambling like this in her sleep? I wondered. I scowled down at the scraps of firelight playing across the gaudy colours of the book-cover. I remembered reading somewhere that sleep-walking is a way of acting out fears that are suppressed during the day. Well, that made sense. Lady Macbeth might well be afraid that the murder would be discovered and she wouldn't be able to talk about that when she was awake.

So far, I understood. But, you see, that's not enough for an actress: she's got to go deeper than that. Do you see what I mean? It was no good just understanding *why* Lady Macbeth was walking in her sleep. I had to know *how* she felt. You're looking blank again. If you're going to under-stand what happened to me, you've got to understand a bit about the job of acting. How can I explain this?

When you work on a role you have to use your own life, your own emotions. You turn inward and ask: do I know what this feels like? Have I ever felt anything like it? It's the only way of really getting inside the character you're playing. Well, those are the questions I had to ask myself that night about Lady Macbeth's sleepwalking.

I took a gulp of lukewarm coffee and I thought: what does it feel like to be unable to share your fears?

And I realized that I knew just how it felt. I remembered that morning under the sunlit chestnut trees, Greg's warm fingers straightening my hair.

'You've not been dreaming again?'

And the immediate, automatic lie.

I thought of the loneliness of not being able to share your deepest feelings with someone you love. I felt the desperate, painful loneliness of Lady Macbeth.

I picked up the book and read the words out loud again into the measured silence. As I did so, a feeling gradually grew upon me that there was someone or something there in the room with me, watching me. I turned round: just shadows, curtains and a bookcase of course. But I still didn't feel as if I was alone. There was something there in the room with me. I threw down the book and ran for the stairs, not stopping to turn off the light. But it seemed as if every step my feet made on the stairs was echoed by another. Afterwards, when I eventually told him about it, Greg tried to convince me that what I'd heard was just the sound of the clock; but I've known that clock for more than twenty years: I know what it sounds like and it doesn't sound like footsteps.

And those footsteps followed me to the door of my bedroom.

It was after that that I told Alan about feeling as if I was being watched when I worked on the part . . .

Greg? Ah yes, in the end I did tell him about it. I was forced into that.

I didn't want to talk to him about it. He hadn't wanted to know about the dreams and I was sure he'd not want to know about this. I managed to keep it from him for nearly a week. I said nothing to him, I got on with my job and he seemed reasonably happy. He didn't mention the dreams and he didn't seem to suspect anything. But then I panicked and told him about that feeling of being watched.

He came in one evening very pleased with himself and announced that he'd had a great idea. I thought that sounded like trouble even before he explained the idea. He wanted Luke to take part in the play – as one of the child actors who alternated the part of Macduff's son. I really felt I had to prevent that if I could. I didn't want my son involved in something that I was sure was ill-fated.

I tried not to upset him. I said something like, 'I'm not sure I like that idea.'

But he was very keen. 'Why not? What's the point of sending him to that school if we're not going to let him go on stage?'

So I tried to find neutral, ordinary excuses. 'I don't think it would be a good idea for him to be in something we're both performing in.'

'Don't see why not. The public would love it – the whole

family working together!' He was obviously intent on having his own way over this and I began to feel irritated. Stupidly, I told him about what I'd felt that night at the cottage.

He put his hands to his face and groaned. I can't even remember now if he said anything then about me being neurotic or ridiculous. He probably did. I know we had a serious row. One of our pointless, painful rows.

It started when he said, 'It needn't give you any trouble, you know, Abby. We can arrange for someone from the school to bring him over when he's needed and take him back afterwards.'

That was it: I was off. 'Trouble! I don't mind taking trouble over my son. I wasn't the one who wanted him to be a boarder.'

He covered his face and leaned back in his chair. 'Oh no, I don't believe this. I'm not going to get drawn into that old discussion, Abby. You know as well as I do why we agreed it was better for him to be away from home.'

I tried to control my anger. 'Greg, please, I don't want to argue about this.'

'Neither do I, Abby, there's no need to attack me so viciously. I just made a suggestion, that's all.'

'Well I don't think it's a very good suggestion.'

'Okay. Fine. I don't mind. I told Luke the final decision would be up to you.'

That was too much for me. 'Oh, that's typical!' I screamed. 'You've talked to Luke about it? You talked to him before you talked to me?'

'Yes.' His voice was still calm. I remember the room was infuriatingly full of his calmness. 'What's wrong with that? I'm allowed to talk to my son, aren't I, Abby? I asked him if he'd like to do it and he was keen. So I said I'd have a word with John but it'd be up to you to decide whether he could audition or not. That seems perfectly reasonable to me.'

'Oh yes, perfectly reasonable.' I hated the shrill sound of my own voice, but I couldn't stop it. 'Now it's up to me to disappoint him, isn't it?'

'But there's no need to disappoint him. Why can't he do it?'

'I've told you. I'm frightened of the play; I just don't want him to be involved.'

'Fine. Then you tell him so.'

'But Greg, I shouldn't have to tell him. He'd never have thought of it if you hadn't put the idea into his head.'

'This is pointless,' he said, standing up. 'I'm not going to discuss it if you're going to be so unreasonable.'

Of course, as usual, I gave in in the end. I just couldn't bear Luke's disappointment and Greg's resentment. Greg was pleased, Luke was ecstatic at the thought of working with his father and, as usual, I was left to feel how thoroughly unreasonable I'd been.

1606

Masters, don't be angry with me. I'm just a weak woman led astray by evil spirits. Doesn't the Bible itself say that all women are prone to sin like our mother Eve because of our weakness? I never meant to do wrong.

As I've sat here day after day in the stinking darkness, with only rats and memories for company, I've wondered a good bit about why I fell into such a great sin. Why was it the devil sought me out? And there's only one reason I can find. It's true what they say in church; some folk are born to be evil just as others are born into sainthood. And if any wench was ever born into evil it was me.

'The old ways,' Mother said, 'have been in our line longer than anyone can remember.'

Do you see, masters? The evil was in my blood. I was born into an evil line.

I understand now. It's as if understanding creeps up
through the stones of this cell with the damp and the cold
and the stench. All my life was tainted with evil; all my life
was leading me towards the cottage in Eldridge's Hollow;
to the room at the top of the stairs and the terrible thing I
did there. I was helpless; I couldn't fight against my fate
any more than Mother could.

She never meant to fall to temptation either, but the
taint was in her blood and she couldn't help it . . .

What did she do? What? Is it possible that you don't
know the things that happened in Berwick? That's sixteen
years ago it happened, true. But with our Scots King come
south to rule in England now, I'd reckoned the story must
have spread.

She too fell into deadly sin, but like me she'd no real
mind for it. If the man hadn't come and tempted her and
threatened us with cruel usage she'd never have done more
with the old things she knew than make a love charm or
say the words that keep the whooping cough away from
the cradle . . .

What, must I tell the story of her fall as well as mine?
She was tried and burned for what she did sixteen years
since. What purpose is there in telling over such an old
tale?

Well then, if I must I'll tell you all I know. It's done with
now and, guilty or not, they can't burn her again.

It was on an evening in early spring that the messenger
came from the Wizard Earl to play on her weakness and
tempt her to sin; raw cold it was, but with the daylight
lingering, and he came to our kitchen door, guided by the
little ragged crippled boy that begged by the forge. Well, a
fine gentleman standing there was a strange sight and at
first Mother spoke civil like, thinking he wanted the master
of the house. But, 'Nay, mistress,' he says with a great
flourish of his white hands. 'It's you I'd like to speak with.
Your neighbours tell me you have some strange skills.'

Well, that was common knowledge you see, always had been. Mother had a bit of a knack for finding lost things and curing sick beasts. And sometimes she'd make love charms for silly girls. Quite a name she had for that, though the truth is they were most of them no more than a pinch of salt or flour tied up in a twist of rag with a bit of ribbon.

But the strange thing was they often worked. I remember one kitchen wench that used one and got her master to wed her. She came back and gave mother a silver piece. Ah, we laughed over that afterwards.

'But it did work,' I said.

'Nay,' she said with her hands on her hips and her head back the way she stood to enjoy something really funny. 'Nay, it's more likely the advice I gave her with it worked. I told her to just trust in the magic and not be tempted to let him have what he wanted till she'd got him into the kirk.'

She was a merry soul, was Mother, and she told me that in the old days at my father's house no one had minded her magic much. She said that it was only after we got poor that folk started to say it was bad and to look sideways at us in the market place. If she so much as haggled with the cobbler over the price of mending my boots, he'd start muttering about the evil eye. 'When you're poor,' Mother said, 'folk start worrying you've got a grudge.'

So she'd got a bit wary about strangers asking questions and she wanted to shut the door on that fine gentleman.

'Nay, sir,' she said, 'I can't do aught for fine folk like you. It's just old simple stuff I know.'

'Indeed, mistress,' he said, talking quietly and looking none too friendly at me where I sat cleaning knives at the table. 'It's something old I've come about. Something very old.'

She looked at him a bit strange like, a bit worried. And her polite smile was sort of dropping away, taking her usual good colour with it. But she said naught. Just waited for him to speak again, door latch still in her hand.

And then he seemed to say something about 'sisters', but it was almost whispered.

I bent closer over my black hands but listened harder. I reckoned he must be talking about her five younger sisters back up in Glenlagan. I'd only ever heard of them like folk in a tale – Mother having left home to wed and never having made the journey back north to visit them. I wondered why this fine gentleman should be bringing her a message from them for I knew they weren't grand folk. My mother was reckoned to have married above herself.

I stopped work so even the whisper of scouring didn't get between me and what the man was saying. But he wasn't talking about Glenlagan. He seemed to be asking a favour of my mother.

'Your help is needed,' he said.

She dropped her hand from the latch and turned first to me and then to the fire. Her face was white and trembling. 'You'd better come in,' she said. 'I don't want my neighbours seeing you there and spreading more stories.' Her voice was all thin and strained as if she was frightened and pretending not to be.

As he took the seat she offered by the fire, he looked over at me. I took another pinch of ash and scrubbed hard at a knife.

'That's my daughter,' said Mother, sitting on a stool and fumbling with the spitted meat to hide some of her fear.

'Your only daughter?'

'Aye.'

'She knows then?'

'Not everything. She's just a bairn. She knows the words but not their meaning.'

'Time perhaps for her to know all.'

'I'll decide that,' said Mother sharply. 'The child's not too clever. But why have you come here?'

'To ask your help, mistress,' he said with another wave of those milky hands. In fact all the time he was talking, his hands flapped round him like a pair of witless pigeons. He spoke slowly, as if he thought his words were very precious, the way some fat men do.

'You know the spell, don't you? You know the curse of the weird sisters?'

'Maybe I do.'

'Maybe? What does that mean, woman?'

'It means I don't know who you are or why you've come here,' she said quietly. 'Why should I trust you? You're a strange messenger to come on the sisters' business.'

'That's true, mistress,' he said, courteous again. 'But perhaps you'll find you can trust the man who returns your property to you.'

He writhed in his seat and pulled out a leather purse that he'd hidden under his cloak. From it he took something and held it out to her.

Just then fat spattered on to the fire from the mutton and in the sudden flare of light I saw clearly what it was in the white cushioned hand. A brooch. Worn old gold with the outlines of three faces and three hunched figures traced faintly on it.

'You should not have parted with it, mistress,' he said. 'It belongs in your keeping. And in your daughter's.'

She looked from it to him, the red creeping back into her cheeks. 'My husband's creditors had not such delicate feelings,' she whispered hoarsely as she reached across the firelight to take it. 'They barely left the clothes on our backs.'

'Well it is back with its rightful owner now.'

'How did you find it? How did you know me?'

'I didn't,' he said and smiled. 'But my master did. He knows many things.'

She stared down at the familiar thing, running her finger

along its lines just as I had done as a baby. 'I am very grateful to your master. Who is he?'

The white hands flapped. 'For the present it's best I don't name him. But he's a great man, mistress. One of the greatest in the land.' He pointed to the brooch. 'How else would he know what that was?'

She nodded. 'What does he want from me in return?' she asked.

'Your help.'

'My help to do what?'

'Let's say he wants you to help him gain his inheritance.'

'Your fine, sly words are wasted on me,' she said, folding her arms squarely across her breast. 'You and I will speak plain; there's no one by to hear us.'

'Nay, mistress, some things are best left unsaid.'

'That's the way my man talked. He was a good man, but he managed his money affairs that fashion – promises half made that others could break when they pleased. And see where such dealings left me and the girl. I reckon plain speaking is better for womenfolk and if you and I are going to do business together we'd both better know what the other's about.' She nodded at the brooch in her hand and spoke as if the little carved faces were real women. 'Your master doesn't want their help to get himself a few dirty acres or a bit of gold. He is trying for the greatest inheritance in Scotland.'

The man squirmed and looked anxiously at the door that led into the merchant's chamber. 'Maybe,' he said in a very low voice. Mother sat in silence, arms folded: just like she used to do with me when I was small and unwilling to admit I'd done something wrong. I felt almost sorry for him; I knew what it was like to have the truth forced out of you by that silence and that stare. 'Yes, mistress,' he said at last, very reluctant. 'That's right.'

'Well then, and what does he want me to do?'

'Just a little information, mistress . . .'

'Nay, tell me exactly what he is about and what he wants to know, or you and I can do no business.'

The hands flapped – like birds trying to escape a net. 'My master is learned in the dark arts and he is gathering together women who have powers.'

'What kind of powers would these be?'

'Dark old things that are best not named.' He writhed under her stare, sweat greased his brow. 'Spells and charms. You know better than me, mistress, the powers that the devil gives to some women.'

'Brews boiled up at midnight, images made out of wax and such nonsense, I'll warrant!' Mother's lips curled up in a kind of grin, but not a kindly one. I knew it well: it usually came with sharp words. 'Aye, I've heard of such stuff and I know there are women in this town – and many of them reckoned good citizens' wives – who deal in such things. But they are not the old ways. Folk angry against the church think they'll try what the devil can give them since they don't much like the way God's treated them. The old ways are different; they've nothing to do with God nor devil, for they come from a time before either were named in this land.'

The man began to bluster. 'Call it what you wish, mistress, it is power and my master is after all the power he can get.'

She turned her face to the fire and busied herself ladling fat from the trough over the meat. She looked so much the housewife, so much the mother I'd always known. 'It's the words he wants, then,' she said quietly – as she might ask the old merchant if he wanted ale. 'He wants the curse of the blind-worm?'

'Yes.' The messenger leaned forward eagerly and perched his flying hands on his knees. 'And he wants the prophecy too.'

'Nay, the time's not come.'

'Ah, but it has, mistress. It has.'

'How do you know?'

'My master knows. He is a wise and learned man.'

'Maybe, but this,' she said, flushed from the heat of the roasting fire and holding out the brooch still clenched in her fist, 'this is older than learning.'

The man smiled, strangely gentle now, as if this house-wife bending over her joint of mutton was a fine lady whose favour must be courted. 'Indeed it is, mistress, but learning will recognize power for what it is, wherever it can be found.'

She shook her head. 'I don't know. I'd not thought to ever use the words any more than my mother did, nor her mother. The curse – and the story that went with it – were just something to be learned and remembered and passed on. Not used.'

'But they were entrusted to you for a purpose. You must know that.'

'But I doubt that purpose is the same as your master's.' she answered quickly. She seemed to make up her mind quite suddenly and she turned the silent stare on him again. He began to bluster once more, but I could see that she didn't like this man and, knowing her as I did, I was sure he'd lost his case. Once Mother had taken against a person she didn't soften.

He sweated under her stare and argued on till the merchant was calling for his supper, but I could see her mind was made up.

In the end he changed and got very angry. 'Mistress, you must and shall help us. I'd hoped my lord's kindness in returning your property would be enough to prove him your friend. But if you'll not believe him so, then we must prove that we can be dangerous enemies to you – and to your daughter.'

When we were alone I couldn't help but stare at her standing flushed and furious by the hissing fire. She had driven the pin of the brooch into the bodice of her rough

woollen gown and the pale gold showed strangely against
the thick blue folds instead of the bleached linen of my
memories.

'What did he mean, Mother? What does he want you to
do?'

She forced a smile. 'Long ago, Jennet, when those words
I taught you were first given to our line, we were told that
they were a curse that would one day be the undoing of
. . . of a great family. We must keep them safe till that time
comes.'

'But who, Mother? Who is it that's to be cursed?'

She paused, flushed red from leaning over the fire. 'Well,
I reckon you must know some time and, I'll say this for
you, Jennet, you're no prattler. You're not clever, but the
secret will be safe enough with you. It's the King's own
line the words were first spoken against. And one day
they'll be their undoing.'

She turned away, seized the spit from the flames and
wrenched the meat on to a board. 'But I'll swear,' she
grunted as she set a knife to the charred flesh, 'I'll swear
the words were never trusted to us for the use of such a
fellow as this, with his nonsense talk of the devil and spells.
That's not the way of the weird sisters.'

1996

I gave in to Greg. I played my part as best I could and kept
quiet about my fears. I even became hardened to seeing
dear little Luke act the part of Macduff's son. And he did it
very well. Most children, given the chance to be stabbed
and die on stage, will try to overdo it, but Luke was
marvellously professional about it – in my unbiased opin-
ion, of course!

Anyway, I carried on; I smiled and laughed when Greg
teased me about being superstitious. But deep down, I was

sure the play was dangerous. I just couldn't get away from the feeling that someone or something was watching me – like a ghost haunting the play. I tried to talk to other people about it, but the only one who seemed to understand was Alan.

He and I somehow fell into the habit of walking in the public gardens behind the theatre during breaks in rehearsals and there, among the ducks and the toddlers and Japanese tourists, I'd tell him how I felt about the play. Alan always seemed glad to get away from the rest of the company – he never seemed at ease in a crowd. And I found him a comforting companion.

He would never look disgusted or call me ridiculous when I talked about my fears; he'd run his fingers through his beard, smile and, above all, listen. Alan was an excellent listener. There was something very reassuring about his huge, dark bulk just looming over me – listening. I explained that it was partly my fear that was making it so hard for me to play the role and one day – probably in the third or fourth week of rehearsals – he produced an old red book with a cracked spine from the pocket of his leather jacket.

'I thought this might interest you,' he said.

We were perched on the ornate parapet of a small bridge beside a pair of Japanese tourists who were videoing the ducks.

'*The Life of Mrs Siddons*' I read, twisting my head to decipher the faded gilt letters. 'Why?'

He opened the book at a place marked by a trailing sliver of torn paper. 'This is her account of learning the part of Lady Macbeth,' he said and began to read aloud, '"I went on with tolerable composure, in the silence of the night (a night I can never forget), till I came to the assassination scene when the horrors of the scene rose to a degree that made it impossible for me to get farther. I snatched up my candle and hurried out of the room in a paroxysm of terror.

My dress was of silk, and the rustling of it as I ascended the stairs seemed like the movement of a spectre pursuing me."' Alan laid a blunt finger across the page, lowered the book and aimed a questioning look at me.

'Yes, that's how I feel when I say the lines. As if there's something there with me. Yes, pursuing me, I suppose.'

'Poor Abigail.' He touched my hand briefly. 'You're obviously sensitive like Sarah Siddons.'

I laughed bitterly at that. 'But nowhere near such a good actress. I think Greg's beginning to wish someone else had got the part.'

'Have you two argued?'

'A bit. We disagreed about Luke doing Young Macduff, but really the problem is me making a mess of my part.'

'You're not making a mess of it. Why must you always underrate yourself? You listen to Gregory too much.'

'What do you mean by that?'

'I've heard him. He's always criticizing your work: belittling you.'

'That's not true,' I said, stubbornly loyal. 'He's just worried about me because I've been ill.'

'Well anyway, you do underestimate yourself. You're very talented, Abigail. Mrs Siddons overcame her fear and went on to give a great performance. I'm sure you can do the same.'

I've thought a lot about Sarah Siddons since then – and about that spectre she felt was pursuing her. She seems to have got away from it.

Perhaps I didn't.

1606

Ah, masters, you are kind to let me sleep, even if it was only for a little while. And I think my mind is calmer for talking about the past. Those last days in Berwick come back strangely clear. I can remember even how I felt in the days that followed the coming of the messenger to our kitchen. Frightened, without knowing what I feared, so that everything that happened seemed to threaten us.

I lay awake at night on the shelf below the onions, watching the dying firelight on the scrubbed table and listening to the chain that held the smoking bacon in the chimney, creaking slowly like a gibbet in the hot draught. And I'd think about what she'd told me.

I'd think about the King as I'd seen him once, the time he rode through Berwick when I was just a little bairn. A fine figure he was, very stiff, on a horse that gleamed with good brushing and stepped very high; but I remember his face too. Too thin it was and sort of hollowed out at the bottom. It looked a bit like the face of old Dougal the water-cart man who used to have the toothache so bad he'd paid the smith to pull every tooth out of his head. But the King's face was smoother and cleaner than Dougal's. Everything about him was smooth and clean – polished up like the coat of his mare.

And I'd think about Mother with her brooch and how she knew strange old things that could harm that polished man on his fine horse. I'd reach out and touch the warm curve of her back and listen to the way she wheezed in her sleep.

Then I'd go to sleep and dream strange, muddled things about the King riding past our back door and Mother standing by with the basting ladle in her hand and shouting. And in one dream the stiff figure toppled suddenly off its horse as she shouted and she hit the hollow face with her ladle – though now the ladle seemed to have turned into a blind-worm that wriggled in her hands. I woke all sweaty and was glad to find her lying still beside me with the shadows of the onions moving slightly on her face.

The raw spring cold turned to driving rain and mud lapped round our threshold. Listening for the knock of the lord's messenger, I'd start every time the wind buffeted the door or spattered rain on the shutters.

'He must have given it up,' Mother said after a few days, her spirits returning. She was never one to stay cast down long.

But our fate was not so easily escaped. The fat man hadn't given up and we were to learn that he and his master were indeed bad enemies to have. We understood that very well by the time he came again.

Four, maybe five, days after his first visit, I squelched through the mud and rain to the cobbler's to get my mended Sunday boots and found the workshop all closed up. When I rapped on the shutters the yellow face of the cobbler's wife appeared at an upper window, grey strands of hair drifting from a cap pinned askew. When she saw me, her face twisted up in anger and she disappeared before I could speak.

A minute later she returned and flung my boots into the mud and filth of the road. 'Take them and get away,' she shrieked.

'What's wrong?' I asked helplessly, shivering on the stone step, my bare muddy toes curling round its edge in fear. 'Why is the workshop closed?'

The face leaned further out from the open shutters, hanging over me, thin jowls shaking. 'It's closed because cobbler can't work with his hands too weak to hold a hammer or needle!'

'What?'

But she'd gone and there was nothing for me to do but to pick my boots out from among a heap of cabbage stalks and night soil and make my way home. I noticed that the hole my growing feet had worn in the toe hadn't been mended.

Mother frowned at the dirty, unmended boots when I got home, but said nothing. Neither of us said anything about it, we just waited uneasily to see what would happen next.

We didn't have to wait long: next day was market day.

We went out early, there being spring cleaning to do in the house, and we reached the stalls before everywhere was crowded. But something was wrong; folk moved away from us as we passed and even the woman at the butter stall who always used to laugh with us and tease me about young men behaved strangely. She tried not to look at us as she cut the yellow pats and when my mother spoke, she turned away quickly to deal with a corner of the sail cloth that was dripping rain on her wares.

Mother was getting paler and she shifted the heavy basket on to an outthrust hip. 'Come on, Jennet,' she said, taking my cold hand in hers, 'we'd better get back home.'

The way between the stalls was narrow and dirty, with the covers spread over the goods dripping water on to the mud and dropped vegetables. We picked our way through as fast as we could, but just by the offal stall a figure appeared, blocking our way through the filthy alley.

She was a tall woman, a prosperous housewife dressed in a good yellow stuff gown with her market basket on her arm. At first we didn't recognize her face for it was all the wrong colour and shape. One eye was swollen and bruised purple and there was another, older bruise on her cheek that was going green. But she knew us.

'That's her!' she said to the offal man. 'That's the witch that the gentleman was asking about.'

'Aye, it is,' he answered, slow and heavy. 'It is; I know her. Got a sharp tongue and a wicked eye. The gentleman's right, those're sure signs of the devil's work in a woman.'

'She offered me a charm to make the men mad for me,' whined the woman to the gathering crowd that was starting to fill the narrow passage. 'But I said I'd have nothing to do with her wicked ways.'

'No, you didn't!' I cried angrily, for I'd recognized her

now. 'You had the charm and it got you what you wanted. You paid silver for it.'

Mother's fingers that were always so warm tightened their hold in the icy rain. 'Nay, child,' she said shrewdly. 'I don't think she did get what she wanted after all. No woman wants blows like that.'

The woman went scarlet behind the bruises and lifted her free hand to her face. 'I fell on the stairs,' she said. 'My luck's been bad ever since I had dealings with this woman.'

'And so has ours,' cried another voice. 'My poor man'll likely be crippled the rest of his life.' The gaunt figure of Mistress Cobbler pushed her way through a throng of ragged little boys that had gathered to watch the fun. 'Fit as a two-year-old he was until this witch came into his shop, wanting him to mend her brat's shoes for nearly nothing. When he said no, she put the evil eye on him. Hammer dropped from his hand straight away and he's not been able to lift his arm since.'

'That's a lie!' cried Mother furiously. 'He was still working when I left him.'

'But it's true, you did put the evil eye on him,' shouted the butcher.

'No,' she said, pulling me close against her hip. 'It's not true at all. The man's just ageing. His joints were swollen all winter.'

She didn't get any further because a great lump of filth and rotting butcher's-stuff hit her face. Very shocked, I watched the disgusting mass slide down her cheek and drop on to the hand that held her basket, spattering on the fresh white linen that covered her butter and eggs. The rest of the crowd watched it in silence too, horrified, but fascinated as well. I turned towards the grinning urchin who was standing, dirty hands already loaded for a second throw. I knew him; it was the club-footed boy that had guided the stranger to our door. I opened my mouth to

speak but before any words came a jeer rose from the
crowd and something stinking hit the side of my own head.

Mother pulled me round and, using her laden basket to
scythe a path through the grinning children, she forced a
way for us back past the butter stall. More stuff hit me,
some of it hard and painful, some horribly soft. A quick
look back told me that it wasn't only the urchins that were
giving chase; the whole crowd seemed to be after us. Even
the respectable matron with the battered face was stooping
to pick up something that had fallen from the fruit stall.

We got home breathless and filthy, with tears washing
clean channels down our faces.

'He did this,' sobbed Mother as she snatched the kettle
from the hearth and poured steaming water into a bowl.
'Ten years we've lived among these people and they've
never treated us like this.' She slopped cold water from the
pail by the door into the bowl and took up a cloth. 'Come
here, child, let me wash your face.'

'But why should he do that?' I protested through the
cloth.

'Oh, Jennet, bless you, surely even your slow wits can
see why. He wants to frighten me. If I don't do what he
wants then things'll go hard for me – and for you too.'

'How hard, Mother?'

She squeezed out the cloth as if it was the fat man's neck
and stared into the smouldering fire. 'Never mind that now,
Jennet. Take off your gown, it'll have to be washed.'

I didn't have another gown so I was wearing an old shift
that'd belonged to the merchant's dead wife when the fat
man came back that evening. He looked at me and at the
dress drying on the pot hook and smelling strongly of wet
wool. He seemed to know what it meant because he smiled
like someone who's got his own way.

'Well, mistress, have you changed your mind?'

Mother, her own dress still stained and damp where
she'd cleaned it and her hair washed and hanging loose to

dry, stared long and hard at him. 'What have you done to us?' she demanded.

'Didn't I warn you my master was a dangerous enemy?'

'The folk in the market all but stoned us.'

'That's unfortunate,' he said taking a seat unasked by the hearth. 'But think on it, mistress, it could have been much worse. They might have gone to your master with their tales of witchcraft. Indeed, they still might. He's a great man in the kirk here, I believe,' he added, spreading the white hands on his knees. 'I don't think he'd like the notion of harbouring a witch under his roof.'

'You're threatening us.' She ran her hands wildly through the clean, straggling hair. 'Look at us! I daren't let my girl out of the house.'

'No, I'm not threatening. I'm asking for your help. And offering help in return. If you're frightened to stay here, well, my lord is a generous man. If you give him the sisters' power, if you'll tell him what you know, he'll see you have enough money to take yourself and your daughter to another town. Enough money to start a new life of some kind.'

She put her hands to her brow and pushed back the tangle of hair. 'And if I still say no?'

'Well then,' he said standing up, slow and ponderous, 'I shall have to say farewell to you and return to my master.' He took two strides towards the door. 'I wish you well with your neighbours, mistress. I suppose if you do find yourselves homeless and penniless, your daughter's pretty face might earn some kind of a living for you both.'

His hand was on the latch when she cried out as if she was choking.

'Wait! Wait, damn you! You know I've got no choice.'

That was how she fell, masters. In the end she told him the spell – and everything else he wanted to know . . .

Nay, masters, I never really understood why the Earl wanted so much to get that spell from her. I only ever knew the words of it; I never knew what they meant. But I reckon there must have been a great power in those words.

Mother was a weak woman who knew powerful things. That's why she died. And that's why I swore I'd never deal in the ways of the devil. Never! In God's name I swore I'd never end the way she did! Squirming in the fire for the pleasure of the grinning crowds.

But there was no chance for me that carried the old taint in my blood, was there? No chance for one that was born a tare of Satan! And in the end the only difference that there'll be between Mother's end and mine will be that you English use the merciful rope, not the flames.

1057

By the time Macbeth and I had got down the stairs from my chamber and out into the yard, the whole house was in turmoil. The thatch of the hall was already alight. Figures ran blackly through the leaping light and the howling of the dogs almost drowned out the cries and the clash of weapons. Drunken and surprised though they were, Gilla-comgain's men were fighting furiously and they outnumbered Macbeth's followers.

'Your woman should be here with the bairn,' said Macbeth as we emerged from the dark stairwell, blinking in the sudden, lurid light. 'Take care!' He took my arm just in time to stop me stumbling over a fallen man.

As I stepped over the body, I caught sight of Morag, huddled against the wall by the gate; the red light was gleaming on her wet cheeks and the hands that clutched Lulach were shaking. The child, securely wrapped in a blanket, was mercifully asleep. Standing guard between them and the fighting men was the mountainous bulk of the one-handed servant who had stood behind Macbeth in the hall. He smiled when he saw us, his teeth gleaming against his great black beard, almost as brightly as the villainous knife that he held.

He gave a great rumble of laughter and barked something to Macbeth across the smoke and tumult of the yard. I missed his words because Morag was upon me then with her shrill, tearful welcome. By the time I'd silenced her, he was saying, 'I've got horses ready to carry away your booty, MacFindlay.'

'Mind your tongue!' said Macbeth and turned to me. 'Lady Gruoch,' he shouted over the confusion, 'there's a house not half a league away will shelter you tonight. If you'll go with my man he'll see the three of you safe.'

'Will you not come with us?' I asked.

'Nay, Lady, you'll be safe enough with me.' The voice of the huge fellow was very close to my ear and the din of battle kept his master from hearing it. 'MacFindlay is not the only one that'd give his life for you. It's not only him you've caught with your other-world charms.'

'Macbeth?' I moved towards him for he'd already turned away from us to the struggling figures in the firelight. 'Will you not ride with us?' I felt as if I'd rather stay there in the burning and bloodshed than go to safety without him.

He stopped impatiently. 'I've other business,' he said. 'You will be safe enough.'

'I know that, Macbeth MacFindlay.' Though the acrid smoke was cutting tears from my eyes, I felt quite calm. 'I'm not afraid if I have your protection. But,' I added simply, 'I don't want to leave you.'

He hesitated, one hand holding his great iron sword as if it weighed no more than a stick. He looked slowly from me to the raging battle, then he shouted to the servant, 'I'll bear you company, Seyton. The lady will ride with me.'

There was a snarl behind me like that of a cornered wolf and I turned to see the big fellow scowling as if he'd like to cut all our throats. But he obeyed the order. Morag was put on one horse with Lulach in her arms and Seyton walked

at its head, the reins looped over his maimed arm, his knife
in his hand.

And I rode out of Gillacomgain's stronghold with Macbeth: my flushed cheek resting against his chest and his
sword pressing on my thigh. As we rode away from the
battle I could feel his heart beating as well as the jolting of
the horse.

1996

John was worried about me.

In fact it would be more accurate to say that John was
worried about my performance, but instead of giving me
hell and a torrent of abuse such as he meted out to several
of the others, he obviously decided that the avuncular
approach would be more effective with me.

'You don't seem happy, Abigail.'

'I'm just tired.'

'You're not worrying about this silly curse business, are
you?' Despite the gentle tone and the plump hand patting
my arm, I knew this wasn't an invitation to confide. I was
meant to say no – or there'd be trouble.

'No, of course I'm not, John.'

'Good, good.' He beamed. 'Well my dear, if there's
anything else bothering you? Anything you want to talk
about?'

'No, honestly.' I tried to get out of the rehearsal room; I
knew Greg was waiting upstairs. But the soft hand weighed
more heavily on my arm.

'Just one more thing, Abigail. I think it might be as well
if you don't spend too much time with my friend Alan.'

'Why not?'

'Well, he's not very good with women. A bit shy, I
suppose. Lovely girl like yourself being too friendly might

give him the wrong idea. I don't want him ... well, disappointed, if you know what I mean.'

'No, John, it's you that's got the wrong idea. All Alan and I do is talk. That's all.'

'What about?' he asked suspiciously.

'The play.'

'Not the curse?'

'No, of course not.'

It was infuriating. No one except Alan was prepared to talk about it and now I was being told not to talk to him.

So I tried to find out what I could for myself.

I began to read everything I could find about the bad luck which is supposed to dog performances. I had plenty of time to do it. The strain of keeping quiet was beginning to show. I was getting anxious and nervous. And Greg was beginning to notice.

'It's not fair on Luke to let him see you in this state,' he said, making me feel that my unhappiness was somehow obscene. 'You know how worried he was when you were depressed last year. He's better off at school.'

So Luke would spend his weekends chasing a ball round the school playing field, Greg would disappear more and more on unspecified business and I'd be left alone in that tall grey house with its dead pretence of a garden choked by the heaviness of the crowded city air. In desperation I tried to find some explanation for what was happening to me.

I haunted libraries and bookshops – some very weird bookshops too – but I still couldn't find out much about the so called 'Curse of Macbeth'.

Have you researched it?

There's a lot about broken legs and bits of scenery suddenly falling on people for no apparent reason – or, more commonly, just missing people. There's a story that the boy who was to play the part of Lady Macbeth in the first production was taken ill, leaving Shakespeare to play the part himself. And there's a reliable account of an actor dying of injuries he received during one of the fight scenes. But there's nothing about a ghost that haunts actresses and, in everything I read, there's only one explanation offered as to why the play should be unlucky.

I read a book that suggested that it's the spell the witches use in the play which brings bad luck. Some people think that it was a real spell Shakespeare had heard witches use in the countryside around Stratford . . .

Ah, you've heard that idea have you?

No, I wasn't sure I believed it either. I still don't know if I believe it. But I was told, very definitely, that it's a real spell.

And it was a real witch who told me so.

At least she said she was a witch, though she didn't look much like one. She looked more like a retired headmistress really, with a tidy perm and spectacles hanging by a cord on a comfortable, knitted bosom. She'd found me furtively reading thin black paperbacks in the 'Occult Bookshop' that she seemed to own and she was quite keen to talk. She told me she was a witch within the first few minutes of our conversation.

'And how did you become a witch?' I asked in bewilderment.

Her pale brow wrinkled. 'Oh I didn't become a witch, dear. I was born one. You either are one or not. You don't choose it, you discover it.' She put on her blue-rimmed glasses and studied me as if she was trying to decide which category I belonged in: witch or non-witch.

It was then that I mentioned the play.

'Oh yes,' she said comfortably. 'It's a real spell, all right.'

'So do you really brew up potions with toads and bats and stuff like that?' It was hard to imagine her soft, beringed fingers tending a cauldron. The sign outside her shop said *Occult Books and Supplies*. I'd wondered what exactly the *Supplies* might be and had half-expected to find shelves of mummified cats and dried frogs, but in fact the place didn't seem to sell anything except books and great tangles of unattractive costume jewellery.

'Oh no, dear. We don't do anything like that. Whatever made you think we did?'

'Because that's what the witches do in the play.'

'Well, I assure you, I don't.' She eyed me sternly through the blue glasses. I felt like an impertinent schoolgirl. 'Have I seen you on the television?' she demanded.

'Probably,' I muttered.

The idea that she was speaking to someone famous seemed to soften her. 'When I said the spell was real, I meant that the words are real, dear. I didn't mean to suggest that anyone dismembers toads and bats.' Her lips pursed in disgust and I guessed she was an animal lover; I could imagine that she was a vegetarian with two or three cats at home. 'It's the words that are important. All the things the spell mentions have a meaning, you see. A symbolic meaning,' she added with heavy emphasis.

'What does it all mean then?'

'Oh dear! I can't tell you that.' She turned away and began briskly rearranging a stand of clanking necklaces.

I went home to read and reread the spell in an attempt to guess what its meaning might be. Bats, toads, dogs' tongues and blind-worm's sting. What could it all mean? Most of the stuff was perfectly harmless. And the sting of the blind-worm didn't even exist! I couldn't make any sense of it at all. But as I thought about it, I began to evolve some ideas of my own and I just had to talk to someone about them.

Of course, I couldn't mention the witch to Greg. God knows what he'd have said about me visiting an occult bookshop. So in the end I ignored John's warning and told Alan instead.

'She seemed very sure that the spell in the play is real.'

'I don't know about that,' he said dubiously. 'It doesn't really sound likely.'

'Why not?' We were in the park again and as we talked I watched the ducks being blown about the little lake. 'It's a perfectly good explanation – if you believe in spells, of course.'

'And do you?' he said.

'I have an open mind on the subject. What about you?'

He was silent for a while. 'Let's say for the moment that I do. I still find it hard to believe that Shakespeare put real witches' magic in.' He leaned back on the bench and stretched long legs across the gravel. 'Do you know the history of the play?'

'Yes, I've been reading about it,' I said defensively. The question seemed rather patronizing. 'I know it was written with a view to pleasing James I. It was 1606 and he'd only been on the English throne for three years, so all the London companies were trying to get in his good books.'

'Exactly.' Alan nodded smugly.

'Well, I've been thinking about it. Of course, James was very keen on plays. Having just come down from Scotland where the church frowned on drama, he really enjoyed the theatre. But he was also very interested in witchcraft, wasn't he?'

Alan nodded again. 'He wrote a book about it.'

'There you are then. What better than a real bit of witchcraft? A genuine spell. That'd keep the King interested in the play.'

'No, hang on, Abigail. You've got it all wrong. James didn't just have an academic interest in witches. He was terrified of them. Back in 1590 a party of witches in North Berwick had been burned for joining with the Earl of Bothwell – the so-called Wizard Earl – in an attempt to kill James through sorcery.'

'Yes, I read about that too, but I find it hard to believe

that he really thought they could kill him with spells and things like that.'

'You've got to see it in its historical context, Abigail. This was the seventeenth century. Most people believed in witches' powers. By the standards of the day, James wasn't overly superstitious. In many ways he was a sensible man.'

'You seem to know a lot about him, Alan.'

'I do. Believe me, Abigail, I know James I.'

He sounded so intense; I wished he'd relax a bit. I pushed back the hair that the wind was blowing in my eyes and grinned at him. 'A close friend of yours, is he?' But he wouldn't return my smile.

'Yes, in a way he is. I've studied him. He interests me.' He folded his arms and avoided my eyes. 'He was an able king really, you know. An intelligent man.'

'Intelligent? I can't agree with that. I've been reading about him. About the things he wrote – the things he believed!'

'Such as?'

'Such as women being naturally evil and inclined to witchcraft. He was taught a lot of rubbish about female beauty being a trap to men by the dour Scottish Calvinists and he seems to have believed it. Even long hair was wicked and dangerous – a snare to men's senses. Or something like that.'

'So he didn't like women. That doesn't make him stupid.'

'Are you trying to start an argument?' I laughed.

'No, I'm just saying he might have had good reason to worry about women. Women can be dangerous. Take these witches in North Berwick, for example. They really do seem to have meant to kill him. They confessed to it.'

'They were probably tortured.'

Alan edged away from me, pushing his hands into the pockets of his jacket and pulling it tight around him. 'They must have been nasty pieces of work anyway, these women the Earl of Bothwell gathered together,' he said with disgust. 'What kind of woman boils up cats and dead bodies?'

'OK, it's nasty. But look at it this way: it wasn't the witches that wanted James dead, was it? It was the Earl of Bothwell who put them up to it. He was James's cousin and he was trying to kill James so he could take the throne himself – it was as simple as that. It was his ambition that really caused the trouble. These poor women were just caught up in the power struggle between James and Bothwell.'

'There's no need to get angry about it, Abigail.'

'I'm not angry – well, not with you anyway. It just annoys me the way men blame women for things. After all, it wasn't some natural evil in women that threatened James, it was power politics. And that's a man's game: or it was then.'

'Yes, but you can't deny these women were prepared to join in. And the point I was trying to make was that James *believed* they were dangerous. You're right he was interested in witchcraft – but not in a comfortable, detached sort of way. It was too close to him. Did you know he talked to one of the women himself when they were brought to trial?'

'Yes, I know. She's supposed to have repeated something to him that he'd whispered in private to his bride on their wedding night. That's fascinating, isn't it? It's little details like that which make history interesting. Much better than all the usual stuff about wars and politics. What do you think she told him?'

He looked exasperated. 'What's that got to do with it?' he said. 'The point is this woman, Agnes Sampson, really terrified James.'

'What?' I laughed, 'just because she knew the royal chat-up line?'

This time he responded and a very grudging smile stirred in the depths of his beard. 'What I'm saying, Abigail,' he went on, 'is that he really believed he'd had a narrow escape from these witches. And James I was not a brave man. Shakespeare would have been crazy to include a real spell in the play. He'd have been risking a charge of treason.'

'Treason? Just writing a few lines in a play?'

'Oh yes. James was very touchy.' Alan had got that sort of euphoric look now that sometimes came over him when he talked about the past. It seemed almost as if history was a kind of escape to him. It overcame his awkwardness and put him on a high, like a drug. 'You've got to remember, Abigail, that those were violent, unsettled times. James himself managed to die in his bed; but his mother – Mary Queen of Scots – had been executed, and . . .' He relaxed and gazed across the park as if he saw the panorama of British history spread on the clouds beyond the ducks and the tourists and ice-cream booth. 'And Charles I was his son.'

'And he was executed too.'

'Exactly. So perhaps he had reason to feel a bit worried about his own safety.' He smiled at me more warmly. 'All I'm saying, Abigail, is that James was no fool.'

'OK, and all I'm saying is that he was a miserable chauvinist.'

He looked at his watch and we both realized that it was time to be getting back. As we hurried towards the blank brick wall of the theatre, I felt strangely exhilarated. I remember looking up at Alan and feeling very grateful to him. He was intelligent to talk to. He made me feel more confident – the whole business of the curse seemed less frightening and somehow more exciting when I talked to him about it.

I took his arm. 'Thanks for the argument, Alan. Don't take it personally, will you? I enjoy a good discussion and Greg's terrible. If I try talking about ideas like this with him, it just turns into a row.'

He pressed my arm closer to his side. 'Yes, I can imagine it would,' he said.

The conversation didn't really answer any of my questions; instead it seemed to set my mind working and produce a whole new set of questions. Why had someone as powerful as King James feared a collection of relatively powerless women? Why did the strong fear the weak? The witches in the play are weak really; just women in a world of warriors and battles. The only power they have is in their words.

My mind, stimulated by the discussion with Alan, began to work on the problem. It occurred to me that men often do fear women's words; I thought of how Greg hated it when I argued with him. And, of course, if you fear something enough it can sometimes be dangerous. That began to make me wonder whether the words of that spell might really have some power. In some strange way a belief in their danger might make them dangerous. After all something must have caused the play's bad reputation. Something had made it unlucky.

And something was affecting me.

1606

I know Mother didn't want to have anything to do with the Earl's man and those strange folk in North Berwick. She loathed the very thought of what they were about. I know that.

I've heard what the street gossips say was done. And in the churchyard too. Which Mother, I know, would have hated. She had always a great respect for the dead. And as for the rest of it, I could never believe she had any part in it. For people say – and the butter-stall woman told me she'd heard it from a man who was there at the trial – that they cut up bodies for their spells and threw live cats into the sea. I never saw Mother hurt a living creature and there was nearly always a stray cat warming itself on our hearth . . .

Aye, I know what it was all done for. She told me about it the night she got ready to join them. And she told me too how unwilling she was. How it was for my sake that she must keep faith with the Earl's man.

'The world's a hard place, Jennet. Harder than you know, and I reckon I must guard you from it. You're not fit to look after yourself.' She'd got a brisk, busy look about her as if she was planning to start baking, or beating the lice out of the mattresses. It was late and the merchant was abed. The meat and onion smell of his dinner still filled the kitchen but the fire had sunk down to a thick pile of grey over a few gleams of red. I was weary and I didn't like the way she was talking.

'I'm not simple, Mother.'

'I know, girl. But listen now. It's best you know what I'm about. I may not come back and if I don't, you must know the old things.' She stopped and ran her hands through her hair. 'I'd hoped maybe I could spare you from it. I thought maybe I could get back to Glenlagan and tell it to one of my sisters' girls. But my hand is forced now. I must pass it on to someone as I promised my mother I would.'

'But I know the words already. The words the Scottish Queen taught my grandmother.'

'Your grandmother? Jennet, it was longer ago than that. But let that be. There is something else you must do.' She sighed and pulled the brooch out of her gown. Then she sat for a moment, suddenly still in the middle of her busyness. She stared down at the brooch and the flat, round faces stared back at her in the dull fire glow.

A terrible thought came into my head. 'Must I make the spell?'

'What's that?' She roused from her thoughts and looked

at me crease-faced, like she looked when I got the kneading
of the bread wrong or let the meat burn on the spit.

'Must I boil the pot with the bat and the toad and . . .'

'Jennet, what nonsense you talk! There is no spell to
make, no pot to boil. Oh! I would the Lord had given me a
child with all her wits about her! It is words, girl. Only
words. Words with a meaning.'

'Are you not going to make a potion to kill the King?' I
whispered. 'Isn't that what the Earl's man has asked you to
do?'

'Jennet! You talk now like the foolish Earl of Bothwell
himself. Sorcery and pacts with the devil and such nonsense. Mummies and the fingers of hanged men. He and
the other fools he has gathered together believe they can
make storms by throwing rotten flesh into the sea.'

I shivered and crept across the hearth till my toes touched
the soft ashes. 'And can they?'

'No. Why, girl, butchers toss bad meat into the water at
the end of every market day. It does nothing but keep the
fish well-fed.' She scowled down at the old faces on the
brooch – rather as if they'd spoiled the dough, or let the
mutton burn. 'That's not how the old ways work.'

'But why does the Earl want storms?'

'Because,' she said, and the creases got worse, 'because
the King is gone to Denmark to bring home his new Queen.
The Earl would have him shipwrecked as he journeys back,
so he can take the crown for himself.'

'And he wants your help to make the storms?'

'There is one among the so-called witches that he's
gathered round him, by the name of Mistress Sampson. If
you and I are not to be stoned from our home, then I must
tell this woman the secrets that our family has kept for
hundreds of years.'

'The words about the toad and the bat and the blind-
worm?'

'Yes, and something else too. I must tell her the Stewart weird.'

I was about to ask what that was, but when I looked at her face it was so ploughed up with creases that I didn't dare. So I waited, listening to the shifting of the dying fire and the faint snore and splutter of the old man in the next chamber. At last she roused herself and leaned over me to drive the brooch pin into the thickness of stuff on my shoulder. 'You must keep this safe for now, Jennet,' she said. 'And you must know this too.

'Long ago that Queen of Scotland who taught the old ways to our Grandam saw in a vision the fate of the Stewart line. A bad fate. Since then every Stewart heir has known it. Every woman that the head of the Stewart clan takes to bed is taught it so she knows the fate that might fall on the children he gets. And every eldest son is taught it when he comes of age.

'But outside their clan, only we have known it. In every generation, one woman in our family has known it.'

'You know it?'

'Aye. And you must know it too, Jennet. I wish it wasn't so, for it's a bad thing to know. Many times they've tried to find and kill the woman who holds the secret. It's a shameful weird that they want kept hidden.'

I was shaking a bit and I remember I asked her not to tell. I put my smoke-blackened hands over my ears. But she told me all the same. She said she must keep faith with the old ways.

Masters, I didn't want to know the fortune of the King's line. And surely just knowing what's ill can't make me bad. I've never wished harm on His Majesty or any of his kin. Nor Mother neither, for that matter. If the Earl's man hadn't threatened us, she'd never have gone to join those bad folk in the churchyard at Berwick.

I don't want to die like she did in front of the grinning crowds, masters. The things she called 'the old ways' have

led me into a great sin. But that was years later and it had
naught to do with that terrible business in the churchyard,
I swear.

I want to confess all, masters. If you'll spare me, I'll tell it
all. I'll even tell that secret weird that she told me I should
repeat to none but my own daughter. I'll tell all.

Listen, it was a strange fortune for a Royal house. But it
was a true one. For half of it is fulfilled already and Mother
said the rest must happen soon . . .

But sir, I want to tell it. I want to confess all and have a
clear conscience . . .

Nay, I beg you, don't be angry with me. If I must be
silent, I shall. If it's His Majesty's will, I'll go to my grave
never speaking the thing she told me that night.

Have mercy on me and I'll speak or be silent, just as you
please.

1996

The questions kept bothering me and eventually drove me
back to the shabby little shop filled with black books and
bangles. I don't think there can have been many customers
there because the headmistress behind the counter recognized me before the cow-bell on the door had stopped
tolling.

'Hello again, dear.' She strode towards me bringing with
her a crisp calm smell of lavender that cut through the
heavy musk that scented the shop.

Feeling compelled to buy something, I turned to the
nearest shelf and chose a dark volume at random. 'I
thought I'd like to read this.'

'You'll like that, dear.' She took it in a plump white hand
and turned back to her till. The gold title on the black cover
read, *The Goddess Inside Us All*.

'You know what you told me before – about the spell,' I began abruptly as I fumbled for my purse.

'Yes, I remember.' A flush crept up her soft, powdered cheeks and I got the feeling she was worried that she had said too much.

'How does it work?'

She frowned. 'It's a spell, dear. That's how it works.'

'Why should it bring bad luck?'

'Because that's its purpose.' She hesitated before dropping my book into a bag (recycled paper, I noticed). 'Part of its purpose at least,' she added.

'But how does it do it? It's just words.'

She gave me a long, unsettling look. Every inch the headmistress. I noticed how her lips pursed, showing up the face powder that clung to the fine hairs round her lipstick. I felt about ten years old. 'I thought you said you were an actress.'

'I am,' I said humbly.

'Then I would have thought you'd know about the power of words.'

And, of course, she was right.

You don't understand; I can tell by the look on your face.

Well, just look around you. Look at this stage. Apart from that ghastly bloodstain, nothing here is real. Nothing. Look at all this stuff: a blunt sword that couldn't cut jelly, with jewels made out of coloured – God knows what – I don't think it's even real glass; a mass of red plastic tubes that are supposed to be guts. It's all fake; all false. But when we step on to the stage it all has to become real. The audience out there who've made their journeys and bought their tickets have to believe in the world here on the stage. They have to care about it.

And all we have to bring it to life with is words.

It's words which hold the magic. It's by saying our lines that we become – for a while at least – the characters we portray. It's words that somehow raise the ghosts of those characters to walk the stage as if they're real. It's through the lines we begin to feel the joy – to suffer the pain – of the characters we play.

Words certainly worked powerfully on me. In the end, the character of Lady Macbeth became hopelessly entwined with my life; on that terrible first night it was impossible to tell where Lady Macbeth ended and Abigail West began.

But looking back now, I can see that there were moments in the weeks leading up to that night that were touched by the same confusion: moments like that time at the cottage, when Lady Macbeth and I drew dangerously close together; when it was hard to tell her feelings from mine. It would happen quite suddenly, usually when I least expected it. It happened once when a group of us were just talking, down in Greg's dressing room.

Have you been downstairs to see the dressing rooms?

Just a row of impersonal doors in a black corridor – none of the stars and glamour people always imagine. I notice Greg's room's still got his name on a bit of curling card pinned to the door. Well it was down there among the costumes and the photographs and the plastic coffee cups that some of us got talking one afternoon about the women in the play.

'Lady Macduff has to be a really attractive contrast to Lady Macbeth,' enthused Greg. 'Her motherliness and loving behaviour are the complete opposite of Lady Mac-beth's ambition and evil.'

'Oh yes,' simpered Chrissie smugly, as if eagerly taking to herself the virtues of her character. 'That's what makes Macbeth's murder of her and her dear little boy so terrible.'

She's small, is Chrissie; fair and rounded with a sort of hazy glow of prettiness and the eyes of a stray kitten looking for an owner. Right now she was looking at Greg as if she wanted him to take her home and give her some milk. (Or give her *something*, at any rate.) Nothing so strange about that, though, in fact all three witches were looking at him in pretty much the same way – even Jo; she's the leggy one with short red hair and half a dozen bits of gold in each thin, lobeless ear.

When you love a man like Greg you get used to seeing yourself mirrored in other women's eyes. I'd think: that's how I used to look, in the early days. But it never got any easier. And this time as I watched him stretch lazily back in his chair, his narrow face lifting into that smile – you know, the one that looks so good on screen – as I watched him, something new happened to me.

'But Lady Macbeth is loving,' I blurted out, surprising myself. 'She's fascinated by Macbeth, obsessed by him. It's for him she's ambitious, not herself. She just wants to make him happy.' Just for a minute, sitting there in the dressing room, watching Greg hold court, I felt closer to understanding the character than I had in weeks of work. 'But it's a weary, bitter kind of love,' I tried to explain as their eyes all turned on me. 'It makes her feel weak and helpless.'

'Hardly helpless,' protested Jo. 'She's too sexy. She uses that to get him to do what she wants – to murder the King.'

'And she's got a powerful tongue,' said Greg. 'She attacks him really viciously. It's verbal castration – "you're not a real man if you don't do it".'

'Yes, she has words,' I said. 'They're the only power she has got.'

'Well, her words are enough to make him a killer,' argued Greg.

'No,' I said quickly. 'She doesn't make him a killer. He's already a killer in the first scene.'

'Don't be ridiculous, Abby,' he said, the smile slipping away. 'That's battle, not murder.'

'Is it?' I had a feeling that Lady Macbeth didn't understand the difference, but I couldn't say what I thought with Greg looking so irritated.

Already the moment of revelation was fading and, try as

I might, I couldn't get it back. But the sense of her presence lingered; I just didn't seem able to get rid of it.

That was the day I saw ... I was going to say, the day I saw the ghost, but that doesn't really sound right. The truth is I don't know exactly what I saw. Just a figure, really. And maybe, after all, it was only Jo or Meg.

We'd all gone back to work after that conversation in the dressing room. I think perhaps it was the first attempt to do a complete run-through of the play and we were here on the stage, not in a rehearsal room.

The scene-builders must have started work because though most of the set was still just chalk marks on the floor, there was a strong smell of newly sawn wood, I remember. It's a smell that always reminds me of that day now. There were problems with the lighting too; it tended to be too strong. Greg had complained loudly about it in his scenes and by the time I got on stage John was irritated and sulky. I didn't like to ask to have it changed again, but it was bothering me. I was struggling not to narrow my eyes. And the sides of the stage seemed black to me. Great caverns of shadows.

I went through the beginning of my first scene – reading from Macbeth's letter, to the point at which Lady Macbeth looks up from the letter and declares her wholehearted support for her husband's ambitions.

'Glamis thou art, and Cawdor, and shalt be
What thou art promised.'

As I spoke the words, I recalled that moment in the dressing room: the sense of a woman lost in the needs and desires of the man she loved, unable to consider anything but this one larger-than-life person who dominates her existence.

It was at that moment, as I looked out of the sickening light into the shadows, that I saw a figure, grey against the blackness, move: move as if it was taking a step towards me.

Shock jarred through me and stopped the words in my mouth. It – or rather she, for the figure seemed to have long hair and a loose kind of dress – raised a hand and beckoned to me.

'For God's sake, Abby, what's wrong?'

John's voice from the auditorium seemed to come from a great distance, echoing as if down a tunnel: very little words, bouncing through emptiness.

I opened my mouth and tried to speak as her hand moved, very white in the shadows, but it was like the dream: no sound would pass my lips.

And then, I suppose, I fainted.

The next thing I knew was Jo holding my head between my knees with a firm hand on the back of my neck.

Struggling up, I saw John's broad cheeks tinged with pink. 'Whatever happened?'

'I don't know. It was really strange.' I rubbed at my aching eyes. 'I thought I saw . . .' I stopped as the faces round me came into better focus and I saw Greg. His cheeks were sort of hollow, drawn in, and his eyes were narrow. He looked . . . disgusted. That's the only way I can describe it. As I crouched there on the floor with people bending over me and my wet eyes smarting, I felt I was doing – and saying – something utterly revolting.

'I think the lights must have made me dizzy,' I said lamely.

1606

So, masters, what is it that you'd have me confess now? Tell me and I'll do it. Anything to win back to the straw and sleep. I'll speak and that fellow who's settling back into his place in the sunlight, he can use scribe's magic on my

words: holding them in the ink he's brewed, sending them
into the future . . .

Mother? Aye, I know she used that spell, those words
about the toad and the blind-worm. And I know how she
used them.

'She plotted to kill His Majesty the King through an old
curse that was worked against his line years ago.' That's
what the sergeant at the gate of her prison told me the
night before they burned her. He was a rough-faced man
with an old scar splitting his nose, but his voice was quite
gentle. 'I should get yourself away from here,' he said. 'I
can't let you in to see her and you'll do yourself no good. If
you're seen here folk might start to ask what you know of
the business.'

'But I know nothing,' I wailed. 'And I don't know what
to do or where to go.' It was a wet night and the rain was
running from the roof, stabbing coldly through the shawl
on my head.

'Know nothing? Why girl, no one's going to believe that!'
said the man, dark in his fire-ruddy doorway. 'Folk are
saying that your mother was a powerful witch that knew
terrible secrets about His Majesty. Things that made him
pale with fear when he heard them.'

I shivered and snuffled, shifting my feet in the slime of
the street as the rain dripped from my nose. The man
reached back and pushed the heavy door further open so
that more of the red light fell on me. He looked at me, from
my bare muddy feet in the wet street to the sodden shawl
from which water oozed down the sides of my face.

His face seemed to be fighting with itself. His lips twisted
back as if he was disgusted, but his eyes were bright and
interested with that sly look to them that I'd noticed men
giving me since my breasts began to grow.

'They say you're a witch too. Is it true?'

'No.'

'Then what are you doing here? Don't you know the

King's likely to send out looking for you? If you're innocent you should get right away. Why don't you go south? Go somewhere no one knows you.'

'But I've got nothing. No money.'

The man didn't answer straight away. His face did battle with itself a bit more. Then he stepped out of his watchman's room and looked to right and left. It was late and there was no one by: just the rain making channels in the rutted mud of the street and a lame dog skulking in the shelter of the opposite wall. His face twisted up sideways, showing his teeth in a half-smile on the unscarred side of his face. 'Come in a bit then,' he said. 'Perhaps you can earn yourself a silver penny . . .'

Afterwards I took his advice and ran to England. And if I did sometimes earn a penny or two the way he taught me that night, it was only to keep myself from starving. Mostly I worked honestly – in other folk's fields and kitchens.

Until the devil came and changed my life.

1996

No one would talk about the Curse of Macbeth in the theatre. In fact most of the cast were very reluctant to talk about it at all, but tough, practical Jo was prepared to give a terse account of her own feelings in the bar of the Blue Dragon.

'A real spell, you think? Yes, I'll go along with that.' She peered thoughtfully into her pint glass, then nodded abruptly. 'Yes. It feels bad when I say it.'

'How do you mean, bad?' I found I was whispering. It was early and the place was almost empty. When the day's rehearsal ended it'd fill with resonant voices and egos, but at the moment there were just a couple of salesmen, looking ludicrously young in unbecoming suits and watching Jo and me curiously as if we were some strange species of wildlife they were observing in its natural habitat.

'Just bad. It feels like something you shouldn't say. Like rude words when you were a kid. You sort of expect something terrible to happen when you've said it.'

'What sort of terrible thing?'

'I've no idea. But I always keep a crucifix handy.'

'I didn't know you were religious.'

'I'm not. But it's best to be careful. I carry a clove of garlic too.' She spoke as if it was part of a tool kit, or a spare gallon of petrol in the back of her car.

Encouraged by her matter-of-fact attitude, I asked, 'Does it feel as if someone's watching you when you say the words?'

She frowned, furrows gathering under the spikes of red hair. 'No,' she said slowly. 'No, I don't think so. I don't see what you mean. Who could be watching?'

I shrugged and tried to look unconcerned, then mentioned the word 'ghost' as casually as I could.

'No. I don't know anything about ghosts. All I have is this feeling that something might go wrong at any moment.'

I gave up then. I think that was probably the last time I tried talking to anyone about what was happening to me – except Alan, of course. In fact Jo and I didn't have the chance to talk any more that evening because just about then the others began to arrive. And, since that was the day that Tony had been hurt, there wasn't any more time to talk about ghosts.

I remember Tony was being brave in a rather self-conscious way. 'It's not much really,' he said, cradling his injured arm as he sat down opposite me and gave a tight smile.

Tony plays – played – Macduff in our production. He was boyish. Good-looking I suppose, but in a strangely unsexual way.

'When did it happen?' I asked.

'The last scene. In the fight between me and Gregory.' He glanced at Greg, then away quickly, as if suddenly very interested in the gas parody of a log fire in its pristine grate.

Alan, clutching a whole round of drinks between his massive hands, stared at the crisp layers of bandage on Tony's arm, through which one tiny spot of red was seeping. 'I don't understand how it happened,' he said. 'What were props doing giving one of you a sharp knife? I thought all the daggers were supposed to be blunt.'

'Mine has to be sharp,' said Greg impatiently, taking his glass from Alan's hands. 'I have to lunge for Tony with it, miss and get it stuck in the floor. It's perfectly safe. He just didn't move the way he was supposed to today.'

'It wasn't Greg's fault,' chirped Chrissie beside him. 'I was watching closely and I know.'

I saw Tony's hand clench on his glass and his lips thin as if he was keeping them closed with difficulty.

'Well,' I said brightly, 'thank God it wasn't any worse. Poor Tony!' I leaned across and put my hand on his uninjured arm. 'Does it hurt much?'

It's interesting that as we sat there looking at that bright new bandage with its minuscule speck of blood, no one mentioned the Curse of Macbeth. But I'm sure we were all thinking about it. And I remember Alan making one of his awkward, unwelcome remarks.

'It's dangerous, having sharp knives around in a theatre,' he said, squeezing on to the crowded bench. 'There could be a much more serious accident if it got mixed up with the others.'

There was an uncomfortable silence and I noticed Jo edge away from him.

1606

Ah! The devil, he is handsome. Very handsome. Not in a way that men would notice, but in a way to weaken women's hearts. He has deep eyes that see things hidden to mortal men and a smile that'd make a virgin saint lift her skirts. Very fine he is in his blue coat with his ring of gold on his finger and such words come out of his mouth as can make a woman believe that heaven has come on earth. Aye, and that she alone is Queen of that heaven.

Ten years I'd been settled in England, in the cottage down at Eldridge's Hollow and though I'd grown herbs and made brews the way Mother taught me, I'd hardly thought on the curse or the other thing since she died. Then one harvest time when I was working in Master Rigg's fields, the devil came to me in the heat of the afternoon and called to me by name. He talked sweet things till I was alive with laughter and then he begged a drink of the ale bottle and I got it for him from its cool hollow under a dark hedge of holly. I handed it over smelling of earth and stone and last year's barley. It was scorching dry harvest weather and the dust of the road was lying on his lips as they smiled slowly in his handsome beard.

'Bless you, Mistress Jennet,' he said when he'd drunk and turned aside to put the jar back in its place.

That was a big field I was gleaning in, but there were other folk not so very far away tying up the sheaves. I remember how their coats were lying there by the hedge and I could hear old Margaret singing shrilly. None will say now that they saw him, then or any other time; but I swear to you that he came in the shape of a man, with a real grey horse that stood blowing hotly and tugging at the grass by the road all the time we talked. And I swear it would have taken a cleverer woman than me to know him for what he was then.

As he put the bottle back under the hedge, we both saw,

on the bank below, a blind-worm sunning itself in loose coils, lying still and silvery in the afternoon sun, the way they do, with ants crawling willy-nilly across its gleaming body.

'Nay, master, don't harm it,' I cried and caught the sleeve of his blue coat. There'd been three killed by the scythes that day and I hate to see any creature suffer for naught.

He smiled down at my hand on his arm. 'Why you've a sweet kind heart as well as a pretty face. Much too fine a lady to be gleaning!'

He stooped down by the coats and, moving slowly, not to frighten it, he picked up the snake. It was a strange thing to do. There wasn't another man in the harvest field that would have done anything but cut it in two while keeping clear of its flickering tongue.

But the stranger held it in his lovely white hands and seemed to know how to handle it. For it's not easy to hold a blind-worm: it's stiff and limp all at once. It'll rise up through your fingers one moment, then drop and slide away the next. But he understood its way. He held it firmly and let it rise up lewdly between us.

'You know the secret of the blind-worm, don't you, Jennet?' Then he explained what he meant by holding his hand to the creature's forked tongue and smiling broader than ever.

I laughed and, to show that I too knew it was harmless (and to tease him a bit) I bent over the thing erect in his hand and I touched my lips lightly on its head. As I looked up he was smiling at me in a bold way.

'So prettily done,' he whispered. 'I see you're a lady with more than a lovely face and a soft heart. Won't you treat me as kindly as the worm?'

Just then the creature rose up higher in his hands and we both laughed out loud – it had such an obscene look there between us.

I was weary with work and loneliness and his eyes made

me feel so beautiful and I liked laughing with him. I slipped my fingers round his and stroked the worm's head.

After that he used to come to me sometimes . . .

Nay, I don't know from where; from London sometimes, I think. I asked him, but he only said he was a gentleman travelling between his properties. I didn't much care where he came from. But I was always glad to see him.

When it comes to pleasing women, I think the devil knows things that God withholds from mortal men.

1996

Lady Macbeth changed me. She gave me a kind of strength.

Did you know that Plato thought actors became corrupted by the bad characters they played? I remember reading that when I was a student and thinking it was a ridiculous idea. But after a few weeks of rehearsing I began to wonder whether the character of Lady Macbeth might really be exercising a malign influence over me.

The confusing thing was, it was exciting too: that feeling that I was close to really understanding her – perhaps better than any actress ever had before. To be honest, part of me longed for those moments when she seemed to take over my whole being.

I remember one particularly exhilarating experience that happened a few days after Tony's accident. Oddly enough it all started with my lucky pendant – the one I always wear on stage.

We'd started the day rehearsing my early scenes, but about mid-morning I'd finished and I'd gone along to wardrobe for a fitting of my costume. I'd taken the pendant off so it didn't get in the way during the fitting and I'd left it hanging on the mirror in my dressing room. When I came back about half an hour later I was rather annoyed to find Alan hunched up in my chair with the pendant in his big paw of a hand. I could see his face in the mirror and he looked excited; above the bulk of beard, where the black hairs streaked his cheeks, he was flushed.

'Abigail, what is this?' he demanded as I walked in.

'Something my father gave me,' I said, holding out my hand for its return. He made no move to give it up.

'But what is it? What's this design in the middle of the pendant? It looks like three faces.'

'Why do you want to know, Alan? What's so exciting about it?'

'Things like this interest me.' He smiled at me in the mirror. 'Go on, Abigail, please tell me. I tell you the things you want to know about the play, don't I?'

'Yes, I suppose you do, Alan. But, to be honest, I don't know much about the thing.' I leaned over his shoulder to trace the outline of the design. 'These circles do look like faces, don't they? And you see the bits round here, I think they're the hoods of cloaks, but they're very old and worn. I've never been able to make it out properly.'

'Where did it come from?'

'The bit with the design on was found under the stone flags of the cottage when they lowered the floor level. My father had it mounted and made into a pendant for me. It was my "something old" when I got married.'

'It is very old.'

'Yes, we thought it might be as old as the cottage.'

'Older, Abigail. Much older.'

'Do you think so?' I was surprised. You know how it is with something very familiar: you forget to think about its origin or history. It's just yours: a part of your life. It was rather disturbing to see him staring intently at my pendant and telling me things about it that I didn't know.

'I've seen something like it before,' he said. 'Carved on a stone in Newcastle Museum. The three figures are probably mother goddesses.'

'And do you really think they're the same?'

'I'm pretty sure.'

'How strange! How old do you think they are, then?'

'The stone dates from the period of the Roman Occupation. But the goddesses are certainly native British, not Roman.'

'Goddesses,' I repeated, rather uncertainly. Goddesses on the necklace Dad had given me! It seemed ridiculous.

'Or witches perhaps,' he said and for the first time since I'd come into the room, he turned his head to look directly at me. 'Is this what you draw your magic power from, Abigail?'

I laughed, but then I saw in his eyes what kind of power he meant. He was looking at me in a way it was impossible to misunderstand.

'You cast a powerful spell, Abigail,' he said.

Because he was sitting down, for once he was looking up instead of towering over me and there was something doglike and hopeful in his heavy face. John was right, I thought, he has misunderstood my friendship.

'Thank you, Alan.' I hoped my voice was discouraging but friendly. I took the warm gold out of his hand.

And then it happened again.

Without warning, she suddenly drew near to me. Abigail West blended into Lady Macbeth and, for an instant, her time and mine were one. That's one kind of power I have, I thought as my hand closed round the pendant, clasping the strange old figures. At this minute I have tremendous power over Alan. This was the strength she had and it was what she used to carry out her plans. And men – strong men to whom killing was a way of life; men who were used to being the ones in control – called her evil because she used the little bit of power she'd got.

1057

You see girl, I found a kind of power the night Gillacomgain died.

No, stop that! I can see your skinny little fingers wrapped in your shawl making the Christian sign. You don't need the Christ to protect you. If this was an evil power, it was one that could harm only men.

That was a strange night. Smoke and ruddy flames boiled over the black walls of Gillacomgain's stronghold, raising a foul stench in the mild summer air, and the moon, almost full, hung low over the sheep-bitten turf as the horse on which Macbeth and I rode slithered and stumbled down the steep path from the gates. Ahead of us I could see Morag hunched on the other horse, with the huge, broad-shouldered servant walking at her side.

'You are very quiet, lady,' said Macbeth when we'd reached the bottom of the rattling track and turned silently on to heath, long-shadowed and silver under the moon. 'Are you grieving?'

'No.'

'He used you ill?'

'I believe so.'

'That's a strange answer, Lady Gruoch.'

'But it's all I can give now, Macbeth MacFindlay. He's all I've ever known. Till I know what it is to be well used by a man, I can't answer your question.'

I felt his chest heave with laughter under my cheek and I stole a quick look up into the dark face that hung over me. His mouth was drawn back in a thoughtful smile. Just for a moment I thought he looked like a man at market who thinks he has seen goods at a bargain price and wonders whether to risk his money.

'The night's getting colder,' he said, 'and you've only your gown to cover you.' He drew his plaid over us both and held it round my shoulders while he managed the horse with one hand. The wool smelled of peat smoke and of horses and of him. I pressed like a contented child into its warmth.

As I did so, I heard a shout from the fellow in front and saw Macbeth's long brown hand tighten instantly on the reins. Looking out from the shelter of the plaid, I saw that a gaunt figure, grotesquely shadowed by the moon, had appeared before us on the narrow sheep track at a place where a few stunted trees writhed against the sky like ugly dancers. Already the maimed man had dropped the reins of Morag's horse and seized hold of the bedraggled creature.

'What's this?' shouted Macbeth over my head.

'A woman, I think, master,' said the fellow, pulling a ragged bit of shawl off the prisoner's head and pressing his knife to her throat.

'A woman with a beard!' mocked Macbeth. 'Nay, hold your hand, Seyton. I think the Lady Gruoch would have the crone spared.'

Without really knowing what I was doing, I'd taken hold of the hard, bare arm that encircled me as I realized who the ancient woman was. She was the only soul in Moray beyond Morag and my child whose life I cared about. 'She's a wise woman who lives in a cave yonder,' I said. 'She's brewed stuff for me.' I leaned my head against his arm and stared into the shifting shadows of his face. 'Stuff that made the blows hurt less.'

'Let her go,' he ordered, but his face twisted in distaste as he spoke, as if he'd found a toad on his bread. And the hand that held the reins moved in the shape of the Christian cross. The one-handed fellow dropped the knife unwillingly.

'Bless you, Macbeth,' whined the woman. 'You are a man who deserves his good fortune and you have done a fine night's work here.' She nodded towards the burning tower behind us. Black smoke was belching over the walls now, carrying gobbets of smouldering stuff with it; screams and shouts and the clash of weapons reached us very thin on the night air. 'For see, you carry away from Gillacomgain's broch not only your father's title but the Crown of Scots too.'

'What?' I felt his body tense behind me. He was like iron. 'How do you know this?'

'She has strange knowledge,' I said eagerly. 'She reads the future in men's faces.'

'Yes, Lady Gruoch,' she whined, 'I have some power. But I think the one who bears the faces of the weird sisters has more. Ah, she has much to offer the man who can win her!'

'We'd best be on our way,' said Macbeth abruptly. The roaring of pent-up fire behind us was getting loud.

'Aye, but first she must tell my fortune too,' growled Seyton, lifting the knife towards her skinny frame.

'Nay,' cried the wise woman, 'yours is a strange face that I'd rather not read.'

'Tell me, woman!' The big man jerked his knife threateningly, his sneering face twisted up worse than ever in the moonlight.

'Nay, it's naught to anger you I see,' she whined, lifting a hand still red with last winter's chilblains to protect her stringy throat. 'I see that you'll be the father of kings, though never more than a great man's steward yourself.'

'Now she talks folly,' shouted Macbeth. 'Come on, we must see the Lady safe and return to the fight.'

But he remembered her words, because when we'd got safe to a farmstead where some old man lived that'd stayed loyal to old Findlay, he took me to the chamber that they gave me and asked, 'What did the crone mean about the weird sisters?'

He was holding the only taper in his hand and I had to stand very close to him because the low, stone-walled room was so small the bed left little space. His plaid was thrown back over his shoulder and the light played along the dark hairs of his arm. He was taut, ready to return to the battle. I still felt that I couldn't bear to part with him. I wanted him to stay with me more than I'd ever wanted anything before.

'I think she meant this,' I said, touching Mother's gold brooch that I wore at my breast.

He lowered the taper to study the design and, scowling, made the sign of the priests' cross again. 'That's an old thing, ' he whispered, 'and some would call it unchancy.'

'My mother was of an old race and never took the church's baptism.'

'There's something strange about you, Lady Gruoch,' he muttered.

'Nay, I'm a baptized Christian; my father saw to that.' I spoke quickly, for he looked almost frightened of me. 'This is just a brooch to me. It's pretty and useful.'

'Useful?' He still looked wary, as if he suspected me of some magic.

I smiled. 'It holds my bodice together,' I said and worked the only spell I could think of to make him stay. I pulled out the pin and my bodice – an open one that I'd worn when I was nursing Lulach – slipped aside to show my breasts, small and brown but pleasantly rounded by the shadows of the light he was holding to them.

For a moment I was frightened at what I'd done and wondered at myself; I looked up and saw him staring. His face framed in its thick black hair was shocked. Slowly his mouth moved again into that calculating smile and I knew that my charm had worked. He raised his free hand and pushed back the gown, the calluses that the sword had worn on his palm rasping on my skin. My body weakened against him.

'Lady Gruoch,' he muttered, 'I didn't mean it to be like this. I thought a priest's words first. I didn't want,' he said, as the gentleness of his calloused hand stirred senses in my body that I'd thought Gillacomgain had robbed me of for

ever, 'Lady, I didn't mean to take you like something
captured on the battlefield.'

'But it's what I want, Macbeth.' I pressed urgently against
the sweet hardness of him and drank in the smell of young,
healthy man. 'I wanted you to take me there on the bed still
wet with his blood. Please. Take me now, Macbeth. I want
you.' I was mad for him. My hands were plucking wildly at
his plaid and his belt. 'Macbeth, my beloved, please!'

'Christ in heaven!' He burst into laughter that shook his
whole body and threw the taper away, but in the moonlight
I could see him still laughing as he undid his belt with a
tug. 'He was a fool to prefer his whores to you, Gruoch.'

He picked me up and his mouth closed over mine. He
dragged the dress down from my shoulders and bent his
dark head to lay his lips on my breasts. 'We've not much
time, little Gruoch, but I'll show you how it should be.'

I clung to him, wrapping my legs round his hard body
and screaming aloud with pleasure; shouting his name out
into the low rafters of the stuffy little room like a blasphe-
mous hymn of praise.

When he rolled away from me, his long hair spilling
round him on the linen, he was gasping and laughing
again. 'Gruoch, my heart! You're not like any woman I've
ever known. I won much more tonight than I looked for.
That is,' he cried, suddenly remembering, 'if the victory
really is ours.'

He leapt from the bed in one lithe movement and
snatched up his clothes. 'I really am like a man that's got
himself into the fairies' realm and forgotten about the
world.' He pulled open the door and shouted 'Seyton!
Bring the horses!'

'Macbeth.' Still aching for him, I reached out and caught
his arm.

'Stay there in the bed,' he said. 'I'll be back. Unless
Gillacomgain's men kill me, I promise I'll be back before dawn.'

'Macbeth, I know now. He used me ill.'

1606

He was like no mortal man and maybe I should have known from the beginning what he was. I'd had enough dealings with men to know their ways and it's certain that there wasn't one man I'd ever known before that could've tempted a woman into the sins of the flesh except by promising her money. But he was different; he knew how to rouse my lust and I hungered for him. He never left me without my longing for his return.

I would sit by my fire times when he had gone, thinking over what had passed between us and wondering when he'd come to me again. And it was at those times – when I was weak with passion – that the old spirit would torment me. It was as if she understood my weakness and took possession of me through it. Maybe a dozen times during that autumn and the hard winter that followed it, she dragged me down into that dark evil place.

The sharp little flames on the sticks, the stone flags and the drying herbs on their hooks would blur before my eyes as if I looked at them through tears, then they'd fade into darkness, as if dusk was drawing in too fast. Her hands would close on mine and then there would be three of us dancing round and round – though I was never sure who the third figure was; I'd see my own terror in her face and know she too was trapped by the old spirit. Round we'd circle, faster and faster, till our hands slipped apart. And then there was a dark room with a twisting stairway. Like the stairway at Eldridge's Hollow but longer, rising up and up into the night. A stairway I knew I'd got to climb, though I was sick with fear at the sight of it.

Climb! Climb! The evil spirit would urge.

Up and up I'd go with my hands clutching at the bare stone walls and the smell of burning clawing in the back of my throat. The stairs were slippery wet and when I bent to touch them, it wasn't the wetness of water I felt, but the stickiness of fresh blood. Blood on my hands. And the spirit forcing me to climb on upwards and upwards.

I'd try to cry out to stop the dream but no sound would come.

At the top of the stairs there was a door. A heavy door, charred at the bottom where someone had put fire to it. It was not quite closed, there was a crack of pale light shining at the side.

Push it open, the spirit would say. Push it open and go in.

And I'd cry out, terrified of what lay beyond that door . . .

Why? Masters, don't you understand? Behind that door was the terrible thing that the spirit would make me do. Behind that door was the unthinkable. The mouth of hell.

Go in, the spirit would say. Go in. It's what we all must face. All three of us. We're joined by fate. Together we have the power I need. You have no choice. We three are the sisters of fate. The weird sisters who together have power.

Go in, she said. And I'd scream at last and wake, all cold and shaking by the side of the dead fire at Eldridge's Hollow. But I think I always knew that one day I'd have to go through that door and do the terrible thing she had planned for me.

All the autumn and through the winter, the spirit tormented me and it was always after my lover had been with me. Maybe I was foolish not to suspect then what he was, but it wasn't till long after that I knew him for the devil. Maybe Mother was right and my wits are slower than other women's; but masters, it's no sin surely to be slow-witted. And I swear it was not hard to be deceived by him. There was nothing about him to show he was evil. He always came in the same guise, the blue coat, the gold ring and the good horse.

Folk now tell all sorts of stories about me – how they saw me fly through the air and change myself into strange shapes. And they swear that they never saw an ordinary man on a grey horse. Well I reckon they must all be blind. They must have seen him. He came to my cottage in the hollow by day as well as night.

But hold! You saw him!

I beg your pardon, masters, the sleeplessness muddles me. I mean there was a man who saw the stranger in the blue coat. One of Master Rigg's bailiffs saw him . . .

Nay sir, I can't remember the bailiff's name. Master Rigg employed a good few fellows to see that the work was done well in his fields. But I know he saw the stranger because he told me he had seen him. 'A fine gentleman on a great grey horse,' he called him and he asked me what his business was at my cottage.

That would have been February then and bitter cold and I was ankle deep in the plough furrows at the very top of the old Five Acre. I was stone-picking and I was working my way as slowly as I could through the sheltered bit where the big chestnut trees keep off the worst of the wind. It's a bleak field and I knew there was trouble brewing when I saw the bailiff stamping through the mud towards me. He was a lazy, short-tempered man and I reckoned it must be something particular he wanted that'd brought him up there to the dreariest spot on his master's lands.

And it was something particular he wanted. He wanted me. That is, he wanted more from me than stone-picking.

'It's plain to everyone,' he said, 'why a man like that – a gentleman on a good horse – comes to a wench like you.' He wasn't angry at first. Just kind of hot and leering.

'It's my business what he comes for,' I said shortly, throwing a handful of pebbles into my basket and moving along sharply out of the trees' shelter, hoping he'd go sooner if he must stand in the wind to talk to me.

He stepped into the furrow behind me and stood close. 'I'd like to do a little business with you myself then, woman.'

'I don't like the sound of your business, master.'

'You watch your tongue, girl. Remember whose land it is you're working on. Aye, and who it is owns the roof over your head. If I speak a word against you, Master Rigg will have you out of that house.'

I set the basket down on the raw red earth and turned back to face him. The wind rattling through the black branches whipped tears into the corners of my eyes and my hair blew its loose strands across my cheeks. I looked at the man: his thick breeches needed washing – or burning – his leather jerkin was greasy with a hundred dinners, his red cheeks stubbled with ginger and grey.

But he was no worse than many I'd done business with before.

I'm no whore, masters. But the truth is I'm not quite chaste either. The guard at the gate of Mother's prison had been the first I'd dealt with in that way and there had been others when hunger drove me to it. I'd rather scrub floors – or pick the filthy stones off Five Acre, for that matter – but when I had to I could bear the grunting and the groping. I'd lie still, holding my breath against the stink of them and promise myself a loaf of sweet fresh bread when the business was done and the money paid. I had borne what I must.

Until the devil came and changed me. Waking my lust and giving me a mind for no touch but his. I don't know why it was, masters, but the body the devil had touched would not yield to another. It just would not, though necessity had never been greater with me.

'I'll have you out of that cottage in the hollow come Michaelmas,' he threatened. And I knew if I didn't give in he'd do it. I wanted to strike the bargain with him. But I couldn't say I'd lie with him.

The hold my lover had on me was stronger than anything else.

1057

Macbeth returned from the broch before dawn and we lay late. But the first thing he did on rising was to send the one-handed servant to find a priest.

'A priest is it, MacFindlay?' sneered the fellow, looming at the chamber door like a giant. 'I think that order comes some hours too late.'

Macbeth grinned over his breakfast. 'I told you to get a priest, Seyton, not talk like one.'

'You let that man speak very freely,' I said, taking the ale cup from his hand and drinking slowly from the place where his mouth had rested.

'It's just his way,' he laughed. 'He's the most loyal man in my company.'

'But he has an ugly, bitter look. How was his hand lost?'

He sopped oatcake in the ale and ate in silence for a minute. Then, setting down the cup, he said quietly, 'I cut it off.'

'In battle?'

'No. I did it with my sword across the smith's anvil. I thought that would make the cleanest cut.' His voice was so calm as he raised the cup to his lips that he might have been talking about dressing a joint of meat. 'He had been caught stealing from the dying on the field of battle. His life was forfeit, but he was a clever fellow and I'd no mind to lose him.'

'And you did the thing yourself?'

'It was hardly just to ask another to do it for me, Gruoch.'

'And now he serves you?'

'Aye.'

'The man who cut off his hand.'

'Nay, Gruoch.' He grasped my chin and turned my face up to his, fingers pressing on the bone of my jaw. 'He serves the man that spared his life. Justice isn't a business for the faint of heart. It needs a clear mind – and a steady hand.'

'Yes.'

'Little one, I never pretended to you that I was soft-hearted. You've certainly no cause to expect that of me. But I promise, I am just.'

I stared at him. The morning sunshine was streaming through the unshuttered window on to the bench where we sat with the food between us. He was still naked to the waist and his long hair flowed on to his bare shoulders. Straddling the bench, he sat straight and alert. The sun striking the hard lines of his face showed that he was younger than I had taken him for in torchlight and moonlight: probably not long come to manhood. A man with authority and powers way beyond his years. So strange to think that it was less than twenty-four hours since I first raised my eyes to his in Gillacomgain's hall.

Now he was everything to me.

I put my hand to his unshaven cheek. 'Whatever you are, Macbeth MacFindlay, I love you.'

Just for a moment his dark face twisted slightly, as it had done when he saw the wise woman on the heath. But the look passed and he put my hand to his lips. 'I'll treat you well, little Gruoch. You'll have no cause to regret this day's bargain.'

The bargain was struck at noon in the old man's hall by a sallow-faced priest who was fussing a lot about burial of the dead up at the broch. Besides the old couple only Morag and the bairn were present – and Seyton, who seemed to mark Macbeth's steps like some great, ugly hound.

When it was all said, I turned away with my hand in Macbeth's hard, engulfing clasp, and for a moment, I saw the strangeness of my position. The household to which I'd belonged were all dead, and I stood here hand in hand with the man who'd ordered their killing: a man I scarcely knew. I had no notion of what might happen next, or where we might go. I didn't even know where I'd lie that night.

I knew only that I'd lie with Macbeth.

The lady of the house held out a thin, loose-skinned hand. 'I wish you well, Lady Gruoch,' she said in a feeble voice that seemed to make every feature of her face twitch. 'I hope you'll find comfort and safety for yourself and your bairn in your new life. It's hard that you should be bereaved twice over just now.'

Macbeth's grip tightened on my fingers and, over the old woman's palsied head, I saw Seyton's sneer twist into an unbecoming smile.

'Gruoch, I'm sorry,' whispered Macbeth against my ear. 'Messengers came from Fife yesterday. Your father has died – peacefully, in his bed.'

I gripped his hand for support and had a sudden vivid memory of my father: his touch on my hair; his ale-bleared eyes; his doting babble about the beauty of the Picts. He was the man who'd gotten me and who'd indulged my childhood. But he was also the man who'd given me into Gillacomgain's hands. In the dark horror of Gillacomgain's bed, all my old feelings seemed to have died. My heart was that of a newborn child: a child born yesterday when Macbeth first smiled at me. No tears came for my father's death.

But why was the one-handed fellow grinning like a boar's head on a plate?

I stared up into the dark face of my husband. 'The messengers came yesterday, you say, Macbeth? But you never spoke till now.'

His face was still and stern. 'I'd other business on hand,' he said calmly.

There was a great unearthly roar of laughter from Seyton. 'Aye, that you had!' he cried approvingly. 'The business of snatching the daughter of the King's heir from Gillacomgain, just as she got to be of value! The old crone was right. You did carry the Crown of Scots with you last night.'

'Silence!' shouted Macbeth and pulled me hard against

his hip. 'I told you, Gruoch. No soft heart, only justice. And besides, you were willing enough last night.'

'And still am willing, my love,' I said. 'All that I have to give is yours.' But Seyton's laughter was like a foreshadowing of the horror to come: a hint that there lay ahead of me a nightmare darker even than those Gillacomgain had devised for me.

1996

As rehearsals went on, those strange, haunting moments when I felt so close to Lady Macbeth came more frequently.

I can't possibly tell you about them all. But there was one particularly disturbing one. Luke rang me one evening when I was on my own in the London house. I remember I was feeling lonely and wishing Greg would come home. I was thinking about him: about how we didn't have enough time together and things like that. I can't recall when it was exactly; it was quite late in the rehearsal period, but I'm not sure if it was before that time Alan told me about the pendant or after. Come to think of it, it was probably after. The opening night must have been looming fairly close because poor little Luke was getting very anxious about his part.

Bless him, he'd rung me from school to talk about his fears. 'What'll Dad say if I don't do well?' he kept saying.

'But you will, my love. You'll be fine.' Cradling the phone in the bland warmth of the grey London house, I longed to put my arms round him. 'You're really good. Just remember not to overdo the dying scene and you'll be great.'

There was a short pause in which I could distinguish echoes and shouts of school life, then a voice that sounded much younger than ten years said, 'I wish I was at home, Mum.'

Tears overpowered me, lumpy in my throat, sharp in my eyes and nose. 'I'll see you tomorrow, darling. Don't worry about anything.'

When he'd gone, I dropped the phone and wailed aloud. I felt stifled alone there in the long room with its sleek radiators and its chairs aligned on the chill face of the television instead of a living hearth. I wanted to be in my real home, with its beams and its fire. I wanted Greg with me. And I wanted my child to cuddle. Luke's absence was like a physical pain; I wanted the feel of him in my arms.

I'm a very tactile person; it's something that really irritates Greg. He says it's childish the way I can't talk to people without touching them; he says it gives men the wrong idea. But I can't help it; it's just the way I am.

Anyway, that evening it seemed terrible that I couldn't touch my child. To comfort myself – or else to make myself feel more wretched, I'm not sure which – I pulled a photo album from under the TV and was soon lost in the magic of it. Luke in the hospital about an hour old, in the awkward arms of his father, who was still looking stunned from the birth; Luke twenty-four hours later with some of the creases ironed out; Luke blissfully grubby at eighteen months in the sandpit outside the cottage; Luke round-cheeked over the candles of birthday cakes in a variety of fashionable shapes – teddy bears, trains, anything but cake-shaped – even one vile green one that was supposed to look like a mutated turtle (I'd been up till four in the morning working on that one). Tears spattered on the plastic film that covered the last pictures: Luke smiling bravely in a stiff new uniform.

Those had been taken just last year when Greg had decided that my depression made me unfit to look after my child. We'd become part-time parents. Which, I thought with a bitter glance at the clock, seemed to suit Greg fine. It was midnight and he still wasn't home.

I flipped back the stiff pages of the album to dwell on the baby pictures. Then he'd been completely mine. There I was proudly breast-feeding him in the hospital. With my finger I stroked the cold plastic of the tiny cheek resting on my breast. Those had been some of the happiest days of my life: lost in the wonder of my child, with Greg sitting by, fascinated, like an adoring shepherd in a nativity scene.

I remembered the softness of the little head on my breast, the demand of the tiny mouth.

And then it happened. Once again, she – Lady Macbeth – came terrifyingly close to me. *Come to my woman's breasts and take my milk for gall.*

The line that I'd wondered about for weeks hit me with a new impact. Before, I'd been taken up with wondering why she should wish her milk to be poisoned. I'd missed the simple and obvious fact of her motherhood. Not only was she a mother; but at the time of Duncan's murder, there was milk in her breasts. So, somewhere in the castle there must have been a baby.

1057

Little Findlay wasn't born until nearly eight years after I wed Macbeth. He was barely three months old (and as bonny a child as mother ever suckled) when Duncan MacCrinan, King of Scots, came to the new hall-house we'd built in Moray. Those were eight years that would have been happy ones but for the barrenness.

Ah, child, how can I describe that time? You're too young to understand. It's barely ten since your mother brought you here in stinking swaddling clothes. You're too young to know what it is to love a man the way I've loved Macbeth. But when I try to remember those times, I can think of scarcely anything except him.

Macbeth, you were everything to me.

Were? You are still. There, I think I can see you in the hell-scene below, stripped almost naked as you toil in the mud with your men. There's more life in you than twenty lesser beings. Even this shell of a heart of mine must move at the sight of you. But is it in love, or in hate? It is all twisted now, Macbeth; my heart's turned as sour as Seyton's leering face.

But then it was all still love, despite the things I was learning about you. It was certainly not for your gentle heart I loved you. Aye, you did well to warn me of that.

It was about a twelvemonth after we wed that more news reached us from Fife. My brother Dunegal and all his family had perished in clan feuding and the rest of my father's land had passed into the hands of Constantine MacGirrick, the husband of Beatrice.

I grieved over the tidings, particularly for little golden-haired Kenneth, my brother's child that I'd loved dearly. But Macbeth said, 'It is the way, Gruoch, when there's feud with the father, the bairns perish too. Men must take revenge where they can. And besides, he's as well dead as orphaned the way things go on now. He'd have inherited your father's title of Tannaisse and who'd let a toddling bairn stand in his way to the crown?'

'Not Macbeth MacFindlay for one,' muttered Seyton, who was standing at his shoulder as usual.

'Hold your tongue! I've no liking for the murder of children. But these are changing times. Feuds prosper because men no longer wish to share their titles. I think we are all taken with the wish for immortality. Men care more and more for heirs they've got themselves.'

There was truth in that. The following year when the old King, Malcolm, died, he'd managed things so that his crown didn't pass to my father's part of the clan as it should have done by the old laws, but to his grandson, Duncan.

And Macbeth, who still looked in vain for his own heirs, became grave. I didn't need Seyton's leers to remind me that I'd failed my husband twice over: that I'd given him neither sons nor the crown that had been promised to my father.

During all that time, life went on about me: Macbeth was busy with the task of securing Moray and holding it against his enemies. But he ruled as well as he fought and soon all seemed prosperous in the mormaership of Moray. He became restless and so anxious for more glory that he healed his differences with the foolish boy Duncan and joined with him in fighting the Norse and the Angles.

But all the while my life followed its own treadmill of hope and despair: of watching the moon and counting days. One day late and I'd hope; two days and the hope would take hold, blotting out everything else; three days and I'd be walking, wrapped in dreams of the future; then always, bitter, bloody disappointment. Time passed and still the only bairn I had was Lulach, growing into boyhood with a haunting look of his father about him.

Macbeth's priests gave me prayers to say and I kneeled for hours in the desolate little chapels that he was having built everywhere. But the words echoed, hollow in my head.

'You should take off that thing,' Macbeth said sternly, pointing to the brooch at my breast, 'if you want the Christ god to heed you.'

A true soldier was Macbeth and his faith was a matter of unswerving loyalty.

'But I can't,' I cried, covering it with my hand. 'It was my mother's and I've worn it ever since she died.'

He scowled but didn't try to force me. He was half afraid of the thing.

Morag (whose loyalty had not yet been given to the priests) used to say to me sometimes, 'There are other powers beside the Christ and his virgin mother. Old things women have been calling on since time began.'

But I'd not listen to her. I knew he'd not like me to turn to them.

And so we went on: month after month, year after year: count the days, hope and despair; mutter empty words in cold shrines that still smelled of mortar and newly cut wood, until the dark day that he said, 'Maybe it really was a changeling that I got myself and the alien blood won't breed with mine.'

'Macbeth!'

'Nay, don't look so, Gruoch. I'm no Gillacomgain that'll beat you for my own disappointment. You can't help being what you are.' And he strode out of my chamber.

I wept as I hadn't wept for years and in the aching blackness of my tears, all I could think was that I must quicken. Macbeth must have what he wanted.

Later I said to Morag, 'You spoke of other powers?'

'Aye. The old wise woman is still alive. She's made herself a home in the ruins of the broch. I'll take you.'

'No. I'll go alone.'

She lived in the old guard room in the base of the tower where a half-burned door still hung askew on its hinges and a small fire of sticks smoked sullenly. The place smelled of bats and darkness. Above our heads sagged the remains of splintered boards that'd once been the floor in the room of my torture; through them the blue sky of May showed in vivid patches. The woman with her red chapped hands and sparse, stringy hair looked impossibly ancient, and was so deaf that I had to shout my business till the dank walls rang with it.

'You've been praying at the wrong shrines, Lady Gruoch,' she croaked when I'd finally made her understand. 'You should take more heed of the one whose face you wear.'

'I don't know anything about her.' My hand covered the brooch.

She narrowed her rheumy eyes and peered closely at me.

'But you've got a Pictish look and should know more of the business than a woman born Scots and noble like me.'

'Can you help me, woman?' I said impatiently.

'You would do better to help yourself. You have more power than I have. I came late in life to the sisters' business for my own ends, but you've got the look of one born to it. What was your mother?'

'I hardly know. She died before I was five years old.'

'Did she teach you nothing of the sisters?'

'No,' I shouted, 'and I have no wish to learn. My husband does not like such things.' I pulled the cloth off my basket and showed the pigs' trotters that I'd brought.

Her milky eyes brightened at the sight of meat and a thin trickle of saliva ran like the track of a snail down her hairy chin. She was near starving, I reckon, for the new Roman priests Macbeth had brought to Moray were getting a grip on folk's hearts and people were wary of her and her old magic.

'I hoped you could give me a charm to make me quicken.'

'Well, maybe I could, Lady Gruoch. But there's no saying it'll work.'

'Give me something, anything that might help.' I pushed the basket closer and watched her sniff the air like a dog.

I left the broch an hour later with a filthy linen rag twisted in my hand. It held some powder or other that she'd muttered words over and told me to sprinkle in my bed. Glad to have it, like a hope in my hand, and glad to be free of the desolate ruin, I broke into a run on the green bank that led on to the level heath.

Our new house wasn't built for defence. It stood on a pleasant, south-facing bank with no walls or ditches. It was a one-storey, timber building of a hall with smaller rooms crowded on either side and a separate block of stables and kitchens across a yard behind. As I approached through the hazy sunshine of the spring evening, I could see the night's first thin trails of smoke rising through the smoke holes in the clay-daubed thatch and stretching lazily on the sweet breeze. Swallows and martins from the nests beneath the thatch swooped and shrieked after insects in the warm air.

I reached the stream at the bottom of the bank where a few shifting birches grew in a cleft of land. A cuckoo was calling languidly further up the little gorge. The stream could be crossed dry-footed at that season and I paused a minute on the stones in the middle to draw in draughts of the soft air and to let hope riot in my head. Tonight perhaps we'd get a son. By the time the cuckoo came next year, I might have a bairn at my breast. Tonight maybe, if he came to me.

'Lady Gruoch, what brings you out alone?'

'Seyton?'

He was standing in the restless shadow of one of the slender trees, arms folded across his chest. The scowl that twisted his face so constantly it seemed almost a disfigurement was deeper than ever and fixed on the rag in my hand. 'What have you got there?'

'It's no business of yours,' I said shortly. I finished crossing the stream and paused on the little patch of shingle at its edge, my eyes fixed on the steep bank beyond him where bluebells were pushing bent heads through even the hard earth of the path. I waited for him to step aside and let me pass, but he didn't.

'Any business of Macbeth's is mine,' he growled. 'And I think this is something that'd make him angry.'

I said nothing. I never knew how to speak to this giant of a man. I could hardly shout and threaten and laugh at his insolence the way Macbeth did, and in company I usually pretended not to hear him. Face to face, alone with him in the cuckoo-calling evening, I felt helpless.

'Evil stuff from the crone up yonder, I'll warrant,' he said nodding at the linen cloth. 'Now that'd really anger a good church man like MacFindlay.'

I thrust the thing behind my back and stared down in determined silence at my hide slippers sinking deeper into the water-seeping shingle.

'Now I don't fear magic myself, Lady Gruoch,' he said reaching up to rest his hand on the pale silvery trunk and hanging over me. 'But I do think it has a strange way of working.'

I was getting more angry. 'I don't care what you think, man. Let me pass.'

'You see,' he went on as if he hadn't heard, 'you've got in your hand there a charm and even a fool could guess what it's for. Now how does its magic work, I wonder? Does it somehow change those vigorous and, I might say, rather noisy matings that you enjoy with MacFindlay? Make them as fruitful as they are lively? Or does the magic instead bring me here to meet you alone in the twilight, to do in a few minutes what he's tried eight years to do?' He reached out and took my arm in a grip that bruised the flesh. 'Well, what do you think, Lady Gruoch?'

'I think Macbeth will kill you for this insult!'

'And I wonder how he'd treat you if he knew of your dealings with the crone? Not death – but a kind of exile perhaps.' His ugly lips twitched upward, showing his teeth like a snarling wolf. 'He's very squeamish about the old magic. This'd likely turn his stomach. If he knew, if some loyal servant felt obliged to tell him what his lady had been about, I think the household might find their nights less disturbed by your cries of pleasure, don't you, my Lady?'

'Damn you! Leave me alone!'

'Come, you know it would be a kindness to him to take what I offer. For in your heart you must know he's the one amiss. You quickened soon enough under Gillacomgain.'

I stood impassive in his grasp, staring down at the water darkening my slippers and feeling the edge of cold slice at my toes. I'd not look up lest even my eyes should admit I'd thought that myself.

The grip of his single hand tightened. 'He has no children, Gruoch,' he said more quietly. 'I know. I know all his whores. There's not one's given him so much as a sickly girl.'

Before I knew I was doing it, my free hand had flown to his cheek and ploughed three hot red furrows with its nails. He laughed and, unable to seize both my hands, he wrapped his maimed arm round me, pressing me hard against his heaving chest. 'Nay, don't pretend you thought he was faithful,' he laughed. 'And if he can stray, well, where's the harm in what I'm offering?' Pressed against him as I was, I could feel his lust. 'Just a few minutes, Lady Gruoch. It wouldn't take long for you and me to make a son.'

Panic thundered in my breast and head, crashing against the bones of my skull and chest like a wild beast imprisoned. 'Let me go!'

'Come, you're a lady with a great liking for the sport. I know that. And your man would be so pleased. Give him a son, Gruoch, and he'll forgive you the weird sisters and your Pictish ways.'

'Seyton, let me go. I can hear horses.'

He held on for a moment thinking it was bluff, but the clatter got louder on the track above us – the track that led to the house. Reluctantly he let me go. 'Think on the offer, Lady Gruoch. I'm always at hand.'

I picked up my skirts and scrambled up the bank, my wet shoes slithering on the earth and stones. On the track above, Macbeth himself was riding homeward in the lengthening shadows with a hawking party. Lulach rode adoringly in his wake and the whole company were spattered red with the light of the sinking sun.

'Gruoch!' shouted Macbeth, wheeling his horse on the track in a spray of small stones. 'What brings you abroad?'

I swallowed and smiled as best I could. 'The pleasant evening,' I said. 'The house was dull without you.'

Seyton loomed up from the stream, blinking in the dying light; his leering face was flushed and bleeding. 'You walk with Seyton?' demanded Macbeth.

'There are always ruffians about, master,' the wretched man said with unusual servility. 'I didn't like to let the Lady walk alone.'

'Your face is scratched,' piped Lulach.

'Ah, lad, I tried to stroke a wild cat.'

Macbeth reached down an impatient hand and pulled me up on to the horse before him. 'Like our first ride together, my love,' I said curling gladly against his warmth.

'Aye,' he said briskly and fell silent. He was never a man to speak his feelings in front of others.

But later that night when he sprawled, sated, in the bed beside me, he said, 'I don't like to see you walking alone like that with Seyton – or any other man. Do you understand, Gruoch? A man can be made to look a fool if his wife behaves like that.'

'I didn't want his company. He followed me.'

'Aye, well, another time, take Morag with you.'

I wasn't really listening, for in the warm darkness there was a certainty growing inside me.

The charm had worked.

'Macbeth.' I rolled over and kissed his mouth. 'I've quickened. We've got a son.'

'What?' His arms went round me, warm and gentle. 'Gruoch, my heart, how can you tell?'

'I just know, my love. I just know.'

1996

My friendship with Alan didn't go unnoticed and it was not approved of. I soon realized that he was not a popular man, though it was difficult to put your finger on exactly what people had got against him. He just made people uncomfortable with his long silences and sudden clumsy remarks. Chrissie, with her usual simpering lack of orig- inality, said his eyes were too close together. And I noticed that the other men tended to exclude him from their conversations and their jokes, talking to him only about work, in strained sort of voices.

Only Jo had the honesty to tell me exactly what she thought. 'He's strange, Abby. Don't have too much to do with him.'

'What do you mean, strange?'

'I don't know. He just gives me the creeps. It's best to be careful.' Jo's the sort of person who carries one of those screeching alarm things in her handbag. She believes in being careful about everything – and especially men.

'He's OK really, when you get to know him.'

'Well, I wouldn't know about that. But I don't like the way he stares at me and says nothing. I find myself wondering about what's going on in his head.'

'It's just his way. He's shy; he doesn't seem to know what to say most of the time.'

Jo shook her head and looked rather warily round the rehearsal room. 'You know about him, don't you, Abby?'

'Know what about him?' I suspected I knew what was coming.

'Well, you know he's been ill?'

I stared at a spot just above the red gleam of her hair. 'You mean crazy?'

'He's been seeing a psychologist or something, I know that.'

'Nothing wrong with that, Jo,' I said, looking her in the eye.

'Oh God! I'm sorry, Abby.' A flush swept up her sharp cheeks. 'I didn't mean . . .'

'It's OK. Forget it.'

I know I should have listened when people warned me

about him. But you see, I've suffered from gossip myself, so I know how things can get exaggerated.

Anyway, I was a bit suspicious when, a few days later, he started to take a sudden interest in my family history. I wasn't so stupid I didn't realize that it was a way of trying to spend more time with me.

I'd been sitting in the auditorium watching Greg and Tony rehearsing their fight scene. I hate scenes like that, actually. They always seem to go on much too long. I mean, what's the point of them? Once a fight starts the only thing you need to know is who wins; there's no point spending hours prancing about the stage hacking at each other. But I was making an effort and watching it because Greg always got offended if I didn't take an interest in what he was doing. Well, the scene had finally grunted and lunged to its conclusion and John was going through it with them, literally blow by blow. I was watching him bobbing around the stage as he talked, when a hot thick finger touched the back of my neck in the darkness and Alan came to squat on the back of the seat next to me.

'Why have you got your hair pinned up, Abigail? It looks better in a ponytail.'

I thought that was a bit of a cheek really, but I just said, 'It gets in the way,' and kept watching John hack the air with an imaginary sword.

He was silent for a while. Out of the corner of my eye I could see him balancing awkwardly on the seat back, his knees close to his ears, looking like a troll or some such thing. Then the thick finger touched the back of my neck again. 'Abigail, I want you to do me a favour,' he said in a whisper.

'What kind of a favour?' I asked uneasily, wishing he'd take his hand off my neck.

He leaned closer. 'Can't you guess?'

I turned to face him, moving away from his touch. 'No, I can't,' I said irritably.

He was smiling in the darkness of his beard. 'Oh,' he said and for a minute or two he just stared. I was reminded of what Jo had said and found myself wondering: what is going on in his head? 'But you do owe me a few favours, don't you,' he said at last. 'After all the help I've given you. Talking to you about the play and everything.'

'Maybe,' I admitted reluctantly. 'What do you want?'

Again he stared in silence for a while and the reply he eventually gave amazed me.

'I want you to tell me about Glenlagan,' he said, very quietly.

'Glenlagan?' I was staring now. 'What about it?'

'Gregory tells me you went there a few weeks ago.'

'Yes, I took my grandmother there.'

'To see the old family home?'

'Well, not exactly. There's nothing there now but a lot of ruins.'

'I know. I was there last year.' He creaked closer in his leather jacket. 'Now about that favour.'

'What favour would that be?' demanded Greg, dropping into the seat on the other side of me.

'I was just hoping Abigail might help me with my research, that's all. I'm working on a book about people emigrating from Scotland; I thought she might know some family history.'

'Her grandmother's the one you need to ask about that. The old girl will bore you to death about it, given half a chance!' said Greg. Then he turned to me. 'What did you think of the scene, darling?'

'Oh fine! It looked good.' I couldn't really remember much about it. It was just another fight scene to me.

Greg was hurt by my half-hearted praise. 'Too busy chatting to Alan to notice, were you?' he asked with a scowl as we walked to the car.

'Greg, you're jealous!'

'Jealous of him? Rubbish!'

I remember I started to laugh. The thought of Greg being jealous was just so funny. And I thought: my power over Alan could be useful. Being jealous might do Greg good.

I admit that's what I thought. It was a cruel idea. And a dangerous one too.

1606

Masters, do you understand what little power a woman has? Do you know, have you ever stopped to think, how helpless a woman can be if she's on her own and poor?

Aye, I know it's God's will we should be so. The Weaker Vessel, as they say in church. But sin comes easy to the weak, masters. It seems sometimes, I reckon, as if the weak can't help but sin. And I sometimes think that if I'd been a man with just a few fields and a house and a chest with a handful of gold coins in it, then I could have been as virtuous as a saint.

But I was a woman: a woman alone without any friends or money. The only thing I had to protect myself was words. They were wicked, dangerous words that the spirit put into my mouth.

Words are always a woman's weapon.

At the back of the church, laid by in the dust and mouse dirt, with the parish bier and the harness for carrying the processional cross at Easter, is that ugly tool of torture that they call the Scold's Bridle: an iron cage to fit a woman's head, with a savage bit, worse than they put in horses' mouths. In my time I've seen a good few women who've angered their husbands with their words have their poor mouths cut to pieces with the thing.

I remember Mother saying once when we saw it used in Berwick, how strange it was that they kept nothing in the church to punish men that beat their wives.

Men must have a great fear of women's words, I reckon,

or they'd not curb them so harshly. Many a woman has been made to regret the words she's used to protect herself. I know I was.

I used words to make the bailiff fear me; to stop him having me turned out of the cottage.

It was a very strange business the way the words came to me from the spirit. It was one of those times when she seemed to take over my will and make me do what she wanted. Listen, this is how it happened.

'You'll regret it if you harm me,' I said when the wretched fellow came one stormy night and tried to force me. I said that in anger. First thing that came into my head, it was. I'd got to do something and I wasn't strong enough to fight him.

He stood on my hearth – the rain running off the sacking on his shoulders and hissing on the hot stones. He was full of bluster and ale that time.

'Come on, wench. You'll like it well enough once we get started, I'll warrant. You're just playing women's games with me to make me keener and push up the price of your goods.' He laughed, so drunk he likely believed what he was saying. He'd no more idea of what I wanted than a bull among the cows. He took a coin from his pouch, snatched my hand and tried to force it, hot and greasy, between my fingers.

I resisted and it dropped, ringing on the stone flags between us. That enraged him and he bellowed, bull-like, again.

'Come on now, girl, or you're out of here come Michael-mas, I swear.'

'No.' I watched the coin spin and settle in the firelight, hating it and him – and the hunger that made me want to stoop and pick it up. I watched it till it was just a blur of gold in front of my staring eyes. And it was then, I swear, that the spirit took possession of me and spoke through me. Suddenly it was her speaking, not me. I swear it was. 'You

won't dare mistreat me,' I cried. 'My mother was a powerful witch that even the King feared and she taught me such
things . . .'

I didn't get any further than that; I stopped and wondered where the words had come from. I swear that until I
spoke them I had no notion of making such a threat. The
words came of their own accord. I didn't mean to claim
any such power. But see how the devil works in our lives:
before I could take the words back, the fellow's face went
pale and he stepped away from me as if I'd hit him. I
thought: I've got my way. And I didn't take the words
back.

But I reckon I was more afraid than he was. After he'd
gone angrily into the pouring night, I stood fearful in the
middle of the room. And I felt the presence of the spirit
there with me. I remember how I turned about feeling
there was something – someone – close behind me. There
was nothing there but the stool and the cooking pot and
the shutters barred against the storm. But still I felt I wasn't
alone. I fled up the stairs shaking and sweating – and I'll
swear I heard steps following me, echoing on the hollow
wood.

1996

Alan didn't give up. Several times over the next few days
he brought up the subject of his research. On one occasion,
I remember, he put his arm on my shoulder and tried to
draw me out of the group in the bar of the Blue Dragon,
muttering something about 'a history lesson'. Much to my
amusement, Greg seized the other shoulder and insisted
that I talk to him about the assassination scene.

To have Greg acting like a jealous teenager was great fun.
It made him notice me, and at that time I craved his
attention.

But I also needed Alan for another reason. My researches continued. Now I was trying to find out about Lady Macbeth herself, but I'd discovered that it was much harder to find material on her than it was to find books on James I. So I got Alan on his own in the usual place and asked him, 'Who was the real Lady Macbeth?'

'Why do you want to know?'

'Because sometimes I feel so close to her. She seems so real. Not just a fictional character. More like . . .' I hesitated, but decided to admit the truth, 'more like a ghost haunting the play.'

'Ghosts is it now, Abigail? What does Gregory say about you being haunted? I should imagine he's a bit squeamish about things like that, isn't he?'

'Yes, he is. I've not dared say anything about this to him. He'd go crazy if I did. You're the only one I've told about how I feel.'

'I have my uses, don't I?'

I put my hand on the sleeve of his leather jacket, 'I don't know what I'd do without you, Alan.' He tossed a stone into the lake to confuse the foraging ducks and I got the feeling he was sulking a bit. 'But tell me about the play. How accurate is it? As history, I mean.'

'You're asking favours again, Abigail,' he said.

'Yes, I know.'

'What about the favour you were going to do me?'

'You mean my family history?'

He nodded.

'What exactly do you want to know?'

'Your ancestors left Glenlagan when the crofters were turned out by the landlords in the 1850s, is that right?'

'Yes, I think it was 1853. My grandmother can tell you the whole story if you're really that interested.'

He had started to pace along the park gravel now and I found myself having to take little scuffling runs to keep up with his massive back. He stopped suddenly. 'Will she? Will you take me to see her, Abigail?'

'Yes, if you want. Though to be honest, Greg's got a point. She really can get pretty boring when she starts going on about it.'

'That's OK.' By now we had come to the bridge at the bottom of the lake. He perched on the parapet. 'It's a deal, then. You promise to take me to see Granny, and I'll tell you about Lady Macbeth.' He held out a warm, square hand and we shook solemnly.

I remember thinking that the deal seemed harmless enough.

Alan took a deep breath, as if he was preparing to give a lecture on the subject of Macbeth, King of Scotland.

'He came to the throne in 1040 and reigned for seventeen years,' he said.

'And did he and his wife really murder the previous King?'

'They might have done. It was a common enough way of getting the crown in those days. But the chronicles from which Shakespeare seems to have taken the story weren't very accurate.'

'I think they did.' I leaned wearily against the gritty parapet and watched curled brown leaves drift, dry as boats, on the leaden water. I was aching from lack of sleep. The dream was coming so often now I'd got frightened of sleeping. 'She must have done something terrible to stop her spirit resting.'

'Dear, dear: ghosts and unquiet spirits! Gregory would be upset if he could hear you.'

'Never mind Greg. Keep your part of the bargain and tell me about the play. Are the events in it basically true?'

'It's hard to tell. As you know, Shakespeare was trying to please King James when he wrote it.'

'By putting in witches?'

'Yes, and Banquo. You know how in the play the witches

tell Macbeth he'll be King and tell his friend, the noble Banquo, that though he'll never be King himself, he'll be the father of Kings?'

I nodded.

'Well that was put in to please James. Banquo was supposed to be James's ancestor – the founder of the Stewart dynasty.'

'Supposed to be? Wasn't he really?'

'No, probably not. The name Stewart was originally derived from "steward". The Stewarts began as stewards to the Kings of Scotland. This Banquo business was just a public relations exercise to cover up their lowly origins.'

'And Lady Macbeth? What do you know about her?' He stared down at the grey sky reflected in the dead water. 'Go on, Alan, please tell me.' I put my head on his shoulder and kissed his hairy cheek.

'Well, I know that "Lady Macbeth" is a misnomer. Macbeth was her husband's given name, not his family name. She wouldn't have taken it. She wouldn't have been "Lady Macbeth" any more than you're "Mrs Gregory".' He put a heavy hand over mine. 'In fact her name was Gruoch.'

Her name! Of course, I thought, she must have had a name of her own. 'That's right! She has no real name in the play. She's nothing on her own – just a part of her husband. Everything she does is done for his sake.'

'What's the matter, Abigail?'

'I know what that feels like.'

'Of course you do.'

I was vaguely aware of his arm creeping round me, but somehow it didn't seem to matter. All I could think about was Lady Macbeth and how that complete immersion in her husband could explain the way she behaved.

1606

The fat bailiff left me alone most of that summer. At least he didn't speak much to me and he didn't try to force himself, or his money, on me again. But he watched me.

I'd see him outside my house odd times. Just watching. And I remember one day at hay-time when old Margaret and I were tossing the grass in the long meadow by the river, his shiny wet face appeared so often over the hedge that Margaret laughed and said the fool must be sweet on one of us. I just kept to my work, hot and modest. I took care that year not to roll my sleeves or kilt my skirts to the knees like most of the women did. Even his looks were unwelcome.

For a while I hoped that the words the spirit had put into my mouth had saved me and I'd hear no more of the wretch's business. But I soon began to fear that though her trick had seemed to save me, the spirit might have betrayed me into a worse danger with her words.

On a sticky hot evening about the beginning of harvest, I met Margaret on the bridge as I made my way home from scouring pots at the inn.

'Have you heard the news, Jennet?' she said. 'Have you heard the news?'

She was a great one for news, was Margaret. I knew she was on her way home now from the Hall Farm after laying out old Master James Rigg. He'd been one of the most important men in the village, had Master Rigg, biggest land owner and a Justice of the Peace and all. But he'd died a slow death, eaten up from the inside and the death smell was heavy on Margaret. Still, they must have given her plenty of ale to get her through the job because she was right merry.

'There's been a man from London at the Hall Farm, that's the news. Came on Law business, he did.'

'What would a London man want up there?'

'A witch,' she said, very full of her own importance. 'That's what young Mistress Rigg told Sally Waller. Only a few days back he came, asking questions about whether anyone in the village had suffered with such things as spells, waxen images and the like of that. With the old man being so sick and all but dead, it was young Master Rigg he spoke to and young Mistress Rigg says she believes it's the King himself has sent this man.'

'Why she's an empty-headed little thing, Margaret,' I said rather quick. I was a bit frightened straight away, though I wasn't sure why. It took a while for it all to make sense and the fear to really take hold of me. 'What's the King care for anything happening here?'

'Well, Sally Waller says that Mistress Rigg was told it by her husband.' Margaret swayed slightly and caught at my arm with clammy fingers. I remembered what she'd just been about and shivered. 'And young Master Rigg wouldn't make a mistake about something like that. He'd know the King's business when he heard it. He's a learned man, is young Master Rigg; five years he went to the Grammar School in town, and Sally says his wife once whispered to her that he's still got the scars on his backside to prove it!'

She laughed hoarsely and, drunkard fashion, seemed to forget what she'd begun to tell me.

'What's Master Rigg's backside got to do with witches, Margaret?'

'He's read a book,' she said swaying upright. 'A book written by the King himself, about how to recognize witches – or some such thing. And the King's right worried about waxen images and suchlike. Thinks women can do all sorts of harm with them.' Margaret leaned over the bridge and spat into the weedy darkness. 'Men are fools aren't they, Jennet? Seems the King himself is as big a fool as the menfolk round here. Do you know, I never knew a man yet that wasn't, in his heart, afraid of women.'

'I hope you're right, Margaret,' I said. I didn't know what

to make of all her talk of books and images. It seemed all muddled in the telling by her and Sally and Master Rigg's new young wife who was little more than a child. It was like that game children sometimes play in a shared bed: whisper a message from ear to ear and see how much it changes by the time it gets to the other side of the crowded mattress.

But the notion of the King hunting witches gave me a fright. It took me back to that wet night at the gate of the prison and the guard's warning.

I remembered too how Mother had told me that the words she'd taught me were a curse on the King's line, spoken long ago when the ancestor of this James who rules now was no more than a servant in the royal house . . .

Aye masters, that what's she told me: a servant who committed a great wrong against his Queen.

I wished with all my heart I'd never mentioned Mother to the bailiff; or claimed to have any powers. I longed to be able to unsay the words the spirit had forced out of me. Supposing the King had sent his witch-hunter to find me. The fat bailiff would have plenty to tell him.

And it wasn't just him I was afraid of either. I remembered how easily folks had turned against us in Berwick once the notion of witchcraft was put into their minds. If I was to find myself homeless at Michaelmas, I'd likely get very little charity from my neighbours.

I struggled through harvest, watching folk anxiously for that look of fear and disgust I remembered from Berwick.

Michaelmas came. Hot and dry it was, more like June than September.

The day passed and no men came from the Hall Farm to throw my pots and my bed into the lane as I'd thought they would. My fear abated and I began to feel a bit happier; no one had accused me yet, though Margaret's wagging tongue had told all the village about the man who'd come to Master Rigg. There were still loaves and pennies for me to earn. And then, maybe about two days past the Quarter Day, my lover came to the cottage.

The unseasonable hot weather still held and I'd spent almost the last of the sunlight pulling weeds out of the herb-beds. The long shadow of the bridge under which the cottage stands crept slowly across the garden and when I'd finished I went down to the stream to bathe my hot, aching feet. I was sitting on the bank, my skirt pulled up to my knees and my toes squirming in the shallow water, hanging just clear of the weed in the stream bed, when I got that feeling – like cold on the back of my neck – as if someone was watching me. I looked up at the bridge, the dark hawthorn hedge and the little dirt path that runs down between them; but I couldn't see anyone. Then, when I was about to go back to the house, there was a sound of hooves, hollow on the bridge. And my lover came on his grey horse.

'Stay there,' he called. And he tied his horse on the bridge, squeezed through the gap by the hedge and came out of the sunlight, down the path to me.

I remember how he came down in the dusk and knelt beside me on the bank. He took one foot from the water and bending down his head, kissed the cold-numbed toes. I remember his hands and his mouth warm and my foot still so cold from the stream. I remember the bend of his long neck above the good linen he wore.

'Let me bathe you,' he whispered.

I laughed and said the water was too cold, but I let him pull the string out of my bodice and bent my head so he could lift off the dress. My face, my hands and my forearms may be gypsy-dark from long toil in the sun and the wind, but the rest of my body's white as any lady's. Like a white flame on the dusk. I stood proudly because I liked the touch of his eyes. I might not be young, but my breasts were still firm, my belly soft and shapely.

Without a word, he took my hand and led me back to

the stream. And I stood with the weed wrapping softly round my ankles while he cupped the water in his hands and poured it over me, trickling it over my breasts till the tips glowed red as roses and smoothing the coolness of it down between my thighs.

Then he bent and licked the drops of water from my breast. He knelt down before me in the dusk. And I stood, white as a goddess, with my feet in the stream and the little fish nosing past my toes. The world was still and lovely in the dusk of the bridge, smelling of water and the nearby harvest field, and the wild garlic that his feet had bruised. In that moment of pure happiness, as if she knew my weakness, I felt the spirit close at hand again; a quiet heavy presence brooding in the weedy shadow of the bridge. I felt her reaching out to join with me, but this time I didn't fear her. I feared nothing; I felt strong and I exulted in my strength.

They say I have danced naked with the devil. Maybe I have. If it was so, then it was a sweet dance and, for all they say, I'd gladly tread that measure again. Even if it opened my heart to the evil spirit. Even if the end of that dance is the noose.

What sin can there be in such kindness as his . . . ?

Nay, very well, I'll say no more of that. But I have another reason for remembering that night. The spirit had taken possession of me and she drove me to a worse sin than lust that night.

When he left me it was dark, save for a pale, lopsided moon that was all but set. I watched the big grey horse fade into the dark lane, the last kiss still sweet on my mouth, and I stood a while by the hedge, breathing in the apple-smell of the sweetbrier and thinking about what had just passed. I felt very calm, very peaceful and full of love for him. Masters, believe me, I'd no notion then that he was anything but a man who came sometimes to love me. Whatever he is – and afterwards I learned something fearful about him – whatever he is, I swear I knew nothing of it then.

As I turned back along the path, I saw a bulky figure standing in the shadow of the hawthorn hedge. It took a step towards me and I recognized the stinking dun-coloured breeches and fat scarlet face of the bailiff. He was watching me and the look on his face was just like that old carving on one of the pew-ends in the church. The one they say is supposed to show the deadly sin of lust.

'How long have you been there?' I asked sharply.

'Long enough, my girl. Long enough to know you for the slut you are.'

I turned away towards the house, my heart loud and frightened.

'Wait!' He stepped forward and took hold of both my wrists. 'I've come to get my rent.'

'It's paid and you know it. I've said I want no other dealings with you.'

His hands twisted at my flesh till it seemed to burn.

'It's not for a whore to choose who buys her wares,' he said, spittle spraying my face. 'My money's as good as any man's.'

Damn him! Damn him!

Damn all you that dare to sit in judgement on me! Why don't you hang me and have done with it? I don't want to tell it all over in this foul, stinking hole . . . !

What did he do? What did he do? I'll tell you what the foul, hang-jowled fellow did. He took what I'd neither give nor sell him! He took it there against the wall of the house, grunting like the filthy swine he was, with his stinking breeches round his ankles.

May he be damned to hell for it!

I cursed him with the first breath I could draw. At least, the words of the curse came from my mouth. But it was the spirit that made me say them.

What, Saintly Eyes, has your companion left us? He must

have a weak stomach. Too weak perhaps to hear the curse I put on that fat bailiff whose name I find so difficult to remember . . .

Nay, my anger's passed now and the curse the spirit made me say isn't something to repeat when the blood has cooled. Let that fellow by the window just write down that I wished the wretch would never be able to use another woman so. That he'd never again have the power to do it.

And I cursed in the name of the toad and the bat and the blind-worm. The old words poured out of me as if they had been waiting years to be said. I felt the fire of the spirit burning on my cheeks and through my sore body; and the words poured out of me till the wretched fellow was pale and shaking. I remember how he started to run before he'd even got his breeches up. I remember his fat backside bobbing very white along the dark lane. And the strength of the spirit kept me standing and shouting till he'd gone.

Then I crawled, sore and broken, back to the big hearth in the cottage.

The sticks I'd thrown on the fire to warm us when we came in from the river bank had scarcely burned away. The little room with my bunches of mint and thyme hanging from hooks on the beams looked just the same as when I'd stepped out to bid him farewell. I crouched by the fire, angry but exulting in what I had done. And wondering if there was any power in the words to make my curse come true. Mother had told me the words had a meaning but she had never told me what that meaning was. Yet the spirit that possessed me knew how to use the power of those words . . .

Did the words make my curse come true? Master, I don't know. Because whatever power there was, it wasn't mine. It was hers – the spirit of the past.

As I crouched there on the hearth, the world darkened round me and she dragged me down and down. The hearth and the room and the herb bundles all faded away and I found myself in that dark place dancing with the two others: the spirit of the past and the spirit of the future.

'The charm's wound up!' cried the voice. 'Now we have all chosen it. Now we have power!'

But masters, it was power to do what she wanted, not what I wanted at all. It was because I'd been angry. Because I'd wanted revenge. That's what gave her evil a hold on me.

Then there was that dream. The stairs to climb. Up and up. And at the top a charred door standing ajar. Go in. Go in. It was the mouth of hell. And I knew that one day I'd have to go through it.

1996

As I expected, Greg was furious when he found that I'd arranged to spend an afternoon with Alan. 'Where the hell are you going?' he demanded.

'To see my grandmother.' The reply hung in the air between us, true but oddly unconvincing.

'Your grandmother?'

'It was your idea he should talk to her, Greg. Remember, he's interested in her story. The one about Glenlagan.'

'You mean he wants to be bored rigid?' he said nastily. He scowled at his watch. He was called for rehearsals that afternoon but I was free. 'You two seem to be getting very friendly. I don't know what you see in him.'

'He's interesting to talk to.'

'Talk? What do you talk about?'

'History, mainly.'

'Sounds fascinating! So when do you think you'll be able to tear yourself away from his riveting company and come home?'

'I don't know. And I don't see why it should matter to

you. I expect I'll be spending the evening on my own as usual.'

His manner towards Alan when he picked me up was far from friendly.

'He's not jealous, is he?' asked Alan as he cleared a pile of untidy papers off the front seat of the car for me and threw them into the chaos of books in the back.

'No, of course not.'

'Thanks, Abigail. You needn't sound quite so sure.'

'What do you mean?' I asked, carefully untwisting the seat-belt before fastening it.

'It's sometimes a bit insulting to be trusted too much.' He put the car into gear and turned his attention to the traffic. I couldn't tell if he was serious or not, so I just laughed to show I'd taken it as a joke.

I thought that was the best way of dealing with his odd moods.

As we crept through the crowded streets, the silence in the untidy car began to feel oppressive. The inside of that car felt very personal, it made me feel I was intruding on his life in a way I never had before: it smelled of musty books and his familiar leather jacket that was lying on the back seat, and of old Chinese takeaways as well. A couple of papers had escaped on to the floor under my feet and I found that the heel of my shoe had pierced them. I rescued them, smoothed them out as best I could and added them to the clutter in the back.

'Sorry about that. I hope they weren't important.'

'That's OK. Don't worry.' He drove in silence for a while, almost as if he was sulking, and I couldn't think of anything else to say. I began to wish I'd never agreed to this visit.

I was relieved when, as we got clear of the city traffic and the shadows of trees began to process through the car, he started to talk, in his usual abrupt way, about the book he was writing.

'Thousands of people left Scotland during the second half

of the nineteenth century, you know. A lot went to Canada, some to the United States and some to Australia. What I'm trying to do is find as many personal accounts as I can. The stories survive in families passed on from generation to generation.'

'That sounds interesting,' I said, glad to make conversation. 'I hadn't realized how widespread the emigration was till Gran and I went up to the Highlands. All those ruined houses! In some of the glens there seems to be nothing but ruins and sheep.'

'Big sheep farms were more profitable for the landlords than the small tenants. That's why the cottages were cleared. Forcibly at times.'

'I hope Gran agrees to talk to you. She can be pretty awkward sometimes. This is the place coming up on the left now. Through the stone gateposts there.'

Gran's nursing home is lovely. It's an old mansion that stands in its own grounds, surrounded by trees. It'd be wonderful living there if you were young enough to enjoy it and you didn't have to share it with a lot of other people that you'd not chosen to live with. Gran hates it. She hates the table manners of her fellow residents – particularly those of the lady who blows her nose on her napkin – and she hates the morals of the nurses. According to Gran there are strange men all over the building at night. She's got a point about the table manners, but I think the strange men have more to do with her sleeping tablets than the love lives of the nurses.

I try to get to see her every week but she's lost her grip on time and she always thinks it's months since I visited her.

'Too busy to bother, I suppose,' she said. She eyed Alan suspiciously as he sat awkwardly on the edge of one of the high, hard chairs in a corner of the commonroom. 'And what's this?' She jabbed a shiny-knuckled finger at the tape recorder he'd put on the coffee-table.

'It's just to make sure I don't miss any of your story, Mrs Granger.'

'There's no need to shout. I'm not deaf. Not like some.' She threw a contemptuous look in the direction of her companions gathered round the TV at the other end of the long room. 'And why should I tell you any story anyway?'

'I explained about it on the phone, Gran. This is Alan Stewart; he writes books about Scottish history and he'd like to hear about your great grandmother and her family being thrown out of Glenlagan.'

But she was in one of her most awkward moods and I could tell that for some reason, she'd taken a dislike to Alan. 'I don't like his name,' she whispered to me . . .

Oh, the reason she didn't like the name 'Stewart' was because the villain of her story was called Stewart. Gordon Stewart. He was the factor – or agent – who acted for the landlord when Gran's great, great grandmother and her family were evicted. (I think I've got that right, by the way. I tend to get the 'greats' a bit muddled up.) Like several other families, Gran's refused to leave their home at first. The factor acted with particular harshness, bringing men to throw them and their possessions out of the cottage before burning it to the ground. My great, great grandmother (or whatever she was) was pregnant at the time and both she and the baby died of exposure as the family huddled in a makeshift shelter. Afterwards her husband took the children to Canada – he had to, there was no hope left for them in Scotland. It wasn't an unusual case; I gather similar things happened all over the Highlands at that time. But the story – and the bitterness – lived on in our family.

Usually Gran will tell the story to anyone at the drop of a hat. She gets so angry about it you'd think it happened yesterday. But it took me nearly an hour to get her to talk to Alan about it that day.

'Stewart,' she muttered after she'd finished her tale. 'There's bad blood between us and the Stewarts.'

'Don't be so silly, Gran. That was more than a hundred years ago. And anyway, I dare say Alan's no relation. It's a common enough name.'

He'd gone back to the car by then, but she kept a chilly hold on my hand and wouldn't let me go. 'You don't want to have anything to do with the likes of him, Abby,' she whispered. 'He's no good; I can tell. Your Gregory's a bit bigheaded – thinks a good deal too well of himself – but he's better than this one. If you must have a man in your life, I tell you, you're better off sticking to Gregory.'

'Gran, I've every intention of sticking to Gregory. You know that.'

'What about this one then?'

'Alan's just a friend.'

'Trying to make your Gregory jealous, are you?'

'No. Well maybe a bit.'

'Up to his old tricks again then is he?'

'I don't want to talk about it, Gran.'

'Well, just don't make yourself ill over it this time.'

I escaped from her and crunched back through the gravel to the car-park, the scent of roses replacing the lingering disinfectant smell in my nose. When I looked back I could see her through the French windows, still sitting aloof from her companions, with her knuckles clenched on the top of her walking stick as she watched me go. She made me feel guilty but I couldn't quite put my finger on what I felt guilty about.

1606

The straw smells of damp and rats and a hundred other prisoners and the snatches of sleep that you allow me in it torment me nearly as much as the endless questions you keep me awake with. But why do you come to wake me,

Blubber Face? What more do you want? Tell me what you want to hear and I'll say it. Anything to get a little peace.

Just tell me what you want to hear!

Forgive me, master. The dream hangs on and my head won't clear . . .

Aye, it's the old dream. I thought confessing would stop the dream. But the evil spirit still calls me; trying to stop me confessing . . .

Your pardon, master. Aye, I see you're waiting. But why have you come alone without your skinny friend and the inky-fingered fellow who says nothing but writes all?

No, master, not to hurt me again! Please! Have mercy . . .

To bargain? But I don't know what you mean. I have nothing of yours to return. No master, I can't help you . . .

When I used the spell Mother taught me I spoke in anger. Forgive me, but if the spell has harmed you, I don't know how to undo it. Believe me. And I'll never tell, sir. I'll never say that you're the man I cursed. I'll not speak your name. You saw how careful I was in front of the skinny city man – I didn't name you, I only said it was a bailiff that'd angered me. I'll go to the gallows without naming you if you have mercy and don't hurt me again.

But here come the skinny one and the inky one. I've not much more to confess, masters, and may it soon be told so I can sleep in the straw till you take me to the rope's eternal nightmare. What have I told you? Of Michaelmas when the bailiff wronged me and I cursed him? And I've told you, haven't I, of how I heard there'd been a witch-finder come from London?

All the village had heard about him. And it seemed as if, all of a sudden, everyone was learned in the ways of recognizing witches. Old Saul at the inn talked about the little marks and blemishes that witches have hidden in their private parts; and the old fool would get himself so excited with his own talk, he'd start to stammer and shake. John Miller said it was a fact that his grandfather had died because a witch had made a waxen image of him and melted it over a slow fire – though that was a story no one had ever heard before and Margaret said she knew full well the old man had drowned when he overturned his cart on the bridge coming back drunk from market.

Once they started thinking on it, folk seemed to be able to remember all kinds of stories about witches. It became quite a fashion. And plenty of them were ready to look a bit warily at me. A woman living alone isn't a comfortable thing in a village, you see.

Folk only needed a word from the bailiff I'd cursed to start them wondering a bit. After what happened at the cottage at Michaelmas he didn't dare come to turn me out. But he could turn other folk's minds against me.

By that Christmas I knew it was just like it'd been in Berwick; I'd made a powerful enemy. There was hardly any work I could get that autumn, in field or dairy or kitchen. Scarce so much as a floor to scrub. Just like Berwick it was; folk were starting to say all manner of things about cures and stuff they'd been glad to take from me for years.

It seemed that what Mother had said was true; the poorer you get, the more folks turn from you for fear you'll ask too much. And even stuff that comes over-plentiful in its season, like the chestnuts that loaded the trees at the farm above the cottage, were grudged me that year, though I'd always been given them gladly before. A poor woman with a grudge that deals in herbs and cures: don't have any dealings with her, she's like to be a witch! That's what folk start to think – once the notion's been put into their heads.

By Christmas I was hungry. And that wasn't my only trouble.

I was sure I was with child too.

I took down the bunch of pennyroyal from the beam to make myself a draught. It's the best cure for that ill and I'd brewed it many a time for other women. But while the leaves were still steeping in my cup, the steam boiling over the pewter rim and drifting on the midwinter air that was nigh freezing even in the house, my lover came. And being no ordinary man (for men usually know nothing about such things) he knew straightway what the stuff was for.

He picked up the cup and smelled it, then he set it down and leaned his head against the beam that comes low over the hearth. 'Jennet,' he said, quiet and gentle as ever, 'I have no son.'

Ah, there was a world of heartache in those words! For a while he didn't seem able to say any more. He just stood with his head bowed over the smoke from the fire, while the steam rose from the cup and the strength of the brew was lost as it cooled in the draught that cut across from the door. There was no sound except the gentle flapping of the flames. Then he roused himself and went on, heavily, 'I'm getting wealth together. Buying honour and titles. But they're barren honours, Jennet, fruitless titles with no son of mine to succeed.'

I put my arms round him and leaned my cheek against his shoulder. 'My bairn couldn't bear your titles,' I whispered.

'No.' I felt him sigh. He was slight of frame; he seemed all restless sinew and bone. His shoulder was hard beneath my cheek. He turned and pulled me against him, his blue eyes pleading as they had over the worm. 'But he'd be mine for all that, Jennet. Nature's copy in which I'd see myself young again.' He rested his cheek against my hair and said something pretty, like a poem:

'This were to be new made when thou art old,
    And see thy blood warm when thou feel'st it cold.'

'Won't you give me that happiness, sweeting? I'd see you and the child wanted for nothing.'

I didn't answer. I couldn't speak the doubt in my mind. I couldn't say, 'I fear it's not of your getting.'

After a minute he took the cup to the door and poured the brew, hissing, on to the ice.

1996

I want to make one thing quite clear. I never slept with Alan Stewart. I never wanted to and I never intended to. There have been a lot of accusations and rumours flying around. And I think Greg started some of them.

But anyone who can believe that I was unfaithful to Greg just doesn't understand. It would have been impossible. Everything I did up till that moment on the opening night when I seemed to go mad and took the knife from the props table: everything I'd done up till that moment had been done for Greg. I took the part because it was what he wanted; I stuck at it because I didn't want to let him down; I kept quiet about the dreams because he didn't want to know about them.

And I spent time with Alan because I wanted to make Greg jealous.

That's the truth. It really is as simple as that.

All right, maybe that's not the whole truth. You sit there with that little recorder in your hand and I can almost feel it forcing confessions out of me. Like an instrument of torture. I admit I had another reason. There were plenty of other men I could have used, but I enjoyed Alan's company. It would be difficult not to enjoy being with someone who listens to you, who seems to enjoy listening and who seems really interested in everything about you. I've never been one of those women with lots of friends who get together to discuss the intimate details of their lives over endless lunches. I don't know why, but I've always got on better with men than other women. Maybe it's because my mother died when I was very young. I never really knew her. Gran was the only important female figure in my childhood: issuing transatlantic advice to my father on the rearing of daughters in long letters and phone calls. I love her dearly, but even after she came to live over here when I was in my teens, I was never really able to chat to her. You listen to Gran, you don't talk to her.

However there are times when you just have to talk. Sometimes talking is as inevitable as sneezing. I hardly saw Greg except on stage, but Alan was always there to listen to me.

After that visit to the nursing home things were somehow different. Until then we'd just met during breaks in rehearsals: now I seemed to start going out of my way to see him. I don't know why really; it just happened. I even went to his flat.

It was a strange place, at the top of a huge old house. All the servants' pokey little bedrooms knocked together, I think. It was all big new skylights and bare floorboards and a lot of the furniture looked as if it'd come secondhand from an office: metal filing cabinets and a big scarred wooden desk. It certainly looked more like the home of an academic than an actor. That surprised me a bit the first time I went. But then I looked around and thought – yes, I should have expected this; he's probably more at home with books than he is with people.

On the desk was a great untidy drift of papers. Papers of varying sizes, all covered in his thick uneven letters and arranged into loose stacks that were sliding into each other. From one of the stacks he pulled out the sheet of notes which was my official reason for that visit . . .

The unofficial reason? Well, Greg had claimed he was going to be working late. I liked the idea of him getting back and finding I was out.

Anyway, Alan had been very keen to show me these notes. 'There you are, Abigail,' he said proudly. 'A very interesting bit of your family history.' He'd researched Gran's story and I have to admit that – whatever his motives for looking into it might have been – what he'd turned up really was very interesting.

Her name, it seems, was Jean MacAlistair and she did die within a few weeks of the eviction, giving birth to a stillborn son. Alan had discovered that from local records. But he'd also found that the eviction was not the beginning of the antagonism between Jean and Gordon Stewart. Nearly twelve months before her death, the factor had arrived in Glenlagan with the notice to quit for the crofters.

And it was the women of the community who went out to meet him, read Alan's thick black scrawl. *For some reason this seems to have been the case quite often when the unwelcome news of eviction arrived. Jean MacAlistair led the women on this occasion. To avoid actually receiving the notice, the women surrounded the Factor and, shouting insults, forced him to hold the paper while they set fire to it. Jean, who had incited this rebellious behaviour, was held to be responsible for his injuries and he seems to have particularly feared her.*

'Why should he fear her?' I asked, looking up from the page. 'She was just a poor woman afraid of losing her home. He was the one with all the power.'

The face behind me was sort of bright. Alan was high on his drug – history. He was very excited about this.

'Ah, but she had quite a reputation, had Jean MacAlistair. Here, look at the next page. I found some old newspaper reports of the business.' He pointed with a thick forefinger.

When there was talk of bringing him to court for his cruel treatment of the MacAlistair family, all kinds of accusations were made. There were rumours of a long-standing feud between Stewart's family and the family of Jean's mother. There were also accusations of witchcraft made against Jean MacAlistair. In the end the matter was hushed up and the MacAlistair family were paid their passage to Canada by Stewart's employer.

It's a terrible story, isn't it? But I think it's probably true. I've thought about it a lot and I can't think of any reason why Alan should have made up those details. Whatever his reasons for wanting to find out more about that old story – and I did eventually begin to suspect that his interest went a bit deeper than just an attempt to get close to me – whatever his motives were, I can't see any reason why the details of his account should be false.

Anyway, whether the story was true or not doesn't really matter. What is significant is that it was about then that my feelings towards Alan began to change. I remember how he hung over me, sweating, as I read the notes, perching on the arm of the hard chair, one hand resting heavily on my shoulder while the other moved across the untidy page. I remember feeling hot and uncomfortable with the evening sunlight on the back of my neck from one of the giant skylights.

'Alan, I think I'd better go.' I removed the big hand pointedly from my shoulder.

'What's the matter?' he said resentfully. 'Will Gregory be wondering where you are?'

Something about his manner made me very uncomfortable, very embarrassed.

In the end the embarrassment overcame my need to talk and even making Greg jealous didn't seem worth that much discomfort. That's why I stopped enjoying his company and started avoiding him.

By the time the play opened I hadn't spent any time with Alan for a week, maybe ten days. Honestly I hadn't. Several papers have tried to make out that I was having an affair with him, but there is no truth at all in those rumours.

Listen. Make sure you get this on your recorder because this is one of the things I haven't told anyone else and I want you to know. I want everyone out there who's judging me to understand this:

By the time the play opened I had stopped encouraging what the papers refer to as Alan's 'attentions'. In fact I had begun to think that maybe it was true what they said: that maybe he really was a bit of a head case. A few days after I

CRITICAL
read those notes I discovered something very strange about

read those notes I discovered something very strange about him.

1606

'You'll know,' Margaret told me. 'As soon as you set eyes on the child you'll know which man fathered it. They all have the look of their fathers at first.'

I said that was not much of a comfort and wished I'd not told her my trouble. But sometimes a woman just has to talk of what's on her mind and I'd got no other friend to turn to. I'd never chattered much over the gleaning and the weeding like some women did. Mine had been a lonely life – leastways since Mother died.

'Look Jennet,' Margaret said. 'You must rid yourself of this load. Make a brew. He need never know you did it a-purpose.'

'But he looked so sad. And he wants the bairn so much.'

'And maybe he does, now. But men are all fools and likely by next year he'll have forgotten all about it – or only notice it to complain about its noise or its smell.'

'Nay. I think he'd keep his word and see it well-provided for.'

'If it's got his looks. Men want to see themselves in their brats. "My nose" they say. "My father's eyes". As if they'd made the child all on their own.' Margaret spat.

'And maybe he will see himself in this child.'

'And maybe he won't. Maybe he'll just see old pudding face from up yonder.'

'But see, Margaret, most likely if I quickened that night I'd have quickened the first time. Not the second time, surely – not when I was standing up – and struggling too.'

'Why girl, there's no knowing. A woman doesn't get a child just when she wants. You ask any woman who's nine or ten mouths to feed and finds herself in trouble again.'

'But most likely it was got before Michaelmas. I'd had no courses since harvest began. At least I think I hadn't.'

I was desperate to believe it was my lover's child. And sometimes I was certain that it was. Three times I made the brew to rid myself of it, but each time, as I set the warm rim of the cup to my lips, I'd be sure it was his and I'd remember the pretty lines:

'This were to be new made when thou art old,
And to see thy blood warm when thou feel'st it cold.'

And I'd think how I could do such a wonderful thing for him. I'd feel weak inside with love for him and I couldn't drink.

It was his, surely it was his. And while there was a chance that it was of his getting, how could I rid myself of it?

He was kind and saw how bad things were with me: how I could get no work. He offered me gold, which he'd never done before; before there had been gifts but never money. I gave it back to him and said I was no trull to be paid for my favours.

'Nay, Jennet.' Kindly he put the gold back into my hand and closed my fingers round it. 'I know you are no such thing. But you're the mother of my child and for your sake and the babe's, I'd see you well fed.'

I wept that day. And I took his money too, because he made me feel there was more dignity in taking than there was in refusing. I could not help but love him. All I wanted to know was that I really was the mother of his bairn.

But try as I might to tell myself it must be his, I could never be sure.

1996

I only went to that garret flat a couple of times: three – maybe four times at the most. At first it seemed fun. Like

student days, I suppose: talking over coffee in the after-
noons. It was certainly better than sitting at home on my
own, wondering where Greg was. But then . . .

Yes, I started to get suspicious about Alan. I saw a
disturbing side of him that I'd not seen before. I began to
realize that his interest in the past was a kind of obsession
and he could get things out of all proportion.

The last time I went to see him was on a wet afternoon a
little more than a week before the play opened. I remember
Greg had just told me that he intended to spend the
weekend in town again instead of going to the cottage with
me as he'd promised. I felt miserable; the rain made me
feel worse and Alan didn't do much to cheer me up.

'I was working,' he said, gesturing towards the confusion
on the desk.

But for all that he stopped work, put my wet coat on the
radiator, offered me whisky and, when I refused, made
coffee. That was the thing about Alan: he always did make
time for me: but he was somehow less willing that day. I
remember sitting in one of the hard chairs with its high
wings enclosing my head. I remember feeling as grey and
damp as the afternoon. I remember how he seemed
unusually sullen. But I don't really remember what we
talked about . . .

Oh no, it wasn't anything he said that made me start to
wonder about him. It was what I found. What I found on
the desk.

I'd been there about half an hour, I suppose, and I was
thinking about going – I was due at rehearsals later in the
afternoon – when the phone rang. He took the call in the
bedroom and I was left with that sort of aimless feeling you
have when you're trapped in someone else's home while
they're busy. You wonder whether to leave and how long
it'll be before they're free; you don't want to seem rude by
behaving as if you're bored, but you're suddenly stuck with
nothing to do.

Normally at such times I start looking at my host's bookshelves, but there weren't any in the room. There was only the desk with its usual load of books and papers.

So I looked at those.

I didn't expect any of it to be private. Just work, I thought. And at first glance that's what it seemed to be. Sheets of notes and books with trailing strips of paper marking pages. He kept everything in manuscript and I know he had an eccentric distrust of computers. Then I noticed that the pages he'd been working on last were different from the others heaped around them.

It was a collection of A4 sheets which seemed to be stacked like the others – until the grey light from the streaming glass in the roof caught the edge of the top sheet and I noticed that these pages were Sellotaped together. Carefully I opened them out and they half-covered the desk. About twelve sheets joined into an irregular shape to accommodate a huge, sprawling, impossibly complicated family tree. In letters thick and black enough to stand out from the crowding notes and names and annotations, the title read THE STEWARTS.

There they were: all the Kings of Scotland, Mary Queen of Scots, James I of England and his son Charles I. But there was much more. One name leapt out at me from the bottom left hand corner of one of the outlying sheets: Alan Stewart (b. 1958). It had been highlighted with one of those fluorescent fibre pens.

I pressed my finger to the name in disbelief, rereading it and making a rough calculation of age. Yes, thirty-eight, that'd be about right. I looked guiltily towards the half-open door of the bedroom: suddenly aware that I was, after all, intruding on something personal. From beyond the door his low voice droned on intermittently, telephone-style.

Too curious to stop now, I began to trace the line back through a maze of generations and found that it wasn't difficult to do. All the relevant names had been underlined. It was clear that they made up the chief interest of the document. In a long and very complex route that involved several dotted lines and question marks (and, by the way, they seemed to me to suggest doubt even in the mind of this very biased historian), the line ran back to one James V of Scotland. I'd never heard of him. A quick look along another limb of the vast tree showed that he was the father of Mary Queen of Scots and grandfather of England's James I. He also seems to have been a man of easy morals and rampant fertility: the tree positively blossomed around him. It was only the legitimate line leading off through Mary and James that had a sparse look to it.

So Alan believed he was descended from the Stewart royal family – illegitimately at least.

I stared down at the complicated diagram with its notes, its question marks and its tentative connections. Was it scholarship or wish-fulfilment? I certainly didn't understand history well enough to know for sure, but I suspected it was a mixture of the two.

'So now you know the truth about me, Abigail.'

Alan was standing at the door, the phone still in his hand and a flushed kind of smile on his face.

'I'm sorry. I didn't mean to be nosy.' I laughed with embarrassment. 'I didn't know you were of royal descent.'

'I've only just finished working it all out.'

'I see.'

He put down the phone and came to join me by the desk, switching on the battered desk lamp and pulling it down to augment the grey daylight. The taped papers lay focused in a circle of yellow.

'Do you see what it means, Abigail?' he said solemnly.

'You're the heir to the throne?'

He didn't return my smile. 'No, not the royal bit. I've suspected that for a long time. But this.' He stabbed at the papers. 'It means that you and I are sworn enemies.'

'What?'

'Look.' He took hold of my right hand and laid the forefinger on his name – not very gently, either. Then he moved it up the page – rather like an impatient adult teaching a slow child to read. 'There.' He pressed my finger to an underlined name that I'd not taken much notice of before. It was his great great great great grandfather (give or take a great or two). Gordon Stewart (1802 to 1875).

I looked up blankly at his face – red above the beard and his lips open and twitching. He was clearly excited about something, but at first I didn't see what he was getting at.

'Gordon Stewart of Glenlagan,' he said slowly, as if I really was very stupid.

'The man in Gran's story?'

'Yes.'

'How can you know that?'

'I've looked into it, Abigail. It's definitely the same Gordon Stewart. No wonder the old lady didn't like me.'

'That means nothing. Gran hardly likes anyone these days.'

'She's got good reason to dislike me.'

'What rubbish! That all happened more than a hundred years ago.'

'Abigail, you and I have the blood of Scottish clans in our veins. Feuds aren't forgotten. They go on from generation to generation.'

'It's nonsense, Alan. I've never heard anything about anyone in my family feuding with anyone called Stewart.'

'Maybe that's because the bloodlines haven't met for the last hundred and sixty years. How could they when your mother's family were living in Canada?'

He'd let go of me by now, but he was still standing very close. Too close. He did that sometimes and it irritated me. I was very aware of him invading my personal space. I moved away and picked up my coat, warm and damp from

the radiator. 'You are joking about this, aren't you, Alan?
You can't possibly be serious about it.'

I remember how he dropped down into the chair by the
desk, swivelling it around and leaning back as far as he
could.

'No, I'm deadly serious, Abigail. It explains everything.'

'What? What does it explain?'

'It explains how I feel about you. How I'm drawn to you
even though you insult me.'

I couldn't believe I was having this bizarre conversation!
I kept thinking he'd start laughing in a minute and admit it
was a joke. But he just kept staring at me.

'I don't know what you're talking about Alan. I've never
insulted you.'

'Nearly everything you say to me is insulting. You treat
me like I don't exist – or as if I was a dog or something.
"Good old Alan, he'll come when I call". And it was just
laughable, wasn't it, when I suggested Gregory might be
jealous of me?'

'Look, I'm sorry if I've hurt you. I never meant to.'

'Perhaps you couldn't help it,' he said, picking up the
taped sheets. He was smiling after a fashion now, but it was
a twisted kind of smile: his teeth showed as if he was in
pain. 'Perhaps,' he said slowly, 'it's in your blood.'

'This is ridiculous, Alan. I'm going.'

I left then and I never went to his flat again.

1606

But what's to do? What are those voices shouting in the
free street outside my prison?

What, Blubber Face? Your friend has gone very quickly.
Did I hear that cry aright? A message from the King? Now
why should the King's messenger come here?

Ah! Your face is as blank as it is ugly. I begin to think

you know no more of what is happening here than I do. Well, let it all be. If messengers were to come from God Himself, they can't kill me more than once. But see, I am glad we are alone, for I've something to say that's for your ears alone.

The devil came here last night, you know. He came here to this cell. I don't know how he came, but there he was in the foul darkness, reaching a white hand down into the rat-ridden straw to take my hand. The same as ever, with his fine blue coat and his ring and his searching eyes. He told me he'd use his powers to save me from this prison. But he gave me something too. He gave me poison and he told me that if he failed to free me I must take my own life. A foul sin to tempt me to!

But see, master, you mustn't tell your London friend, because the devil told me something else as well. He told me how to cure you: how to restore your manhood . . .

Aye, it's all true. Last night he came here, with the poison and the charm to cure you. And if I'd not known before that he was more than mortal, I'd have known it now. But I did know. I learnt it too late, but I knew it before last night.

At first, master, when you brought me here, I couldn't believe that it was the devil I'd lain with. Though you told me yourself about his ice-cold seed and the unnatural acts he made me perform, it was all much more than my poor wits were able to remember. Maybe if I'd been wiser I'd have known him for what he was when the spirit began to trouble me. I reckon maybe I was slow to believe it because it was something I didn't want to believe.

But I believe it now. I have good cause now to believe it! The day you first brought me to this prison I found out something terrible about that fine man on his grey horse.

Listen. At first when the jeering crowd came to Eldridge's and would have taken me to the river to swim me, I didn't believe he was the devil, though I knew I was bad and fit to die.

'It was a spirit possessed me,' I told them as I crouched by the cold hearth, still sore and weak from the birth. And I knew it was true, for what else but an evil spirit would make me do what I'd done in that chamber at the head of the stairs.

And it was you, master, all red-faced and sweating in the middle of my little room, the bunches of marjoram and sage swinging about your ears, it was you, as you held back the crowd a moment with your arm, like Moses commanding the Red Sea, you said, 'It is the devil, woman, that has corrupted you through the lust of the flesh.'

The devil! No, that I could not believe. I had lusted, it was true, and that was a sin; but it was only for a mortal man. I'd swear he was a mortal man – and a good man too. And even while they were pulling tight the biting cords and bending me double till my back felt like to break, so they could tie my wrists crosswise to my feet, even then I was thinking: nay, they lie about him. There was love between him and me and it was the one good thing in my life. They lie about him. Through the pain and the fear and the strangeness of those familiar faces twisted awry with hatred, I held on to that thought.

It was only later, after the skinny London man had come to stop them, his big horse dancing and trampling the green growth of the river bank into clogging mud, it was only then that I began to wonder if there was any truth in your words.

'There must be a trial!' shouted the London man. 'The King wishes it.' And the curses and the jeers all along the river bank were stilled so that the little sounds of the wood pigeons and the weir crept back. 'She must stand trial at the assizes. Justice must be done according to the King's law.'

So they brought me here and I found that I was not to

die straight away as I would certainly have done at the hands of my neighbours, but to face questions and questions and the certainty of the gallows in the end. So then I thought, I must know: I must prove to myself that he was man, not devil.

That was the last night of peace I ever had, for you didn't start your questions till morning; but I couldn't sleep. There was no getting away from the coldness of the stone. It battered its way up through the straw, no matter how I wadded the filthy stuff under me, and there was nothing else, not so much as a stool to put between my backside and the cold. There was a moon up, painting the bars in shadow across the merciless stone and I sat in the patch of light, listening for the first time to the prison sounds: the rats squealing and fighting somewhere in the darkness, groaning from another prisoner in a different hell somewhere close at hand, laughter and the rattling of dice from the jailer and his friends. Through the bars came the scents of a herb garden: mint and thyme and the rank smell of chives. And I thought: somewhere near there's another woman who keeps a garden like mine at Eldridge's Hollow. Does she grow her herbs for the cooking pot only, I wondered, or is she too a maker of brews and potions? Is she too in danger of being called evil by her neighbours?

And that set my mind to wondering in the coldness of the cell what it was that'd made me evil. Was I gotten evil? Had I sucked the poison from my mother's breast? What had caused the spirit to possess me and make me kill? Was my lover in truth the devil? Was it my desire for him that had led me into evil?

See master, I didn't want to believe that and I thought of a way to prove that it wasn't true. I thought: I'll see his fortune and in that I'll see his end and I'll know for sure that he's a mortal man like any other.

It's a simple enough thing to do, the way my mother taught me, with the charm of the Three Sisters. You must

hold the brooch with their faces on it in your hand until
it's warm, then picture in your mind the face of the one
whose fortune you will see. Then you must lie down to
sleep with the charm under your head.

I took it out of my gown where I'd hid it and the three
familiar faces looked strangely calm in the moonlight. I
remember thinking how they seemed to care naught for
my misery. I stood by the window where the scent of herbs
crept in to relieve the prison stench and I thought on his
face as I'd seen it in the harvest field: smooth cheeks and
high forehead, a straight, long edge of nose, blue eyes
under high arching brows and a small mouth that was
never still. I remembered him laughing over the blind-
worm. Then I bundled up the straw as best I could and lay
me down to sleep with the brooch clutched under my
head. I dreamed his fortune and when I woke, I knew for
certain that he was no mortal man.

There was no end to his future.

I saw him and his words living for ever in the hearts of
men and women as yet unborn. And I knew then that you
must be right. It was none but the devil that had taught me
how to love. I was a woman who'd lain with the devil; little
wonder then that an evil spirit had taken possession of me
and made me kill.

And to kill where I loved most dearly.

Here, Blubber Face, stop crossing yourself. The devil
means you no harm. Didn't I tell you that he has told me
how to get back your manhood which the curse took from
you?

This is what you must do to be free of the curse: take the
brooch. Nay take it; it won't hurt you. Not if you do with it
exactly what I say. Take it back to Eldridge's Hollow and
hide it in the cottage there. The stone flag at the side of the
door is loose; it's where I always hid any little bit of money
I ever had. Put the brooch under that stone, close the door
and come away. If you do that, Blubber Face, and tell no

one about it, you'll be cured. You'll get your manhood
back . . .

For what it's worth!

Well, the fat fool's gone to do it and I hope the devil
spoke true and it works.

'Tell him to do something. Anything. No matter what,'
the devil said. 'If he believes that doing it will cure him,
he'll be cured.'

The devil's work is a strange business indeed!

He said that with this fat one on my side, it might be
possible to get me freed. But I don't think so. The thin city
man with the eyes of a saint is more powerful, I reckon,
and I can tell he wants me hanged.

He's a strange fellow, with his quiet ways, his fine silk
doublet and his messages from the King. I have wondered
for days now why he has come all the way from London to
bother with the trying of a poor woman like me. And why
does he want so much to see me hanged? He doesn't say
much. He sits by mostly, while the fat one talks about the
evil things I've done, and he nods and he tells his clerk to
write it all down. But all the time it's as if he's knocking
nails into my gallows.

And this morning I learned something that surprised me:

This London man, with his fine clothes and his fine ways,
fears me as much as the fat oaf I cursed. He is full of
learning, but it seems his learning makes him as afraid of
me as the other fellow's foolishness.

He came here early when this cell was just light but at its
coldest and the pigeons were just beginning to call beyond
the bars, and he brought the barber with him. To shave my
head.

The shears jabbed my skull in a dozen places, though I
stood as still as I could. I stood and watched the long black
hair drop and curl in the patch of light the window puts on
the stone beside the straw. There was a lot of it, a great soft

heap, dark beside the greyish straw, and the barber had a mind to take it away to make a wig.

'No' said the London fellow, catching the barber's sleeve as he stooped to gather it. 'It must be burned.'

'But why? I'll pay for it.'

'The woman is a witch. Everything about her must be destroyed – the evil must be cleansed.'

Then he stirred the black curls with the toe of his shoe and his face went thinner and tight with thought. 'His Majesty does well to warn us of woman's alluring beauties. It is their vanity that leads them into evil and their beauty tempts men to sin. But what is this, this beautiful long hair that acts like a snare to men?' He kicked the pile of hair as if it was a dog that had bitten him. 'Just rubbish to be burned. And what is she now to tempt godly men to fornicate?' He turned to look at me, dirty from the straw and my shorn head bleeding. And he gave a kind of fearful smile. As if the shears had made a dangerous thing safer – like a strong chain fastened round a wild animal.

He fears me, I thought. He – aye and his master, the King – for all their wealth and learning, can fear a weak, poor woman. And because they fear me, I'll hang.

Let the devil say what he will to torment me with false hope, I know I'll hang. For here they come now: the London man in his russet doublet with a handkerchief held against the prison's stink and, trailing behind him, the pockmarked man with inky hands comes scurrying, his arms full of parchment and his quill between his teeth. And I must tell them the end of my story. I must tell them about that night down at Eldridge's Hollow when the spirit drove me to kill.

I'll hang. And maybe it's right that I do. Perhaps they are right to fear me. I have done an evil thing.

But at least Mother's brooch is safe. I didn't want that to fall into their hands. Let it lie in the cottage and maybe a cleverer woman than me will find it. One that can understand its power. Mother always said I should pass it on to my daughter with the words, as it had been passed on for generations. She said it must remain in our line.

But I have no child and I know no kin to give it to. It grieves me to leave it so; Mother would be angry with me if she knew I'd failed. Sometimes in my snatches of sleep I dream of her face furrowed with anger and of her voice scolding me. But what can I do? I know of no way to get the brooch or the things she taught me to her sisters' folk in Glenlagan. So let it lie in the cottage; let the old powers sleep there.

Come then, master, I'll tell the end of my tale and yon fellow can write it down. I'll put my mark on it gladly and then let me hang.

I'm not frightened any longer. I have gone beyond fear now.

But I was frightened then. When the time came for my child to be born I was more frightened than I'd ever been before. I beg you'll remember that, masters. Fear's like madness; it makes folk do strange things. It wasn't because of the pain I was frightened; I'd seen others through it and I reckoned that what other wenches could stand, I'd manage too. But I was afraid of the baby; afraid of what it'd be like.

'Nature's copy,' he'd said. But who would this bairn be a copy of? Which was the man that'd stamped its features?

Fear, masters, fear and loneliness seized me. For see, I'd no friends in the village and if my lover'd not stand by, things would go hard with me.

So I lay alone in the bedroom at Eldridge's when the time came. It was three months since I'd laid out poor old Margaret for her grave after the sweating sickness took her. And there wasn't one other in the village that'd stand friend to me by then. The rumours of witchcraft had got such a hold on folk. There wasn't one that'd offered to help, though my state was plain for all to see. I lay under the sagging ceiling about two days past midsummer, watching dawn break, grey as tears, through the straggling branches of the crab-apple tree, listening to the pigeons call; waiting as the pains got stronger. And I thought, I'll know. When I see the child, I'll know for sure which man fathered it; whether it was a fat ugly fellow with a face carved out of lard, or a man with a look that'd turn your heart weak.

I'd know.

But what then? If I'd got a bairn that my lover could never see himself in: if this was not his son, he'd know too. And what would become of me?

The June day grew hot under the apple trees and the bees droned among the herbs. From time to time, one would crawl stupidly over the sill and blunder about a bit before finding its way back to freedom. The day wore on and the pains got stronger. And the fear grew. Better, I thought as I sweated through noontime, better it dies than lives without the look of the man that'd provide for it. Better it dies.

Shadows stretched themselves slowly from the trunks of the trees as I lay in pain on the soiled bed. And the bulge in the ceiling seemed to billow before my eyes. From time to time now the bees' hum and the bubbling of the wood pigeons faded into blackness as I tired.

I knew I'd have to keep my wits clear if I was to deal with this all alone. I'd have to stay awake. But by the time moonlight crept over the sloping floor, I could feel myself sinking, sinking down into darkness. And I knew the spirit was fighting to possess me again. All muddled with the moonlight and the smell of the blossom now were those dancing faces; the voices whispering in that other place.

Then there was one great pain tearing through my body and searing through my head like a white-hot flame. The moonlight and the blossom were all swallowed up in the darkness of that other place.

And so was I.

Her hands seized mine.

Now! I could feel her triumph as she took possession of me . . .

What happened next? What happened? You sit there with your pig eyes all bright: eager to drive another nail into my gallows! You'll never understand if I should talk from now till Christ comes again what happened, or how I tried to fight against that evil spirit.

I tried to fight her, but she was stronger than me.

For a long time there was just darkness and pain and then the dream. The same dream of the stone stair twisting up to a half-open door. I stooped down, touched the stone treads and felt the blood, but this time I remembered why there was blood on my hands. I knew what was happening to me. But it made no difference, I had to climb those stairs. Up and up to that charred and broken door, my heart beating thickly because I knew that this time I had to go in.

Then I could feel the wooden latch in my hand, all sticky with blood. I didn't want to open that door. I knew it was hell that lay behind it. But she was making me do it. I tried to scream, but the sound wouldn't come out; it just choked my mouth. And all the time my bloodied hand was pushing open the door . . .

Yes, I saw what lay beyond it. I saw . . .

Damn you! You know too! You know as well as I do what lay beyond it.

It was the bedroom at Eldridge's that lay beyond that door. With the light of dawn falling square on the bed: a grey twisted cover all soaked in water and blood and the smell of it mixing with the scent of blossom from the window. My baby lay with his tiny cheek resting softly on my breast. And my hands were at his throat . . .

Aye, he was dead! Have I ever said it was not so? Have I ever even said that it was not these hands that choked the life out of him? There were no other hands in that room to do it. These hands, all bloody with his birth, had strangled him. But it was the spirit that possessed me, made me do it. She did it. And yet . . .

No, I'll not think that! He was my baby. My own sweet son that I loved the moment my eyes fell on him, even though he had the fat ugly look of the man that'd fathered him. So small he was in my grasp. So slippery. I remember how, limp and still as he was, I pressed his blue mouth to my breast in some mad hope he'd suck. He was my bairn. Unless the spirit possessed me I could not have done it. I couldn't. And yet . . .

Ah, how eagerly you watch me! You know the doubts that torture me. You know the terrors that haunt this cell of mine. So write it down, hang me and may the devil take you!

I had wished him dead. I am evil; I must be. It was the evil in me that gave the spirit her chance.

1996

Alan behaving so strangely, the dreams disturbing my sleep and a ghost haunting my work. By the first night I was nearly out of my mind with worry.

As you know, the opening of the Maypole was a circus of publicity. There were television cameras about for days and microphones like soft toys. And journalists – were you there?

Oh, you were there for the kiss, were you? Yes, I remember that clearly. Greg enjoying the cameras: looking his full six foot: with more life and enthusiasm in him than is natural – or safe. I'd no idea he was going to embrace me like that. But that's Greg – always ready with the perfect gesture. The dramatic touch to make everyone see us as the perfect team – the perfect couple. Not just a couple

either: the perfect family. Did you see the picture of the
two of us in costume with Luke?

That was on the day we opened and by then things were
not good between Greg and me. In fact he could barely
bring himself to talk to me when the cameras weren't on
us. I was desperately tired and worried.

The final days of rehearsal, which are, of course, always
hectic and strained, had been almost intolerable to me this
time. I was tortured by lack of sleep and twice during those
last few days I had seen that strange figure standing in the
wings when I was on stage: her hand raised as if she was
beckoning to me. And there was no one I could talk to
about it. After that strange episode over the family tree, I
was steering clear of Alan's long dark stares. And I didn't
dare breathe a word of my fears to Greg – even supposing
I'd had a chance. He was never at home long enough for us
to have much of a conversation.

Of course my performance suffered. 'You're doing OK,
Abby, but I get the feeling you're not quite giving it all
you've got,' said John.

'I'm sorry.'

He patted me comfortably. 'That's all right, my dear. It's
sometimes best to hold back a bit in rehearsal. Just so long
as you pull out all the stops on the first night.'

'I'll try,' I promised wearily. But I wasn't sure I'd have
the energy. It seemed ages since I'd had a decent night's
sleep.

Then, the night before we opened, I had the dream three
times and it frightened me more each time. It was different,
much worse than usual. And after I dreamed it for the third
time I just could not go back to sleep again. I was terrified
of what might happen if I did.

I'd gone to bed early that night with a hot drink and a
Jane Austen novel – that's my usual recipe for calming
nerves. But I was finding it very difficult to relax. I couldn't
get away from this feeling that there was a ghost waiting

for me in the theatre. And then there was the empty space in the bed where Greg should be.

I couldn't make much progress with *Pride and Prejudice*; I just lay there wondering where Greg was. I turned off the bedside light and lay for what seemed a long time, staring at the sickly light filtering from outside on to the ceiling, longing for the real darkness of the countryside, and listening tensely for the sound of his car.

Then, more suddenly than such things should happen, the dream began. I was standing somewhere dark and cold with two other icy hands clasped in mine.

'Peace,' said a hoarse voice. 'The charm's wound up.'

I looked to right and left: two figures darkly hooded in the darkness. 'Go on,' said the voice. 'Climb the stairs.'

Then suddenly I was alone and there was a narrow flight of stone stairs before me; they twisted slightly between stone walls, but the door at the top was visible, black at the bottom, slightly open. Moving against my will, I set my foot in the hollow of the first step and began to climb. I could smell stone and fire, scorched wood – and blood.

Blood on the steps beneath my feet. Stooping down with my heartbeat thudding through my whole body, I touched it. Sticky on my hands. But I had to go on. Beyond the door was something I must see, something I must know about.

Inside me the scream was building, choking in my throat. My hand reached for the door – and I didn't wake up as I always had before.

The door crept open with a dull groan and I stepped into the room beyond.

Moonlight from a window fell across scorched boards and in its track lay the body of a woman, face down in a welter of blood, faded fair hair straggling down her back, its loose ends dangling stickily in the dark pool. Beside her, with small hands still clinging to her long skirt, was the body of a little girl barely toddling age. Close by, half in and half out of the moonlight, lay what seemed to be a boy a few years older. There was blood everywhere: on the floor and on the walls; bedding, roughly made toys and a roll of wool were scattered about in confusion. The place stank chokingly. The smell rose even from my own hands. I was sure I was going to be sick. I retched – and the scream burst out of me at last, dragging me back to my half-empty bed under the light-smeared ceiling.

I lay sweating and gasping as my scream rang and faded through the dismal, empty house, then I raised myself up on the pillows and scrabbled for the light. The little green figures of my clock showed 1.14. By the clock lay the open paperback and an empty mug ringed in cold froth. Beside me the bed yawned emptily.

Quarter past one and Greg was still not home.

I leaned back against the pillows and pushed the quilt off my sweating body. I still felt sick; the scene of carnage had been vivid. The stink of it had brought it unbearably close, making it quite different from a scene in a film. I had to gaze around at the little familiar things: in an attempt to erase the horror; to get reality back into the right shape. I stared at gaudy tissues unfurling from a box on the dressing table; at Greg and Luke smiling from the photo frame beside the bed.

So this was what lay beyond the door, I thought: blood, death and destruction. But why did the dream haunt me?

And then, with no warning, no sense of encroaching sleep, I was dreaming again.

The same figures dancing; the same voice. And the thought: not again. I can't go through it again.

There were stairs before me, but they were different: bare wood with a handrail, rising only a short way, no more than a dozen steps. I knew this place.

I was standing in the living room of the cottage, facing the stairs to the bedrooms. It was familiar even in the half-light, but the fear was the same as ever.

'Go on. You must climb the stairs.'

No! Not again. My own voice seemed to echo in my skull. I have done it. I have seen. I won't go up again.

'But you must.'

And my feet were already moving on the wooden stairs. Up and up. Ahead was the door of Luke's room. The room that had been my own when I was a child; a room I loved dearly, with its sloping floor and its low irregular ceiling. But I was shaking with terror at the sight of that door. Something terrible lay beyond it; something unbearable.

I won't. I can't.

But my hand was on the latch of the door and it was swinging open as the scream gathered inside me. I stepped in.

It was grey dawn in the room; light from the open window fell on a low bed under the bulging ceiling. A bed with twisted covers soiled with blood and water. On the bed lay a woman soaked in sweat, with her newborn baby in her hands. She was small with wild eyes under black tangled hair. I stepped closer to see what she was doing. She lay on her side, her breasts bare and ghost-white, and the child lay on the filthy mattress beside her. Its creased face looked strange, greyish-blue with something more than the dreary light. It was choking. Then I saw that the woman's hands – red and cracked, with black-rimmed nails – were at the child's throat.

At the sight of those red hands on the frail white newborn flesh, the scream burst out and woke me, dragging me back into the safety of familiar things. But familiar things didn't seem so safe any longer.

I was still sweating on the bed, my hands still holding back the quilt and the little green figures had processed only to 1.32. This time I really was going to be sick. I stumbled through into the bathroom, just in time. As I washed afterwards, I peered at myself in the unhealthy mirror light. My face was pale with black lines gouged under the eyes.

'God! What's happening?' I demanded of the sickly reflection. But the sound of my own voice wasn't comforting. I was in that state of stretched-out fear that comes when you're tired and alone. It's rather like being afraid of yourself.

'Where's Greg?' I asked the white face, hoping that the normal, natural question would sound better. 'It's nearly two and he's not home.'

That felt a bit better. Think about that: not those stairs, those terrible choking hands. I padded back through the bedroom and out to the landing, flicking on all the lights as I went. The landing opens out into a kind of gallery overlooking the ground floor which lay in darkness beneath me now, familiar furniture contriving sinister shadows. But at the back of the landing a flight of stairs leads up to the second floor where Luke's bedroom and Greg's study are tucked into the old attics. Under the stairs, a window overlooks the drive at the side of the house and it was to this window I went now to see if his car was there.

I pushed aside the blind and looked out. Street lights smeared the darkness. Out on the street, car tyres whispered wetly and greasy tarmac gleamed, but the drive was empty.

'I hope he's not had an accident,' I said, speaking mechanically to fill the emptiness. But I didn't really think it was likely that he had.

I crept back to the bedroom where the book, the empty mug and the open bed gave the place a stale kind of look – like a bedroom when you've had a day in bed with 'flu. There was nothing to do but to crawl back into bed and lie with all the lights on, wide-eyed, waiting for the sound of his key in the door.

Though his presence is no protection, I thought. The dream comes often when he's lying next to me in bed. But all the same, I thought, I want him to come home. I want him here with me. It's dark and lonely.

It was so dark I could hardly make out the stairs in front of me. But they seemed broader than they had in either of the other dreams. Broader and shallower with a shiny black handrail. And there wasn't exactly a door at the top but a kind of dark tunnel with a light somewhere beyond.

'Go up,' said the voice. 'Go up. There is something up there that you must do.'

Slowly I began to climb for the third time and as I did so, I realized where I was. I was in the Maypole, climbing the stairs from the dressing rooms to the stage. The dark tunnel ahead of me was the back stage passage with the stage lights showing beyond. All I was doing was walking upstairs to the stage. And yet I was terrified. This dream was much worse than either of the other two. Ahead of me there was something more frightening than either of the other doors had revealed. And yet I had to go on.

'Go on. Go on,' urged the voice. 'You must do it.'

And I had to do as the voice said. I had no control over my actions. I reached the top of the stairs and moved into the tunnel beyond, heading towards the terrible light.

'Abby! Abby! For God's sake! What are you doing up there at this time of night?'

Light flooded in on me and I struggled to take in what it showed. A flight of pale, carpeted stairs below me; Greg at the bottom, white shirt open, jacket on his shoulder, face turned up to me in bewilderment – and irritation.

'What are you doing? You look awful.'

I was standing at the top of the second flight of stairs, by the door of Luke's room. I dropped down on the top stair and pulled my knees defensively up to my chin.

'I don't know what happened,' I whimpered. 'I must have walked in my sleep.'

He strode up the stairs two at a time and put an impatient arm round me. 'Christ Abby! You're soaked in sweat!'

'Greg, I feel awful.'
I leaned on him and let him lead me down the stairs.
His shirt smelled of perfume.

1606

They're building a gallows in the street outside. If I squint up sideways from the little barred window I can see the foot of it in the dust, and all morning long I've listened to one of the fellows whistling as he hammers in the nails.

I knew the devil only tormented me with his talk of freedom. What use was it if Blubber Face took back his accusations? The city man has come here to see me hang and see me hang he will, no matter what anyone else says. He told me that last night and I know now why he has sat by so patiently waiting for my confession.

'You'll hang, Mistress Jennet, for all that fat oaf talks of letting you go free. And you know why, don't you?' His smile made him look harder and skinnier than ever. A dried out skeleton jerkily playing a man's part.

'Aye, I know why I'll hang. I killed the bairn. The spirit of the past made me kill my own child.'

'Hah! We'd find ourselves a mite short of womenfolk, I reckon, if we were to hang up every drab that strangles an unwanted brat.'

'It's only the devil that tempts me to think I shouldn't die.'

'Yes, your devil! He's a strange fellow. What did he tell you of himself? That he was a gentleman journeying between the city and his country home? Ah well, he lied to you. He is no gentleman. He's a man of business and his business is debauchery. A devil indeed! But did you ever tell him the spell?'

'Aye, maybe I did. He was always asking questions. There wasn't anything that didn't seem to interest him. I told him all the old things Mother taught me – the tale of the old Queen of Scotland too. But I didn't tell him the Stewart weird. I swear I didn't tell him of the shameful fate of the King's line.'

'But you told him the words? The words you called the curse of the blind-worm?'

'I did, but what does that matter? I see now that he'd know it all without being told.'

'Did you ever tell anyone else?'

'Nay. Who else would I tell? Mother said I should pass it on to my daughter, but I have none.'

He smiled then and turned away to the locked door. 'That's well. At least you'll hang alone. His Majesty will be satisfied.'

'His Majesty?'

'Indeed, Mistress Jennet, you are an important woman. The King waits eagerly to hear that I've done his bidding and you are hanged. Tomorrow he will lie easy in his bed.' He gave a sharp nod with his sharp chin and hammered on the door for the jailer.

1996

I have to arrive in good time for a first night. I can't rest at home because I'm convinced the car's going to break down on the way to the theatre or something.

So when Alan came to my dressing room half an hour before the curtain went up, I was already dressed and made up, though I won't say I was exactly ready for the performance. I was sitting at the workbench with my lucky pendant clutched in my hand, trying to avoid the sunken eyes of the reflection in my mirror. And trying to prepare myself mentally. I wanted to do well. Not so much for myself, really, but for Greg; I wanted the play to be a great success for his sake. Or maybe I wanted to prove to him how much he needed me. Anyway, I sat at the mirror, telling myself the same things over and over again.

I can do this. I can produce a performance that's better than 'intelligent and adequate'. There is no ghost waiting for me in the shadows beyond the stage lights. I can get into the part without letting her take me over completely.

Then Alan came.

He stood by the door, very tall in his costume of leather tunic and rough leggings, and I felt embarrassed. As I said, I'd done my best to avoid him since that strange business over the family tree. After a minute or so of silence, he said abruptly, 'You look wonderful, Abigail.'

'Thank you.' I thought he must have forgotten all that 'sworn enemies' nonsense and I felt relieved.

I gave my reflection a quick glance. Not too bad. The black dress was flattering, cut low at the neck and clinging tightly down to the hips. The heavy mass of fake red jewels made my skin look very pale. My hair was loose and the bright light of the dressing room was giving its brown a pleasant red sheen. In the mirror, I saw Alan take a step closer behind me. His face was intent, as if he had seen something fascinating but slightly frightening. One enormous hand rose and reached towards me, then fell heavily to his side.

'Your hair, Abigail.'

'What's wrong with it?'

'When it's loose it makes you look – different.'

I caught his eye in the mirror. 'Different in what way?'

He shrugged. 'I don't know. But it's good. For the part it's good. You look – irresistible. The perfect evil temptress.'

'Thank you! I don't find that very flattering.'

'I didn't say it to flatter you. I said it because it's true.'

'Alan, I'm very busy, will you excuse me?' I started to fiddle about with make-up and hair brush, willing him to go away. I could feel his eyes on the back of my neck like the chilly edge of a knife.

I heard the castors of the costume rail squeal as he pushed it impatiently aside on his way to the door. Then: 'Oh, I nearly forgot,' he said. 'I looked in on Gregory just now. He said he'd like to have a word with you when you've got a minute.'

I got up quickly, glad of an excuse to get away from him. He stood in the doorway, forcing me to squeeze past him. As I did so, the speaker by my mirror hissed into life and the voice of the assistant stage manager announced: *Half an hour. Half an hour.*

Out in the corridor things were quiet, but you could feel the electric atmosphere of first night nerves; it filled the air like an invisible smog. A few warriors with grisly wounds were sprawled on some chairs, drinking out of plastic mugs from the coffee bar and playing chess against a pocket computer. The door to one of the larger dressing rooms was open and I had a glimpse of Luke perched at the long bench between two nameless thanes. He was already dressed as Young Macduff in a loose white nightshirt that would show the fake blood when he was stabbed. His little round face in the mirror looked very young and tight with excitement and worry. I longed to go in and cuddle him, but I resisted the urge. He'd hardly welcome such maternal attention in front of the men.

Greg's door, the only one labelled, was just beyond. The best dressing room. As I reached it, Alan who was still standing by my door, called 'See you later, Abigail,' and moved away.

I pushed the door open on the usual bright confusion of costumes, photos and junk – and stopped short.

It sounds clichéd, I know, but it's perfectly true that if I close my eyes now I can see the scene in that dressing room: gaudy colours from cloaks and cards and bright lights stabbing reflections deep into the mirrors. And Greg wrapped hungrily round Chrissie's soft little body.

To make it more memorable – almost ludicrous – he was

in costume for the battle scenes while Chrissie (whose only scene came after the interval) had not yet changed. Bulky tartan engulfed synthetic silk blouse and a big hand with a heavy leather wristguard rested on a fluorescent lycra thigh.

I wanted to laugh. I don't know why, but I could feel laughter rising sharp and hard inside me.

'Shit!' Greg unravelled himself, colour burning on his cheekbones. 'Abby, wait a minute. For Christ's sake, Abby!'

I stumbled back along the corridor, my hand over my mouth, hysterical laughter trickling out through my fingers. Past Luke's door, past the wounded men who had now been joined by a warty witch, to my own room. I dropped down on my chair by the mirror, shaking and giggling uncontrollably.

'Calm down, Abby. You've got to calm down.' Greg blundered in after me, slammed the door and stood with his back to it. Pale now except for two patches of red high on his cheeks, he loomed by the door, hands resting uncertainly on his heavy belt. He was frightened. 'Abby, please try to get a grip on yourself.'

'I'm OK. I'm OK. Just leave me alone.'

'You're not OK.' He came and crouched down by me. 'You're hysterical.' I tried to speak, but with him close to me, the shaking got worse. 'I didn't mean to upset you,' he said.

'Well thanks very much! How considerate!'

'Christ, Abby! What do you expect me to do? Grovel? Apologize?'

'Apologize?' My voice came out sort of strangled. 'No, I don't expect that. Why should I? It'd be the first time you'd said sorry in ten years!'

'Abby, we can't argue now. You've got to pull yourself together. If you break down now everything's ruined.'

'Don't touch me!' I shrieked as he tried to take my hand.

Twenty minutes, said the speaker, as calm and oblivious as

God speaking from the burning bush. *Twenty minutes. Mr Mortimer to make-up please.*

'Go and put your beard on, Greg. That'll stop you kissing for a bit anyway.'

'Shouting at each other is pointless. We can talk after. Right now what matters is the play.'

'Yes,' I snarled. 'That's what matters, isn't it? Never mind how I feel. Never mind if you've made me look a fool. What matters is the critics calling Gregory Mortimer's Macbeth one of the greatest. What matters is you proving that you're more than a pretty face and sexy body. That's what matters, isn't it, Greg? God! That's what matters!'

'Calm down, Abby. Please calm down. Isn't this play important to both of us? And to Luke. If you won't calm down for my sake – then think of him. He can probably hear you screaming.'

'Oh yes! Drag Luke into it! Well perhaps you should have thought of Luke before you started groping that little tart.'

Mr Mortimer to make-up please.

'Abby, my love, please calm down. And for God's sake do your best.' With a nervous eye on the black-rimmed clock above the door, he pushed back the hair that fell in several streaks of damp gold across his brow.

'You're really frightened, aren't you, Greg?' I said, beginning to calm as I watched his terror. 'You think your mad wife is going to spoil your great success. But I'm not mad, Greg. I get a bit depressed, that's all. And is it any wonder when . . .' I was getting less calm so I avoided that. 'I've had plenty of cause over the years. You know I have.'

'I know, Abby.' His face was placating. Anything to keep me quiet. 'But please, don't let me down now. I've worked so hard for this. We've both worked hard.'

He was pleading with me! 'I've never seen you grovel before, Greg.'

'Abby . . .'

'No, it's all right. I won't let you down.' I felt a surge of exaltation. Now he was in my power. Right now he needed me desperately – more than any other woman. I liked that. I liked watching him suffer. I'm not sure if it was love or hate that made me take his face triumphantly between my hands and whisper:

'Thou shalt be what thou art promised.'

'Abigail . . .?' He put up a hand uncertainly to cover mine; he looked half hopeful, half frightened.

Mr Mortimer, your last call to make-up.

He unfurled himself with a creak of leather and took a step towards the door. (Moses inevitably obeying the commands from the bush.) 'I'll make it up to you, darling. I promise I will.'

'Just go now, Greg.'

I turned back to face myself in the mirror. 'Ghost or no ghost,' I told the reflection whose painted cheeks were gouged with two long tear tracks, 'I'm going to do my best. And I'm going to show them all just how good my best can be.' Mechanically, with perfectly steady hands, I set about repairing the damage to my face.

I felt surprisingly composed.

By the time I came up here to the stage for my first entrance I was deadly calm. I had walked through the electric atmosphere, the hand kissing, the smell of make-up, hot feet and a dozen clashing perfumes, thinking only of the part I must play and of how good I could be. Everything else was deliberately blocked from my mind. It was the best way to get rid of that vision of his hands crawling up the soft, bright thighs, those yellow curls frothing against his bare shoulder. I forgot everything but my role; I even forgot my fear of the ghost in the shadows.

I climbed the stairs like a sleepwalker and made my way along the passageway behind the stage where small props were laid out on carefully labelled benches: daggers and lanterns and goblets, all meticulously arranged. Near the end of the bench I paused, picked up the yellowish letter from its label: *Act 1 Scene 5 Lady Macbeth* and walked towards the stage.

And then out of the darkness of the wings into the stage lights – and a kind of escape. The charm of acting took hold of me. Now Abigail West, deceived, unloved wife, could be left behind completely. Lady Macbeth with her letter stepped out into the spotlights and the familiarity of her lines.

'They met me in the day of success . . .'

Familiar, safe words. But they weren't really alive until that moment when, at last, the ghost came out of the shadows. Lady Macbeth drew close to me and took control.

'. . . Come to my woman's breasts
And take my milk for gall, you murd'ring ministers . . .'

The words poured out of me but it was her saying them; it was her calling for the help of the spirits. It was Lady Macbeth's overwhelming need for her husband's success that made her prepared to do anything.

She had taken over now. She and I were one. I felt her emotions. From that moment on it becomes difficult to explain exactly what happened because I seemed to be two people at the same time. The character was so strong. It was as if my anger and jealousy had done away with my defences. I'd held her back for weeks but now she took over and I found myself feeling things that I didn't really understand.

From the shadows strode the tall figure of Macbeth. Arms and shoulders bare but for the loose plaid he wore over his left arm. Every inch the hero, yet his eyes fastened on mine anxiously as if he was afraid – afraid of me. But that was a strange thought for this was not just the figure of Gregory Mortimer that I had seen with one hand greedily clutching at a shiny thigh. This was also the great Scottish thane returning to his adoring wife . . .

'Great Glamis, worthy Cawdor,
Greater than both by the all-hail hereafter,'

I held out my arms in greeting.

1057

'My dearest love,' muttered Macbeth as he embraced me and took his son awkwardly into his arms for the first time.

It was the day that he came back from fighting for the King's party, bringing with him half the thanes and mormaers of the land – and their families too – to celebrate the victory in our house. He was delighted with the honour he'd won in battle. And I was proud too – as if the child was a great prize that I'd won for him. And, for a little while, he was pleased to cradle against his battle-gear the little silky head of the heir for whom he'd waited so long.

'Hello, young Findlay. You're going to be a fine man, aren't you? The women say you've got my looks. Do you think so, Gruoch?'

'Macbeth, of course he is like you! See there, his smile is just like yours. I never saw a bairn that looked more like his father.'

He held out a hand, its wrist roughly bandaged from the recent fighting against the Norse, and watched the tiny, fat fingers curl round it. So proud he was! Happy – but still not quite content.

Remember this, girl, no matter what you give, a man is never satisfied. He'll take your soul and still ask for more. You look at me so innocently under your braids – I only hope you never have to learn that the bitter way I did.

Macbeth was never quite content, damn him! Whatever I have done for him has never been enough. He has never trusted me. Just an hour ago, down there in the hell-scene, an ox floundered horribly in the mud. I could see Macbeth, whip in hand, cutting free the harness and shouting to the men. And I could see, as clearly as if I stood beside him, because I know it's his habit when anything goes amiss, I could see his hand moving in the shape of the Roman cross. Ah! And then I saw the turn of his head. His face with the long hair blown about it turned palely this way.

He looked to see if I was cursing him!

Damn him! Does he fear me so much? What have I ever done to harm him? What have I ever done but try to give him what he wanted? And he was never content. Even the bairn couldn't keep a smile on his face for long.

'Little Lord of Moray,' he mused that night, stroking the baby's soft, dark hair, but his eyes wandered to the open door of our chamber, through which poured the red light of the hall's huge fire and the din of preparations for the feast. 'But what else will there be for you, while this great fool Duncan sits on the Throne of Scots with no more wits than a Hallows-fire dummy?'

'Hush, my love. The King's own party are in the house!'

'Nay, I say no more than plenty of others say.' He lowered Findlay into the depths of the ancient cradle. 'He is a fool, Gruoch. Last year he marched against Durham and won nothing but the deaths of his own men – their heads set up on poles in the market place for a mockery. But now, when I lead his armies against the north, it has been a very different tale.' He pushed back the plaid from his bare arms and held his battered hands to the chamber fire. His face glowed with more than the ruddy light. 'Men are willing to follow when I lead, Gruoch; they'd rather follow me than . . .' His voice trailed away but his eyes turned expressively to the hall where the household were busy preparing to receive Duncan. 'Nor do they forget,' he said more quietly, 'that I'm wed to Bodhe MacKenneth's daughter.'

He turned to me and seemed to study me, so gravely that

I feared the birth had marred my looks worse than I'd thought.

'I was not ready to use that when Malcolm died,' he muttered, more to himself than me. 'He died too soon. But now . . .' Again his voice wandered into silence.

'My love, let me see the wound on your arm.'

'No, it's healing, leave it be.' He brushed my hands away impatiently but continued to stare at me, the firelight heating his face and showing up the lines of weariness round his mouth and eyes. 'Gruoch, do you remember that woman? The crone with a beard that we met on the heath?'

'Aye, my love.'

'Do you remember what she said – about the crown of Scots?'

'I remember.'

He was staring at me as I stooped over the cradle; staring almost as if he wondered what I was. 'She mentioned that brooch of yours. And said you'd got a lot to give a man. Gruoch, do you know what she meant?'

'Nay, I've told you before, I don't. But my love, I swear I'll give you everything I can.'

'Aye.' He dropped his eyes to the flames and, leaning over the fire, chaffed his hands together. 'I know that, my dear. But do you think she was just foolish with age?'

'No. She had – and she still has – a name for speaking truth. And,' I glanced at the cradle, 'her charms are good.'

'Then maybe . . .' With his face still turned from me, he gazed into the fire and was silent. From beyond the room came the clatter of benches and trestles; within there was only the sound of the cradle's rockers on the hard earth floor. 'But no,' he said, standing up at last. 'There's honour to remember. I've no cause against him.'

His face was fallen, the light of pride and victory all gone from it, as he bent to kiss me. Only the weary lines remained to tear my heart.

'My love, don't look so sad. Aren't you pleased with your son?'

'Aye.' He nodded, almost sulking, the way Lulach did when he couldn't get his own way. 'He's a fine lad, but that little halfwit bastard of Duncan's stands to get more than him!'

It was terrible to see him so unhappy.

'I thought the baby would make him content,' I told Beatrice later that evening.

She and I had escaped early from the feast at which nearly all the highborn folk of Scotland were gathered. We'd gone to her chamber to talk quietly together; it being many years since we'd met and like to be as many more till another gathering such as this brought us together again to gossip about our bairns – and our men. It was soothing for once to have someone to whom I could talk about such things. Usually there was only Morag, and her understanding was small.

I remember Beatrice shaking her head wisely when I told her about Macbeth's unhappiness. 'He cannot help but be ambitious, Gruoch. They say he is a great leader of men.'

'Aye, they will follow him to the death. He's a man that can win the loyalty of everyone that knows him.'

Beatrice laughed at my eagerness. 'I think you're happier with your second husband than your first, Gruoch.'

'I am. But what of you, Beatrice? Are you happy?' I pitied her her man.

Constantine MacGirrick, now the undisputed Lord of Fife, had not improved with the years: still sour and grim-looking, he seemed well-suited to the new name he had adopted. Macduff, he called himself now after his famous great-grandfather, Duff (The Dark One). Son of Darkness, I'd heard his own servants calling him in the kitchens and I was sorry for Beatrice, wed to a man who was despised even by his own grooms.

'I'm happy enough,' she said. 'In many ways MacGirrick

is a good man. He's got more of a liking for his home and bairns than many men have.'

'And for you, Beatrice?' I wanted her to be loved. I wanted her to know something of the passion I'd found that night the broch burned. Though it seemed unlikely with such a man as the priestish Lord of Fife.

'He likes me well enough, I think.'

'But does he love you, Beatrice?' The darkness of the little room, with light and faint laughter spilling across the yard from the crowded hall, reminded me of our chamber in my father's house and the nights when we had shared secrets in our bed. 'Do you love him?' I whispered.

She sighed and stood up, shifting the baby she'd been nursing from her breast to her shoulder. 'Gruoch, I am a real woman, not a lady in a storyteller's song. MacGirrick is a good husband. And kindly to his children.'

'But you do not love him.'

'I have never wished for another husband.'

'Neither did I when I was married to Gillacomgain. I knew no better. But, Beatrice, to be wed to a man you truly love . . .'

'Hush, Gruoch. Don't talk so.' The bairn started to grizzle shrilly and she walked about the room to comfort it. As she stepped into the dim glow from the hall that filled the open doorway, I saw how she had changed over the years. Her face had got blotchy and worn and she wore a bag-like headdress that engulfed her lovely fair hair.

'I'm sorry Beatrice, I didn't mean to make you discontent.'

'Nay Gruoch, I'm content enough. You and I were always different. It wasn't me,' she said with a smile, 'that used to want to tease poor Ban into kissing and suchlike.'

I laughed. 'I had forgotten Ban!'

'No,' she went on quietly. 'I would not have MacGirrick a lusty lover. I'd much rather he listened to me than kissed me.'

'Doesn't he?'

'Not on important matters. In all our years together he has never taken a word of advice from me.'

'He's a fool then. You've always understood men's business as well as any man. Why, when we were just bairns my father would listen to you. Do you remember how you saved the sheep from the foot-rot by persuading him to move them to drier ground?'

'Aye, but if they'd been my husband's sheep, they'd have stayed in the bog and died.'

'Why?'

'Because he will take no advice from any woman.'

'Why?'

'I don't know really. All I know is the rumours I've heard from some of the older women in the house.' She rubbed the bairn's back till a thin trickle of milky vomit ran down her shoulder.

'Tell me the rumours, Beatrice, I promise I'll not repeat them.'

She laughed and wiped her shoulder with the baby's shawl. 'Like the old days isn't it, telling secrets to each other?'

'I've missed you, Beatrice.'

'And I've missed you. It's hard having no one to share secrets with.' She sat down again with the baby on her knees. 'Well, the women in our kitchens say that Mac-Girrick doesn't trust women because he killed his own mother and he's under a curse for it.'

'Killed his own mother!'

'That's what they say.'

'Do you believe it?'

'I don't know, Gruoch. But if he did he must have done it when he was very young. No one in the house remembers her. But what I do know is that MacGirrick distrusts women and will take no notice of what I say.' She scowled under her linen bag of a headdress and absent-mindedly kept rubbing too vigorously at the bairn's back.

'What advice would you give him if he'd listen, Beatrice?'

'I'd tell him to keep peace with his fellow thanes. Have you not seen how he is at odds with nearly everyone but the King? Gruoch, surely even you must have noticed how he and Macbeth cannot agree?'

'I saw they didn't speak much in the hall.'

'Aye. But they sat on either side of the King and both tried to gain his ear.'

'It's just the way men behave, Beatrice. There's no use in us worrying about it.'

'But what if there should be feud between Moray and Fife? Think on it, Gruoch. You and I would not be able to meet like this.'

'They would not feud.'

'I'm not so sure, Gruoch. My man is not ambitious for glory and power like your Macbeth. It's land and gold he wants, but if he thinks Macbeth is too ambitious there can hardly be peace between them.'

'Nay, Macbeth has no wish to be at feud with anyone.'

'He may find he has no choice. Can't you see that?'

'Beatrice, I'm not like you. I don't understand the business of battle and feud. All I want is to see Macbeth happy.'

She sighed and gave up trying to make me understand.

'Then if you want your man happy, perhaps you'd better get to your chamber and be ready for him. They will finish their drinking soon.'

'No use in that,' I said sadly, 'he won't share my bed. He's taken all his gear off to another room. He says he's afraid of souring my milk.'

Beatrice just laughed. 'Men are always more careful with the first. I only wish MacGirrick would take such care now.' She looked down ruefully at the bairn in her arms: a sturdy girl about six months older than Findlay. 'The births get harder, Gruoch and since this last one I've had a pain in my side.'

She looked almost old. Ten years and eight children had

dragged down the youthful curves and put them all in the wrong places and I saw now that the few wisps of hair straggling from her headdress were not the bright gold of her youth but the dull colour of dead grass.

'You must take care not to have another bairn too soon, Beatrice.'

'I will,' she said feelingly. 'I'll keep this one at the breast as long as I can; that helps a bit. And I reckon that our men may all have found themselves some Norse women in this latest fighting.'

'Battlefield whores!'

'Why Gruoch, I do believe you're jealous,' she said. As if I cared anything about such wretches! Why should I care about them? Wasn't I the daughter of Bodhe MacKenneth who'd brought her man much more than yellow hair and a straining bodice?

I was taken suddenly with an idea: tomorrow, I thought, I'll go to the wise woman and see if she will tell me more. Maybe I can learn something that'll bring back Macbeth's smile and win him once again to my bed.

1996

'Abigail, are you all right?'

The backstage gloom swam rather uncertainly around me, as the character of Lady Macbeth relaxed her hold on me. Then things focused. Flats off to my left, figures waiting for their entrance silhouetted against the light; bare brick wall; wooden benches with paper labels and assorted props. As reality came back I realized that I hardly knew what had been happening while I was on stage. It really felt as if a spirit had been in possession of my body.

But now I was myself again and Alan's arm was round my waist.

'Just for a minute everything seemed a bit confused,' I muttered, trying to move away.

But he held tighter. 'Poor Abigail,' he whispered, mouth close to my ear, beard brushing my cheek. 'He's a bastard, isn't he?'

I glanced up at the face hanging over me. 'I don't want to talk about it, Alan.' He pulled me closer. 'Let go of me!'

He released my waist but took hold of my wrist instead. 'What have you got there Abigail?'

'The letter . . .' I glanced down and saw to my amazement that it wasn't.

It was a dagger: a stage weapon from the bench with a red and gold handle and a blade polished up to catch the spotlights. And my fingers were clutching it so tightly my knuckles were white.

Behind me Duncan and his entourage swept on to the stage. In a minute it would be time for my second entrance.

'What are you doing with that?' whispered Alan.

'I don't know. It wasn't me . . .' I began, but stopped myself just in time. I'd been about to say that it wasn't me but Lady Macbeth that'd picked it up while she was in control of me. And that sounded crazy. 'I don't know what I'm doing with it.' Hastily I dropped it on the bench.

'Careful,' said Alan. 'That's the wrong place. This is the sharp one Gregory has to drive into the floor in the last fight.' He picked it up and turned it to show me the blob of red paint the props department had put on the hilt to distinguish the one dangerous knife from the blunt, folding daggers that were used in the murder scenes.

It was time for my entrance. I had no time to wonder why, without knowing it, I'd picked up a sharp knife. But before Lady Macbeth entered to welcome Duncan to her home, I did notice, with a sick jolt, the place where I'd accidentally dropped the dangerous weapon. It was on the label that read: *Act 4 Scene 2. Young Macduff's Murderers.*

1057

What? What did I say?

Child, you should not have let me sleep. There is no time for sleep. Quick, bring tapers and let's have light. There'll be darkness enough in Dunsinane after tonight. Darkness, aye and sleep too. Eternal, dream-maddened sleep . . .

The dream? Aye, it was the same as usual. Always the same dream: a stone tower and narrow stairs wet with blood, stairs leading to a half-burned door with a reddish light beyond it. Stairs that I must climb again and again. Up and up to the door; to the murky mouth of hell. But what did I call out?

'The Thane of Fife'? Oh, that's nothing but an old rhyme Beatrice and I used to chant when we played hiding when we were children. Aye, but we little dreamed then that Beatrice would one day be that wife: the wife of Macduff MacGirrick, Thane of Fife – and that I'd one day seek her desperately and in vain.

'The Thane of Fife had a wife. Where is she now?'

Ah yes, girl, of course you know what became of Macduff's wife and bairns – all the world knows of their terrible fate. But what I need to tell you is how I brought about that fate. If it's true what your mother told me and you are kin to me – and I think it may be true, for all she was dim-witted and a slut. Your eyes meet mine sometimes like the image in my mirror. If it is true, it's only right you know how the curse fell on our house. For if you are of my kin then you too are caught in the curse. It goes deep into the blood and between my bloodline and the line of the man I hate there will always be feud.

But I was talking of Beatrice. Poor Beatrice! I couldn't tell her that I planned to visit the wise woman, and I had to creep away from the house next morning without her seeing me, as if she was my enemy. With all the King's

followers in the house, it was easy enough to slip away
unnoticed in the confusion.

The cuckoo was calling again as I made my way across
the heath to the ruins of the old broch, though May was at
her darkest and cruellest, with the sky overcast and a
savage wind thrashing the young growth. In the rubble-
choked guard room there was the same fire of green sticks,
smoking worse than ever with the draught that blew down
through the broken tower.

'Why do you come to me, Lady Gruoch?' muttered the
crone when I'd made her understand what I wanted. 'It's
you that wears the faces of the goddess. Ask her what you'd
know of the future. Did your mother not teach you the
way?'

'I've told you before,' I shouted impatiently. 'She died. I
hardly remember her.'

'She taught you nothing?'

'No.'

Under the straggling hair two eyes, like wet pebbles,
were turned upon me shrewdly. 'Well, the way of future
gazing is easily learned. See here.' She came close, bringing
the smell of extreme age with her, and wound chapped
and smoke-grimed fingers round the brooch that I was
once more wearing to fasten a bodice cut for nursing. 'Hold
the charm tight in your hand as you go to sleep and think
hard on the one whose future you'd know. You'll see in
your dreams whatever there is to see.'

'But you said before that Macbeth would be King.'

'What's that?' she said, pursing up her hair-fringed lips.

I began to wonder if she was foolish as well as deaf with
age. 'You said, that night we met you on the moor. The
night the broch burned. You said he'd won the crown of
Scots.'

'Aye. I did.'

'So will he be King?'

'He has it in his power.'

'But will he?' I screamed so loud that a couple of jackdaws clattered up from nests somewhere above us.

She tapped the gold charm on my breast. 'Ask the weird sisters,' she said. 'They know better than me.'

I sighed and, with my foot, pushed towards her the clammy basket I'd brought.

'Meat!' she gloated over the sheep's liver. 'You're a kind lady.'

'If it's true, what you say about the brooch, I'll send more.'

She folded her hands over the soiled cloth that covered the stuff and stared up blearily. 'The Lord of Fife is yonder in your hall, I think,' she said suddenly.

'Aye. He came with the others that follow the King.'

'What sort of a man is he?'

'Macduff? Sullen and silent for the most part. His wife tells me he has the soul of a merchant and reckons everything according to its price.'

'Does he?'

'You know him?'

'Nay.' She turned into the shadows and picked up a charred stick. Taking the liver from the basket she skewered it and held it over the flames. 'I've not set eyes on him since he was a squalling, red-faced brat. But I knew his mother. And his father too.' She stared into the fire as the blood from the meat splashed and hissed on the flames. The dank room filled with the smell of charring flesh. 'Girrick of Fife, he was another one like your man that thought an heir would make him happy.'

'And did it?'

'I doubt it,' she said, eyes fixed on the roasting liver. 'Though he was prepared to do anything to get his son born.' Her mouth lifted into an ugly grin showing spongy gums and stubs of black teeth. 'Tell your man to beware of Girrick's son,' she said. 'Beware the Thane of Fife. Constantine

MacGirrick has as good a claim to the crown as anyone. Tell your Macbeth to be sure he doesn't lose it to him.'

'I'll tell him.'

But I reckoned it was needless. Beatrice said the man had more or less sold his claim to the crown for lands and empty titles. I was thinking more of the brooch. Could it enable me to see Macbeth's fortune? And if I dreamed good things, would he believe them? If only I could see with certainty and make him believe. If I saw it, it would be almost as if I had made it happen.

Too much daylight lingered for my liking on the heath and in the little valley below the house. I was impatient for the night. But the men were not even returned from the day's hunting when I reached home and first I must think of feeding my baby.

The cradle was empty and Morag wasn't in my chamber. I found her in the hall, helping to prepare for the night's meal — or rather clearing away the mess of last night's feasting. She'd got a damp sack of river sand and she was throwing it in handfuls on some of the messier places in the rushes. Beside the usual trouble of men being sick, they'd set some of the smaller dogs to fighting last night and there was a good deal of blood about. She needed plenty of sand, and to help her lug the sack around, she'd got a wench I'd not seen before.

'She's called Ingid,' said Morag sourly with a jerk of the thumb towards the girl, who was half a head taller than me, with butter-coloured hair twisted up in a ragged crown and breasts and hips that looked like fat creatures struggling to burst out of her patched blue dress. 'The men brought her back with them.'

'You're fortunate, Ingid,' I said. 'My husband isn't known for his kindness to enemies.'

'But this he knows, I am no enemy me,' said the girl, chanting the Gaelic awkwardly in Norse singsong. 'Just a poor woman taken prisoner by Sweno's men. And Macbeth

MacFindlay he is fair. He says if they use me badly, then I am friend to Scots. He is kind and orders the common men of his not touch me. I am not for common men, me.'

'Where's the bairn?' I asked Morag, turning my back on the silly girl's red face and whining voice.

'He was peevish. The Lady Beatrice took him to her room.'

I started to the door and then was taken with a pleasing thought. 'Ingid,' I said to the wretched girl, 'Morag can finish here on her own. You get yourself to the kitchens. There's a pig been killed and they need someone to wash out the guts.'

It was the foulest task there was. I felt a bit happier as I set off to find Findlay.

In fact Beatrice had taken him not only to her room, but to her breast too.

'I hope you don't mind, Gruoch. It was just a little to settle him.'

'No, I don't mind,' I said, picking him up from the big bed where he slept curled beside her little girl. She was the only person that I could have allowed to do it. 'I'll miss you when you go, Beatrice,' I said pulling the brooch loose and settling the baby to feed. 'It's been good having you here with me. Like the old days.'

'Well, we'll all stay a few days longer, I think. Stay till your storehouses are empty I fear, Gruoch. The King likes it here and is pleased with your man. Besides, the hunting in Moray is good.'

'Aye, there's no sign of them returning yet,' I sighed. 'And I'd hoped to see the meat on the table soon and the whole household settled to sleep early.'

'Are you tired, Gruoch?'

'No.' I fingered the brooch, warm in my hand. 'But I want to sleep soon.'

I knew not what to expect of such dreams; I knew

nothing of future gazing. And what happened to me was a disappointment – at least when I first woke it was.

I had no trouble making sure it was Macbeth that I was thinking of as I drifted into sleep under the wolf pelts, with the sound of slurred shouting still coming from the hall, and closer to me, the sweet wheeze and snuffle of Findlay in the cradle by my bed. His face was almost always my last waking thought. Clutching the warm gold I thought of that face as I had first seen it across Gillacomgain's board, lit by the smile that had made me feel like the only woman in the world. There was sweet content as I thought of it, warmly blotting out the drunken clamour from the hall.

And then, nothing.

Or so it seemed when I first woke in a cool bright dawn. Nothing. I could remember no dreams. Sleep had come to me thicker and blacker and deeper than it used to when I drank the old woman's brew. I'd dreamed nothing. I'd nothing to tell Macbeth.

But as soon as I thought of him, something came to me. Not a memory of any dream, just a certainty. A wonderful certainty.

'Morag,' I shouted distractedly, 'watch the bairn. If he wakes bring him to me. I must see Macbeth.'

I ran through the waking, yawning household and found him sitting alone on the sunny bank in front of the house, his shoulders hunched sullenly as he honed his dagger on a whetstone. He looked a bit bleary from last night's drinking and the well-water he'd used to revive himself still spiked his hair. His expression didn't brighten when I joined him, and when I mentioned the wise woman, his scowl only deepened. He glanced quickly behind us to see we weren't overheard, then back at me with a look that was hardly approving. 'You went to her, Gruoch?'

'Aye. I thought you wanted to know more about what she said.'

He turned his attention to the blade in his hand. 'Maybe,'

he said reluctantly, but his face twitched with distaste. I was suddenly reminded of an old tale Morag used to tell us of a cat who, though she longed to catch the fish in her master's pond, disliked the feel of water too much to make the attempt. Macbeth wanted to know his fortune, but the priests had got such a grip on him, the mere thought of the wise woman was as repellent as the touch of water on a cat's paw.

'Well,' I said sitting down beside him and laying my hand on his arm. 'She said again that you could be King, but told me nothing new, except that you should be wary of MacGirrick.'

'MacGirrick?' he echoed. 'Are you sure, Gruoch?'

'It's what she said.'

He scowled down at the knife. 'I thought the wretch cared only for goods. But I will beware of him. Perhaps he plans to sell us all to the devil if he can get a good enough price.'

'But Macbeth,' I burst out, unable to wait longer, 'I have seen your future.'

His hands stilled on the blade. 'You, Gruoch?' He turned to face me, blinking in the light of the sun that was rising behind me. 'How?'

'By this.' I touched the brooch.

He quickly made the sign of the cross – but asked me what I knew, for all his piety!

I put my cheek against his shoulder and gazed across the sheep-cropped grass where our shadows stretched, seemingly endless, and here and there a dew-jewel sparkled. 'My Macbeth, I know that you are invincible.'

'What?' He bent over me, kissing my cheek and murmuring against the bone of my face, 'What do you mean, little one?'

'I know two things, my love. I know that there's not a man born of woman who could kill you. And I know you'll never be defeated until the forest walks.'

'But how do you know these things, my love?'

'The weird sisters told me.'

'Nay, Gruoch, I don't know. Sometimes you frighten me.'

'My love, I only said . . .'

'Nay, it isn't what you say, woman. It's the way you look. There's a wild strange look that comes on you when you talk such stuff. Your eyes are enough to turn a man's insides to water.'

As he spoke he leaned away from me, his face tight with distaste. And then, to my horror, his look stiffened into a mask of pure loathing. I was terrified till I saw that he was no longer looking at me but down at a place near my hand.

'Don't move,' he whispered, his lips twitching up in a grimace. 'There's a blind-worm by your hand.'

Sure enough, beside me, gleaming silver-grey on the sheep-cropped grass was a blind-worm, sunning itself. Its scrap of tongue flicked sleepily. I laughed aloud. 'Fie, my Lord! You a soldier and afeard of a worm!' I moved to touch its triangular head but he struck away my hand.

'They're vile, dark things with venomed tongues.' His voice was full of disgust – just as it had been a moment since when he spoke of the sisters. The knife in his hand flicked into the air and with wonderful aim pinned the thing, squirming, to the grass.

I laughed again. 'Well done, my Lord. But it is not true. The blind-worm has no poison.'

He shrugged and stood up, his face relaxing as the unreasoning terror melted. He turned away as if he'd dismiss the shameful memory of his fear – and maybe too the memory of the other business that frightened him.

He turned back towards the hall where folk were beginning to stir, but then he stopped and burst into laughter. 'Why here's as strange a sight as your walking forest!' he cried.

I followed his gaze and was annoyed rather than amused

to see Seyton shambling toward us, his plaid trailing loosely and his hair still ruffled from sleep. And with my baby held awkwardly in the crook of his maimed arm.

'What, man, have you turned nursemaid?' roared Macbeth.

He grinned sheepishly across Findlay's red face and fat, thrashing arms. 'Old Morag said the Lady wanted him brought to her.'

I reached up and took him, warm and soft, in my arms and felt that wonderful power of motherhood as he quieted just for being near me. But Seyton didn't turn away immediately, he hung over me while I avoided his eyes as usual.

'He's a fine lad, isn't he?' he said, smoothing the silky black hair with a coarse, clumsy finger. 'Dark. Just like his father.'

'Aye he is,' said Macbeth.

'And just three months old, I think.'

'Aye, but I've never known you take notice of a bairn before, Seyton.'

'No more I have, master, till now.' He still stayed watching the child. I could feel his presence though I would not look up at him. I sat quite still on the grass, watching the sun gain power over the little tree-lined vale below. A cuckoo's call rose with the sound of the stream by which Seyton and I had met just a year ago.

Macbeth stirred irritably behind me. 'Get yourself to the stables. See how the horse goes, the one that fool Duncan lamed yesterday.'

I felt the dark presence withdraw and drew a breath of relief. I opened my bodice and put Findlay to the breast.

'Macbeth, my love, do you often think of what the old woman said?'

'Aye.' His voice was cold. 'I'm thinking on it now.'

I stared up at him – dark against the sharp blue of the morning. 'And what say you?'

'That he's a man I thought I could trust.' With a sneer of disgust he bent down, pulled his knife from the worm and cleaned it on the grass.

'What do you mean, my love?'

'Nay, it's nothing. Just a foolish thought. You meant what she said about me becoming King.' He kicked away the broken body of the blind-worm and gave me a forced smile.

'Aye, of course.'

'Then I say, Gruoch, that the King of Scots lives, weak of mind maybe, but strong enough in body. And almost ten years my junior. That's what I say.' His voice was dull and heavy with disappointment. He crouched down beside me and put his finger under my chin in his old manner. 'But what say you, my changeling wife? What says the one who wears the charm of the old goddess and sees the future in her dreams?'

I couldn't tell if he was pleading with me or testing me; but I knew he looked sad. He looked as if he longed for me to put into words what he'd not talk about himself. But would he hate me for saying it?

'I say, my love, that you would make a better King than Duncan – or any man living. And . . .' I avoided his eyes and looked down at the child. He was half sleeping now against my breast, one little leaflike hand curling and uncurling in milky contentment.

'And what?'

'And I would do anything, anything at all, my love, to help you to the crown.' The bairn stirred in my arms as I spoke and his mouth, still white with my milk, moved in one of his slow, new smiles; his eyes focused on my face as if he'd ask me what exactly it was that I'd do. The tiny frailness of his body seemed terrible and, just for a moment, I was afraid, as if I had had a glimpse of another future: a dark terrible future, in which the promise I had just made must be kept. And kept in a way too fearsome to imagine . . .

Macbeth dropped his hand from my shoulder, hope, distaste and fascination still warring in his face. 'Gruoch,' he said quietly. 'Help me to the crown.'

I took his hand and, holding it over the baby's silky head, kissed its battle scars. 'I will, my love.'

1606

There's horror in this cell far worse than the gallows outside in the street. There's the memory of a tiny cheek resting like silk against my breast, the memory of my hands on the soft flesh of his throat.

Oh God! The foot of the gallows out there in the moonlit dust looks like peace compared to the hell inside me. I daren't close my eyes to sleep. The picture of his pale dead face seems to wait in the darkness. I stand in the draught of the window to keep myself awake; so tired that at times I find myself longing for the closing of the rope around my neck.

But can the hangman release me from my nightmare?

Why should death end my suffering? I think the dream will go on for ever and I'll walk again and again up the stairs to the room where my child lies dead in my hands. Again and again for ever.

I stand here, my legs aching with the need for sleep and the night air sharp against my face. I force myself to listen to the scratch and rustle of the rats in the straw, to the bawdy song of the drunken guard and the low sobbing of another, unseen prisoner. Anything to keep my mind from sleep and memories.

I care nothing for the ending of my life. It's been hard and bitter. My child is dead and the one good thing that I thought I had – the memory of love and gentleness – was a sin, it seems. The only thing I want now is rest.

If I could only be free of the guilt of my baby's death, I'd walk to the gallows with a high heart. But I'm still in the power of that spirit of the past. And she has no pity.

1057

It was plain to me that there was only one way for Macbeth to win the crown. Duncan was young, and so fearful a soldier that he was unlikely to die in battle. A weak man he was and his weakness made other men discontent. I have no regrets over the killing of Duncan MacCrinan. I was no Beatrice who could understand the ways of power as well as a man, but even I could see that had Duncan reigned long the land would have been torn asunder with battles as every thane fought for lands and glory. I knew that morning when Macbeth asked my help that there was only one way for him to get the crown of Scots. And that was the same way he had got Moray. He must deal with Duncan the way he had dealt with Gillacomgain. Who would mourn him? His grandfather had won him the throne the same way – with the murderer's knife rather than the soldier's sword.

All I had to do was overcome Macbeth's doubts. And I must do it before the King's party left our house. Once he left Moray, Duncan MacCrinan would be out of our power and God only knew when we might have such an opportunity again.

Those were crowded, busy days with Duncan's soldiers and followers and thanes thronging our new house which had not been built to hold such a company. Macbeth spent his days riding and hawking and hunting with the King while I was kept busy seeing to the baking of loaves, the slaughter of fowls and the clearing up of filth from the hall floor. At night I slept alone in the wide, sagging bed. The only time I could be sure of seeing Macbeth was in the evenings when the whole company gathered to spend three hours or more eating and drinking in the hall.

On the last night that Duncan planned to spend under our roof, I made sure that the food was good and plentiful. And I gave orders to the boys to pour the liquor freely. As I had hoped, all the men ate and drank deeply that night – except for the King.

Duncan MacCrinan was a sickly figure with thin legs and hair like badly spun flax. He picked at his meat with skinny fingers and drank his ale watered. He barely looked a man though he must have passed his twentieth year. Beside him sat MacGirrick, dour and priestish as ever, but I was courteous to him for Beatrice's sake.

'It was good of you, my Lord of Fife, to bring your family to our house. It's many years since my cousin and I had the pleasure of meeting.'

He nodded curtly. 'A man should keep his family about him as much as he can. And now,' he said with a quick look at Duncan, 'now this fighting is over we can perhaps all return to our homes.' He picked up his cup and threw another wary look along the table, this time beyond Duncan to Macbeth. 'Now perhaps we can raise our sons and tend our own lands in peace.'

'But the fighting is not over yet,' said Macbeth quickly. 'We've unfinished business in Northumberland. That is, you have traitors to deal with there, sir.' He turned courteously to the King and forced the scowl off his face.

'Nay, sir, you would be well advised to leave that hornets' nest alone.' Macduff turned a servile leer on MacCrinan.

'That would be a disgrace to your grandfather's memory, Lord King.' Macbeth tensed beside me as if his hands were already on the sword hilt. 'Let Fife hide his head at home among the women if he chooses. The rest of your subjects have blood and honour in their veins, not water!'

MacCrinan sat silently between them; for all the world like the Hallows-fire dummy Macbeth had called him.

But the Thane of Fife had a look of fury on his long face. 'Honour!' he spat. 'What honour is this you talk of, Moray? The kind of honour that repays your cousin's hospitality with a knife in the back?'

Hastily I leaned across Macbeth to play the good hostess to Duncan.

'You eat too little, sir. I hope the table we keep does not displease you.'

'Thank you, Lady. The food is good,' he muttered, seeming to talk through his nose as much as his mouth. 'I never eat heartily.'

'Macbeth my love,' I whispered, taking the opportunity to rest my head on his chest and pretend to eat from his trencher, 'remember you are the host. Don't speak so hastily.'

'Nay little one,' he muttered into my hair. 'There'll never be peace between me and MacGirrick. Remember he was Gillacomgain's ally.'

'That's all past now.'

'Not in Fife's mind. And now he tries to work on the King with his foolish words. Look how Duncan listens to him; he will make peace with Northumberland. And then what will become of me? I am a warrior, Gruoch; it's in battle my glory lies.'

'Nay, beloved, you and I both know you're destined to be something greater than a warrior for this fool Duncan.'

'What's that you say, my love?'

'Hush now. We will talk later. But keep peace for now, my heart.' I kissed his cheek. 'Come to me after they are all abed and we will talk.'

'Talk of what, little one?'

'Of what the weird sisters have promised you.'

He put up a big, hot hand and pressed my face closer to his. 'I'll come, beloved.' He was heated with the ale and wine. His voice slightly blurred with it. His eyes were fixed on me.

I rose, bade farewell to the King and left the table.

As I made my way through the hounds that crowded round the door I looked back and saw the flaxen-haired dummy sitting between the straight figure of Macbeth and the stooping shape of MacGirrick who was leaning forward saying something to him. Macbeth was holding his cup to his lips and gazing at me across it as he had the night we met. I smiled at him and went to my chamber to wait.

It was late when the house finally subsided into silence and Macbeth came to join me. The liquor was heavy on him then, though there was never anything sottish about Macbeth. The stuff seemed to make him bigger and easier – and to make him forget a bit about his priests. He remembered my words in the hall and he was very anxious to talk about the weird I had seen for him.

'You say that I'm invincible?'

'Aye my love. No man born can kill you!'

He stooped over me, and kissed me.

'No one can defeat me in battle?'

I smiled at his eyes burning with ale and hope and – yes, with something else that I was very glad to see. The talk of power had fired him. 'No, beloved, no one can defeat Macbeth MacFindlay, unless he can press the forest itself into his army.'

He paced back across the room again to where I sat beside the embers of a burnt-out fire; bending gently, he cupped a hand around my cheek and lowered his lips to mine in another long, ale-flavoured kiss. 'My heart, no man can do that, can he?' he asked with the trust of a child.

'Nay my love, no man can do that. You need fear nothing, my love. Everything you want is yours for the taking. You only have to have the courage to take what you want. Nothing, no one can stand in your way.'

'I don't lack courage, my little one.'

'I know that, Macbeth. There is not another man like you.'

This time the kiss lingered much longer on my mouth and I reached up hungrily to him, clutching at his hard body, longing for what I'd been denied so many months.

He drew back his head. 'My Gruoch, we must think of the bairn.'

'It'll do him no harm, dearest,' I whispered. 'Stay with me, beloved. Don't go to your Viking slut.'

'Gruoch.' I felt him hesitate. His eyes wide – maybe a little afraid. I ran my fingers into the long dark hair and lowered my lips to his neck. I felt him weaken; felt his body move against mine. This was the moment; I knew he was in my power. I pushed his hair aside and set my lips close to his ear. 'Stay with me tonight,' I whispered, my hands on his belt. 'Stay with me, King of Scots.'

He clutched me to him and I could feel I'd won. I'd won what I wanted – and what he wanted too. Afterwards it was easy to persuade him to take the knife and do what I knew he must.

1996

'Art thou afeard
To be the same in thine own act and valour
As thou art in desire? Wouldst thou have that
Which thou esteem'st the ornament of life,
And live a coward in thine own esteem,
Letting "I dare not" wait upon "I would",
Like the poor cat i' th' adage?'

I faced the tall, bare-armed figure, standing above him on the steps at the back of the stage. I had ceased to wonder whether it was Greg Mortimer or Macbeth I spoke to. I knew that in some strange way it was both; just as I knew that Gruoch was joined with me. Glowering up at me, the dark eyes showed fear and fascination. He threw back his cloak and seized my shoulder.

'Prithee, peace,'

he cried, tormented by the taunts.

'I dare do all that may become a man;
Who dares do more is none.'

His hand squeezed my shoulder; his face, close to mine now, showed a strange mixture of fear and trust. The dark eyes clung to me, demanding my support and yet fearing that dark part of me that he couldn't understand.

Gazing into that narrow, handsome face, eyes reflecting the sharp light above high cheekbones, I felt weak with love for a moment. Present love and love from the distant past. But it was a bitter, stubborn kind of love that survived all the things I knew about him and forced me, almost against my will, to get him exactly what he wanted. To help him win the crown, the success he craved.

And, with a lurch of terror, I realized that, to show my determination, I must face the worst imaginable thing – to stare into the very pit of hell. Stiffly my lips – the lips over which Lady Macbeth had control – moved in what I now understood were the most terrible, most powerful words of the play. There was enough of me, Abigail, left to think: this is it. This is the dark part of the play that has caused so much bad luck through the centuries. Not some strange occult practice, but the real, human nightmare of a woman facing the worst imaginable act. And I felt myself caught in words more terrible than any spell or incantation.

'I have given suck, and know
How tender 'tis to love the babe that milks me.

I would, while it was smiling in my face,
Have plucked my nipple from his boneless gums
And dashed the brains out, had I so sworn
As you have done to this.'

1057

My baby!
  There's blood on my hands! Blood I'll never be rid of . . .
  Aye girl, it was the same dream. Always the same.
  The brew I drank is taking hold too soon. I must not
sleep again. If I sleep now I may never wake and there's
still the end to be told. I must tell you all. I must explain
the curse of the blind-worm to you.
  It all went wrong for me, you see.
  Findlay sickened the very day they chose Macbeth for
King.
  He lay in his cradle flushed and feverish, his little blue
eyes staring as if they saw nothing, while the house was
ringing with the shouts of acclamation.
  And Morag was sure she knew the cause. 'Your milk's
turned to gall and I reckon we both know the reason.' Her
face folded in disapproval and her watery eyes wandered to
my bed. 'A nursing woman should sleep alone.'
  'That's foolish,' I said quickly. It would just be too cruel
if my love for my man was poisoning the milk in my breast
and making my bairn sick. It was unthinkable that what I
had done to get that which Macbeth's ambition demanded
should prove the death of my child. And it would be
terrible if Macbeth were to lose the heir of his greatness
now, when everything he had wanted was within his grasp.
King Macbeth. I was so proud of him.
  But now that he had got what he wanted; now that I'd
helped him as he'd asked me to, there was a terrible change
in him. He seemed to become a different man.

Look at Macbeth now, girl, toiling in the light of the torches that are wan with the coming of dawn. Working like ten men in the mud and the cold with Lulach there at his side, trying as always to match him – and failing. There's still not a man in Alba that can match him.

My husband! He's all but a stranger to me now. And I lost him at the very moment that I'd thought to bind him closer to me. For the killing of Duncan preyed on his mind. Even when they had proclaimed him King and we were actually preparing ourselves to travel down to Scone for his coronation, he could not forget Duncan's death.

Just when everything he had wanted was in his grasp, he changed. I could not understand it. He became anxious and troubled, like a child with nightmares. Yet there was no need to be uneasy. Duncan had died quickly and quietly and all the company believed our story that it was his own servants who had done the deed. Within days it was agreed that Macbeth was the obvious successor. Everything he wanted was within his grasp. But he was not content; I could tell he wasn't from the look in his eyes, though at first he said nothing to me about it. Indeed, he hardly spoke to me and he didn't seem able to speak civilly to anyone else. The victory I had gained for him seemed somehow hollow and meaningless.

I told myself that all would be well when the child was better and Duncan laid in his grave. But it was on the very day that the funeral party set off that things got worse. I have good cause to remember the day Duncan set off on that final journey.

They took the body on the long road south and westward to the Isle of Iona, the most sacred Christian site, where the bones of Alba's Kings are stored. He'd probably been about a week dead by the time the funeral party gathered in the yard to begin the journey. I remember how the priests were making a great fuss with grand prayers for the immortal soul – and incense to cover the smell. It was hot in the yard, although it was still early in the day. And crowded too.

I remember the scene so clearly. The lords who were to accompany the bier were gathered round it, bare heads bowed in the sharp morning sun, while thin, restless hounds threaded their legs. The boys from the stables were leading out the ponies and women were loading loaves of hard-baked bread on to the mules. At the back of the yard an old man and a lad were arguing over the best way of fixing a squawking cage of live chickens on to one of the pack-beasts.

I had taken up a position a little apart. Standing on the steps to the hayloft at one side of the yard, I watched the men gathered around the mounded white linen wreathed in sweet-smelling herbs. A still point at the centre of turmoil. I watched the two figures that stood side by side at the head of the litter: Macbeth's straight, broad-shouldered figure, black head gracefully bowed, and the gaunt, stooping frame of MacGirrick. The Lord of Fife had elected to travel with the funeral party to Iona instead of going directly south to Scone with us. He seemed determined to show more devotion to the dead King than the living one.

But now he and Macbeth stood together, eyes closed, probably the most devout of all the lords, listening as the priest droned prayers in tedious Latin.

Why Latin? I wondered impatiently. The Christ was not Roman; neither are we. Surely God understands Gaelic. It was because I was feeling irritated with the Christian ceremony (as I often did) that I kept my eyes open and my head unbowed. So I saw clearly what happened in the yard below me.

A figure appeared at the open gate: a thin old woman in a ragged skirt, with a threadbare grey shawl pulled over her head. I saw her disappear among the horses and thought she was probably making her way to the kitchens to beg. But then, to my surprise, she emerged from the shifting hooves and flanks of the horses. She stood for a moment among the solid backs of the praying lords and seemed to look about her, searching for something, or someone.

I leaned forward to see her better and the heat from the yard rose up to hit me with the smell of the horses and the incense and the herbs and the sweet, sickly smell of death. I could see her sunken face now turned upward like a questing hound's and I could see the grey ratstails of hair straggling from the shawl.

At last she seemed to see what she was looking for and then, to my amazement, she dropped down on her hands and knees. Everyone else was busy with prayer or packing and no one seemed to notice the old woman as she began to thread her way stealthily among the sturdy legs of the assembled thanes. And the men, anxious to show loyalty and devotion – and used to the passing of the dogs among them – didn't look down as the crone crawled to the head of the bier – and to the feet of the Thane of Fife.

There, with her bent back actually touching the trestle that supported Duncan MacCrinan's hearse, she turned up her withered face and, pushing aside the shawl to see better, she stared at the dour, pious expression of Mac-Girrick. I waited. I thought any minute she'd be discovered and thrown out of the gates, but I was fascinated to know what she was about.

When she had looked her fill, she seemed to nod and then, without any show of haste, she took something from her tatters and laid it carefully on the cobbles of the yard, just in front of MacGirrick's boots, in the little space left clear beside the trestles.

I strained forward to see what it was she'd put down but I couldn't quite see the ground beyond the shrouded bulk of the corpse. However, I could see her making her way, more quickly now, back among the legs and the horses to the gate. She was out on to the track beyond the walls before the priest stopped droning, before the men opened their eyes. Before pandemonium broke loose in the yard.

With his head bent, the first thing MacGirrick must have seen when his eyes opened was the stones at his feet – and what now lay on them.

He gave a great roar of fury, pulled his knife from his belt and shouted for the gates to be closed. 'Seize the woman!' he shouted. 'Lay hold of the witch!' But he turned with his knife in his hand and faced Macbeth. 'What trick is this, MacFindlay? How dare you let this happen?'

People were running around the yard and pressing forward, trying to see what ailed the Lord of Fife. As I stepped down into the crowd the guards were swinging closed the high gates and the priest was steadying the bier that had been almost knocked from its trestles in the confusion.

'Peace, man! What's the matter?' Macbeth's voice cut powerfully through the babble. 'And what is this?' He bent down to retrieve the thing from the cobbles but MacGirrick stepped forward, the blade still in his hand.

'If you lay a hand on that, MacFindlay, I swear by the cross, I'll cut your throat.' He bent down himself and quickly snatched up the thing, hiding it almost protectively in his big hand.

But I was by his side now and I'd seen what it was. Or rather I'd seen what it looked like – I couldn't imagine what it might actually be. What it looked like was nothing but a bit of dried pig's bladder.

I could see the anger, white on Macbeth's face, but I doubt if anyone else in the yard could tell how furious he was at the insult of that drawn knife. 'I've no wish to touch it, man,' he said calmly. 'I only want to know what it means – why you fear it so much.'

MacGirrick slowly slid the knife back into its sheath. 'I did not mean to threaten you,' he said stiffly. 'But I don't like your house. There's evil at work here. Evil and witchcraft.'

'I don't understand what you're talking about, Mac-Girrick.' Macbeth was as formal and as furious as his guest. 'But tell me who has harmed you and I'll have him punished.'

'Search the house. Search for a woman. An old woman with the devil in her. Search for a witch, Macbeth.'

Macbeth beckoned to some men from among the watching crowd and told them to search out any strangers within the gates. As he spoke to them his eyes caught mine. 'Gruoch?' he said, very quiet and very cold. 'Do you know aught about this witchcraft the Lord of Fife fears so much?'

'No.' The denial came quickly – from my heart, not from my head. Until that moment I'd meant to say something very different. I'd crossed the yard to tell them what I knew, what I'd seen. But then Macbeth had turned that look of accusation on me.

Faced with talk of evil, he turned to me. 'Gruoch, do you know aught?' He seemed to fear me like Fife feared that bit of dried skin. And I could not, I just could not reply 'Yes, this is what I know . . .' I couldn't even admit that I'd seen the woman in the yard, let alone tell him that, when she'd turned her face up to Fife, I'd recognized her. Even when it had been for his sake, he had half hated me for visiting the old wise woman. He'd feared my dealings with her. I could not bring myself to tell him that I'd recognized her in the crawling figure whose strange gift had so terrified MacGirrick.

Besides, a few minutes' thought told me that it was perhaps best for me to act as ignorant and innocent as Macbeth. The Lord of Fife seemed to suspect us of plotting against him. Best, I thought, to deny everything, not stir up the threat of feud which Beatrice had seemed to fear so much.

But though I held my tongue, I meant to get the truth

out of her as soon as I could. I was determined to find out what she was about.

I turned away from them and, leaving Macbeth still shouting orders in the yard, I escaped back into the chill loneliness of my chamber on the far side of the hall. I sat down on the edge of the bed and pressed my hands to my face. From the yard I could still hear voices calling and the hurried footsteps of the searchers echoed around the house. My room was still and dead; it smelled of old fires the way it always did on summer days when the hearth was cold. I cupped my burning cheeks in my hands and wondered what the old woman had been doing by the bier. I was angry with her for making trouble between Macbeth and Fife, though I still could not believe as Beatrice did that there was any real danger of feud.

I hadn't been alone many minutes when the door swung open, letting in hot air and the smell of chickens. Macbeth stood in the doorway, stooping and resting his hands on the low lintel. 'Gruoch,' he said looking coldly at me, 'what does all this mean? What has angered the Lord of Fife?'

'My love, I don't know.'

'Is it witches' spells?'

'How should I know, Macbeth?'

'By that thing you wear.'

'Why do you suspect me, Macbeth? I swear to you I know nothing about it. My love, why are you looking at me like that? What have I done to offend you?'

'A great deal, Gruoch. You've ruined my honour, brought dark powers into my house. Must I stand by while the Lord of Fife insults me for what I'll swear was my wife's doing? And . . .' For a while he seemed unable to go on. He just stood leaning on the doorframe and watching me as if I was something strange he could not understand. Then his eyes slid coldly from the great sagging bed to the cradle that was now yawning, dark with painful emptiness. 'And then there is the business of the child.'

I felt as if he had hit me. 'What of him?'

'What man would trust a woman that could give up her baby to another breast?'

'You know I had no choice. My milk failed, Macbeth. I had to let him go,' I cried wretchedly. The empty cradle was like a pain to me. It was only the day before that I had given in to Morag's persuading and stopped trying to feed him. In the end my milk, poisoned or not, had stopped flowing. Giving Findlay into the care of another had been terrible to me. Macbeth could not know how ashamed I was of my dry breasts, nor how I ached for the child now. He'd not speak to me like that if he understood.

'They say it's a sure sign a woman's been faithless to her husband if she can yield the bairn to another,' he said.

'My love, you cannot think such a thing of me. Whatever else you may think of me. You might think me a witch or a murderer. But you cannot, Macbeth, you cannot think I could ever betray you.'

He made no answer to that but continued to watch me as if he loathed me.

'Macbeth, how was I to feed the bairn with dry breasts?'

'And why were they dry, Gruoch? Tell me that?'

'Nay, I don't know. There's no knowing such things.'

He left the doorway and took a step towards me – standing close, but making no move to touch me. 'The women say,' he began slowly, 'I've heard Morag say it: that a woman with a child still at the breast should keep herself away from her husband.'

'My love, that's nonsense. Many women lie with their men and their bairns are none the worse for it.'

'Careful women who want their children to thrive are more cautious. They'll check their passions a bit. A woman that's waited seven years to get her child might spare a little thought for that child before she acts like a bitch on heat.'

'Macbeth!'

'But nothing cools your lust, does it, Gruoch? I remember how you saw your man killed before your eyes – your household slaughtered and within the hour you were ready to play the whore.'

I felt sick. 'No, my love. That's not true. All I wanted – all I've ever wanted – is you. Don't you understand?'

'Nay Gruoch, I know not what to think of you sometimes. You're not like other women.'

'I love you more than any other woman ever could.'

'You talk of love! You who put the knife in my hand when I was full of ale and sleeping in your bed! You have destroyed me with your evil ways. Don't you see that?'

'Macbeth, I don't understand. You killed Gillacomgain and never thought about the business again.'

'Don't you see the difference, woman?' he said. 'I'd got a feud with Gillacomgain. I had none with Duncan. You should not have goaded me into it. I should have waited till I could kill him cleanly in battle.'

'What's clean about battle?' I protested. 'In battle there'd have been a hundred men killed besides; women widowed and children orphaned. A single stroke of the knife was surely cleaner than that.'

'Damn you. Do you know nothing of honour?'

'No, I only know love.'

That old look of disgust was stronger than ever. I was reminded of the way he'd looked at the worm the morning I told him of the prophecy. 'You are a changeling,' he muttered.

'Macbeth, don't look so. I only did it to get you what you wanted.'

'Aye, and what did you do, Gruoch, to get me a bairn in the cradle?'

I looked at him in horror. That was worse than anything that had gone before. It was as if all the fear and disgust he'd held back was loosed now. His face was flushed and he looked somehow different from the man I'd always

known, in the saffron-dyed kilt and fine gear he'd donned
for the gathering of thanes. 'Macbeth, what do you mean?'

'I mean I've not forgotten the rest of the crone's words.
It wasn't me that was to father Kings, was it?'

'That's a foul thought, Macbeth!'

'Is it? I'm minded of a day about twelve months back
when you had a fancy for walking alone with Seyton.'

'No!'

He turned away from me without another word and
went to deal with the Lord of Fife.

When I was alone in the room, tears oozed from the
corners of my hot, swollen eyes. I ached with weariness.
What with watching the baby and worrying over the
change in Macbeth I'd not slept more than bits and snatches
since the night of Duncan's death. I curled myself tightly
on the great old bed that he now refused to share with me.
My head felt as if it'd burst with misery.

So now I knew what was in his mind. Now I knew how
much he despised me for doing what I swear he wanted
me to do. Now he trusted me in nothing. I slipped from the
bed and crouched beside the empty cradle, resting my head
on the edge of it and breathing in the faint smell of baby
that lingered in it. I couldn't bear it. I seemed to be losing
everything I loved.

1996

If I – or any woman – had set out to imagine hell, I couldn't
have thought of anything closer to it than those words of
Lady Macbeth's:

> 'I have given suck, and know
> How tender 'tis to love the babe that milks me.
> I would, while it was smiling in my face,
> Have plucked my nipple from his boneless gums
> And dashed the brains out . . .'

They are like a glimpse into the very mind of the devil himself. And I tell you, if there is something in the play that has exercised a dark power for hundreds of years, it is those words – that little touch of hell. I know: I have said the words and felt their power.

In those words lies the Curse of *Macbeth*.

That night when I spoke the lines it felt as if they were dragged out of me: as if I was making a promise that I did not fully understand; but a promise which I would be forced to keep and keep in a way too terrible to imagine.

I remember a little while afterwards stumbling down to the dressing room, shaking and wondering what was happening to me. My feet felt too heavy and my head felt too light. I remember Jo – or was it Meg? Someone in a witch costume anyway – holding out a hand as I passed her in the corridor and saying, 'You're marvellous!'

I remember a porter handing me a note from John, scribbled on a page torn from a diary: *You're brilliant Abby, I knew you were holding something in reserve for the first night.*

Then I remember the cluttered stillness of the dressing room and how it seemed years ago since Greg and I had argued there. A grey, dead place it seemed. Life was upstairs, under the stage lights.

I sat down by the mirror because enough of Abigail, the professional actress, remained to prompt me to check my make-up. The face, very pale between black dress and red-brown hair, stared out at me: too small, too thin, too heavily shadowed.

Why did everything seem wrong?

Like a toddler groping for her security blanket, I fumbled among the heavy costume jewellery at my throat for the lucky pendant I'd hidden there. I clutched its familiar shape in my left hand while with my right I dabbed powder on to my damp cheeks. The gold was soon as warm as the sticky hand that held it.

I concentrated on the face, trying to repair the damage that little oozing tears and sweat had done at the corners of my eyes. But it kept blurring in front of me. I seemed impossibly weary.

I remember thinking, 'I'll just close my eyes a minute, then I'll feel better.'

As I thought that, the face in the mirror went completely out of focus for a split second. And then it swam back into sharp, close focus. There was my face, with the little lines and blobs of tears under its eyes, the powder fresh on its cheeks. But now, behind that face, there streamed innumerable others, as if this was a kind of trick mirror reflecting my image over and over again into mind-numbing infinity.

I turned quickly, expecting to see someone holding another mirror behind me; that was the only reasonable explanation for the effect. But I saw no one behind me – just the dull, dead busyness of the place; the white nightgown laid out ready for my final scene, discarded shoes, red roses in a yellow plastic bucket.

I pressed the pendant to my lips and, with a great effort, turned back to the mirror. There it was still, that long line of faces stretching unbroken into the distance. They all stared out of the mirror towards me, eyes very wide with my look of fear and bewilderment repeated over and over again. But now I looked more closely and saw something more terrifying. Those faces were not all just reflections of mine. They were like mine. But they were all different.

In the play the witches show Macbeth a vision: in a mirror he sees the line of Kings who will succeed him. Well, I seemed to be seeing something similar, though whether it was the past or the future I was seeing, I'm not sure. Just this stream of faces, repeated into infinity.

Then it changed and one face rushed closer – eyes wide and terrified. A small dark figure with hands raised like the ghost in the wings. But now the hands she held out to me were deep red: blood dropping from them in great glistening drops.

And the fear that slipped into my mind at that moment was definitely for the future, not the past.

Something unthinkable; something that could exist only in the mind of the devil, was about to happen to me. I raised my own hands to cover my eyes, to protect myself from the thing in the mirror. Sticky with sweat as they were; it felt, just for a minute, as if my hands too were bloody.

Miss West. Your call.

Slowly I took my hands from my face. All the mirror showed besides my own terrified face was costumes and roses in crisp plastic wrappings.

1057

The old crone laughed. She laughed in my face when I went to her and asked what her business had been in the yard.

'So there's feud brewing between Moray and Fife, is there?' She sounded pleased about it.

'No. Not feud. There must not be feud between our house and MacGirrick's.'

'Do you fear for your man?'

'No, of course not. Macbeth will not be beaten by the likes of Fife!' Or by anyone else, I thought. I clutched the prophecy to me like a lucky charm. 'No man born of woman shall harm Macbeth'. But there were other things to fear. 'My cousin is wife to MacGirrick of Fife. I fear for her – and her bairns.'

She didn't answer that. It almost seemed as if she'd not heard. The ruined broch was different today: the fire was out and the place smelled of cold ashes and the woman's own filth, of bats and damp stone. A dead place. And she sat on a dirty bed of bracken, not stirring in the ragged sunshine that fell through the broken roof.

I'd come there as soon as the funeral party and our other guests had left the house. I was determined to get the truth out of her. But at first she'd say nothing about her business with MacGirrick.

'Did you give your man my warning? You told him to beware of Fife?' She rocked herself on the bed.

'I told him, but Macbeth has no need to fear . . .'

'And now MacFindlay is King?'

'He was proclaimed so by the thanes when Duncan MacCrinan was found murdered in his bed. In three days' time we will go to Scone for the coronation.'

She nodded. Pleased – very pleased with that. 'I judged him well that night we met. An ambitious man. I knew then that he was the one who could destroy the line of Girrick of Fife. A tool in my hands.' The hairy lips curled into an ugly grin.

'You've done this on purpose? You have made feud between us and Fife?'

'You're a fool, Lady Gruoch!' she cried. 'You've come here with your baskets of meat – as if I was a dog! "Give me this," you say, "Give me that." Asking for my help and all the time without the sense to use the power you've got. Or the wit to understand what others are about.'

For all her fury she made no attempt to move from the heap of filthy bracken and I realized that it was because she hadn't the strength. Her body crouched like a dry husk against the clammy wall, a patch of harsh sunlight on her pale, withered cheeks. Only her voice seemed to be alive. And what it was saying had a deadly power over me.

'What have you done?' I demanded. 'Have you made spells? What spell have you put on Macbeth to make him seek the crown and destroy himself?'

'Nay, you talk like a priest trying to frighten bairns. Spells and charms indeed! And you a woman that wears the face of the Goddess. I made no spell to tempt your man. The ambition was already in him when we met on the heath. I said aloud what he'd thought. And that excited him. He was like a man with his lust aroused by a whore's bawdy talk.'

'But you bewitched MacGirrick. It was a charm you left at his feet. Why else would a grown man go pale at the sight of a bit of dried skin?'

'I gave him his own, that is all. It was the terror in his own mind turned him pale. It's the evil inside men that destroys them,' she muttered. 'Though they'll always look for something else to blame. And usually it'll be a woman.'

'Tell me what your business was with MacGirrick or I'll tell Macbeth what I know and have his men come to fetch you.'

'Send who you will, Lady Gruoch,' she spat. 'They can't do much but hurry my death a little. I have what I want. Your man will destroy the house of Fife. He's got the power now to do it – and MacGirrick drew his knife on him yesterday. Macbeth MacFindlay's not a man to forgive an insult like that.'

'You've used me!' I cried angrily. 'You've used me to brew feud between my husband and my cousin.'

'Aye, Gruoch, daughter of Bodhe, I've used you. Just as you tried to use me. Paying me in offal for the things you want.' She drew a rattling kind of breath and stirred in the dead bracken. 'But I didn't give what you wanted. I gave what I wanted to give. And what I wanted was a strong hand raised against the house of Girrick.'

'Why, you wretch?'

'Revenge,' she said quietly. 'What else spawns feud?'

'Revenge? What is MacGirrick to you?'

'He is my grandson.'

I stared at her in the broch's ruined stillness. Above our heads a jackdaw cursed in the broken tower. 'Who are you?' I asked.

She coughed and spat in the direction of the filth-heap by the wall. 'That's a question you should have asked long ago, Lady Gruoch. Did I not tell you once that I was nobly born? But you didn't hear me, did you? It didn't matter to you. Nothing mattered to you except that fool man of yours and what he wanted. If you'd asked then I'd have told you all and you might have escaped. But you didn't ask. To you I was just a filthy old woman. A beggar woman to be fed on the rubbish of your kitchens! But I am as well-born as the daughter of Bodhe. I too am descended from Kenneth MacAlpine. The royal blood runs in this dirty old body too and you'd have had to treat me differently if Girrick had not made me outcast.'

The heat of the day, the stink of the hovel and my own terror were choking me. 'And that is why you want revenge on Girrick's son?'

'Nay, I want revenge because he killed my daughter.'

She told me the whole story then: rejoicing in the telling, gloating over my rising fear and pausing now and then to say, 'You're hearing it too late now, daughter of Bodhe. There's nothing you can do now.'

According to her tale – and I have too little cause to doubt she told the truth – this hag had once been wife to a mighty thane and she had borne one child, a daughter who had been of course a pattern of virtue and beauty. At sixteen this wonderful girl was married to Girrick of Fife. A widower 'well nigh her father's age', his first wife had left no surviving sons and Girrick hardly thought of anything but getting himself an heir that'd keep his name alive.

'As if,' said the crone, 'the world would be the poorer for losing the name of Girrick of Fife.'

Well it seems the wench soon quickened and bore the child to term.

'For three days I tried to get that damned brat born. Three days and her so brave all the time, but getting weaker and weaker. Arse-first the wretched thing was coming and

I couldn't do anything.' Her withered hands clenched on the bracken and a thick rheumy tear gathered slowly in the corner of one eye. 'Three days; then the priest said she was dead.'

The ruined tower was silent for a minute and the disturbed birds began to settle back on their nests. 'I told them she was still living,' she whimpered. 'But Girrick and the priest were ready with the knife. Girrick was desperate to have his heir born, no matter what. In the end they had to drag me off her before they could do it; Girrick had his men get me out of the room. And the priest said it was God's will the bairn should be cut out.'

Suddenly the hovel rang to the ghostly sound of dry, unearthly sobs. 'I heard her scream,' she gasped through the sobbing. 'In Christ's name, the whole house heard. Damn you, Girrick and every one of your line. I heard her scream.' The sobs got louder, racking her body so it jerked wildly on the damp bracken. And through the sobs she kept repeating, 'I heard her scream, I heard her scream,' over and over again.

There was something terrifying about her weakness and her anger. Something terrible about her lying there ragged and filthy on a foul bed, cursing the mighty house of Fife. Her voice was a cry from the dark, hideous places. The blistering curse of all things ugly, helpless and despised that breed their venom secretly: the untold power of the weak and the wronged.

For a while the woman was sobbing so much over this old grief that I couldn't get her to go on with her tale.

'What happened after?' I asked. 'What magic did you use to make Girrick's son fear you so much?'

After a while she became calm enough to tell me how Girrick had made her outcast. He feared she'd harm his son and he probably had good cause to fear it. She certainly hated the bairn for causing her daughter's death. It seems the child's nurse had been an old servant of hers and from this nurse she somehow stole or bought the thin caul of skin that had been on the baby's head when it was born.

'When they knew I'd got that there was great commotion. The superstitious fools believed I'd have power over the child because I'd got something of him. You'd have thought it was his soul I'd taken!'

Constantine MacGirrick grew up knowing that his grandmother had sworn revenge on his line and knowing too that she possessed a part of him. The superstitious believe that witches can make spells against them simply by using a nail paring or a lock of hair – or even a bit of linen that's been worn and fouled. How much more might be done through the skin the child was born with?

And MacGirrick was a superstitious man.

He'd turned to priests for comfort and had never trusted women, but always he'd believed that a woman who hated him had a supernatural power over him. Then, in our courtyard, that withered skin had appeared at his feet, like a threat.

'And he blames Macbeth for it,' I said furiously. 'He thinks we have plotted with you.'

'And because he fears Macbeth, Macbeth fears him. Now they are set to destroy each other.'

'No,' I said quickly, 'you can't harm us.' She must not. I remembered Beatrice as I'd bidden farewell to her a few hours ago in the litter with the baby in her arms and the children gathered round her. Fear twisted inside me like a pain in the gut. Whatever happened I must protect her from the feud.

'You'll not succeed. I swear you won't. I'll see no harm comes to Macbeth – or to Macduff's brood.'

'And how will you stop me?' Spittle showered on to the stones from her loose mouth. 'You can't even get your man to do what you want. Lady Gruoch, you have no understanding of men, or men's ways.'

'I know this, though. My man won't be destroyed by Macduff of Fife or anyone else.'

'And how do you know this, my Lady?'

'I saw his future. The sisters told me he'll never be defeated. "No man of woman born can harm Macbeth." '

The words hung shrilly in the silence of the broch. They repeated themselves in my head and my heart began to pound.

Slowly, the old woman's thin, colourless lips rose into a hideous grin and she began to laugh – like a devil might mock the tortured in hell. I backed away, out into the sweet fresh air where the sun was warm on the sheep-bitten grass and a rabbit was scuttling for shelter under the fallen stones of the gateway. I turned and ran down the slope, each step jarring through my body. When I reached the stream and stopped for breath, I found that I was weeping. Weeping with terror.

I stood shaking and sobbing on the sinking river shingle, clutching for support at the papery trunk of a birch. Gradually the truth trickled coldly through my brain. The prophecy which I had given with such pride to my man was like a knife in his back. Macduff was not born of woman, but torn by a priest from his mother's dying body. He had the power to kill Macbeth.

And I dared not confess my mistake.

Have you ever held a blind-worm, girl?

Don't be foolish. It has no sting. All the slow-worm has is a tongue that men fear. But when a woman holds it in her hand, it feels like . . . Ah well, girl, you're too young to be told what it feels like, and my mind is wandering from the business. The sleeping draught'll get the better of me if I don't tell all quickly.

Now it matters more to me than anything else that you understand it all.

I think I knew as soon as I saw you in your swaddling

clothes that you were the one who must carry the tale into the future. Your mother was just a slut from the clansmen's hovels, but when she brought you here claiming Lulach had fathered you, I believed her, because it seemed right. Right that there should be a woman of my blood to carry the memories.

It's for this I've raised you, girl. Listen well.

We all travelled south for the coronation and, by the time we got to Scone, I hardly dared to speak to Macbeth. He glowered darkly and seemed to suspect everyone around him of treachery – except for the one who seemed to me to most deserve suspicion. Despite those cruel words to me, he still kept Seyton at his side.

On the journey, moving slowly and muddily south through uncertain summer weather, his horse was always next to Macbeth's. And when at last the trudge and the muddle and the tedious packing and unpacking were over and we were all gathered in and around the abbey, Seyton was named Steward, with authority over all our household. So as the preparations were made for Macbeth's coronation, Seyton loomed beside him like an ill fate all the while. Why, I wondered, when he was so impatient of everyone else, did he allow so much freedom to this fellow whom he did not even trust?

'Ah but I have my uses, Lady Gruoch,' the man gloated. 'And I know more and see more than any in his company.'

It was the night before the coronation that he managed again to trap me alone. On the green mound at the abbey's heart, the Stone of Destiny stood blackly waiting the morrow's ceremony. In the monk's herb-garden to the south of the kitchen quarters, there was a stillness I welcomed after the turmoil of our lodgings; and I lingered there a while, busy with my own thoughts in the damp chill of the summer dusk. Till he came like the boor that he was, crushing fragrance out of the mint and thyme with his clumsy boots.

'The more suspicious a man gets, the more he needs someone like me,' he said. 'Someone who has his ways of learning others' secrets. Knowing what others want hid gives great power.'

I turned away, not to the dark path that led back past the church to the guest house, but straight towards the ruddily lit kitchen doorway, from which voices spilled.

'Wait, Lady.' He caught my arm. 'You see, Lady Gruoch, I know your secret.'

'Then you know more than I do,' I said sharply. 'For I didn't know I had one.'

'Aye you have, though you may pretend to yourself that you haven't. The fact is, you've hidden your bairn from your husband because you fear what he'll do to it.'

'What do you mean? Why should Macbeth harm his own son?'

'Because he fears it's not his.'

'That's a lie!' My voice rang out too clearly in the close garden and I forced myself to speak more quietly. 'My milk failed and the child was put to nurse.'

'And you told Macbeth where he was sent?'

'Yes. No, perhaps I didn't. But such things are women's business. Not his concern.'

'Ah.' He let me go and smiled, ugly and treacherous. 'Maybe that's so. It's strange, my Lady, isn't it, how things are not always as they appear?'

I took an uncertain step towards the kitchen door, but couldn't leave him. The treacherous sneer held me as surely as his hand on my arm. I had to know what he was about.

'That's something your man doesn't rightly understand, Lady: how appearances can deceive. He saw you and me just walking together alone and he doubted you. He saw me carry the bairn and suspected me of fathering it. He's easily convinced by appearances, isn't he?'

'You meant him to be, damn you! He's forgotten it now.'

'Ah, but it would be so easy to remind him.'

'Damn you to hell, Seyton! Leave me alone!' I picked up my skirts, poised for flight in the herb-scented dusk; but he caught me again.

'But I can't leave you alone, Gruoch. You see, Lady, I was at his side when you cast your spell across Gillacomgain's board. The magic you used, Lady, to ensnare Macbeth, trapped me too. I've waited nine years, Lady, while you treated me like a dog.' He was gripping my arm again and every time he sneered 'Lady', he jerked me closer, till my face touched the shoulder of his leather jerkin and I smelled his sweat.

I looked wildly round the little green space between its three walls of reddish stone, hardly knowing whether I longed or feared to see other folk about. There were still voices in the kitchens. From beyond the church where some newly arrived thanes were setting up camp came shouts and the sound of posts being driven home with stones. From his trampling feet, the scent of mint rose sharp and clean. It's a smell I can't abide now and I never come near it without remembering that night: his painful hold on me; his vile closeness; the weakness and the anger inside me.

'Remember,' he said, his breath hot on my cold face, 'appearances can be confusing. You and I can easily enjoy each other's company a little with no one seeing or suspecting anything. On the other hand, I can make sure there's plenty to see and suspect without you so much as touching me.'

'You're a fool! What do you think he'd do to you if he really believed . . .'

'Ah, but I can be away to his enemies before he can take his sword to me again.' As he spoke, he thrust out the maimed arm and, with his face twisted in a grin like that of a man in pain, he clutched his loins obscenely. 'It'd be much more than a hand his famous justice would have sliced off for that offence, wouldn't it, Gruoch?'

God! There was bitterness in that voice. I thought how blind Macbeth was, not to see the sheer hatred that was all twisted up with this fellow's allegiance. He was like a great ugly dog that fawned upon its master, licking servilely at his hand, while all the time, behind the slavering tongue were the strong teeth, just waiting for the moment to strike.

'And there's this to remember too, my Lady,' he went on. 'If I'm driven out of MacFindlay's household, I'll take with me the very interesting story of Duncan's sudden death. There's plenty would be glad to hear about that. Macduff of Fife for one.'

'I don't know what you're talking about.'

'Of course not.' He let go of my arm. 'But Macbeth does well to be wary of that one. So think on it, Lady. A little kindness to me is all it takes to stop the Lord of Fife knowing your man's secret. And,' he whispered, horribly damp against my ear, 'and to protect everything you care about most . . .'

There was a heavy tread on the dry gravel that the monks had laid between the orderly herb-beds and I saw a figure move in the gloom; a figure with hair so fair, or else so white, it gleamed pale in the dusk.

Seyton turned impatiently towards the fellow, a shambling figure, dressed for, and smelling of, the stables. 'You've no business here, man. Get yourself off.'

But the fair-haired man stood his ground with a determination that suggested simplicity. 'Pardon, Sir, but I came to tell the Lady that her horse is lame.' He turned to me, ducking his head respectfully. 'What would you have me do, Lady? Shall I prepare another horse for you to ride in the ceremony tomorrow?'

I sighed with relief. 'Take me to the stables now. I'll look for myself.'

Seyton cursed as I moved safely away towards the lighted kitchen, but as soon as we were out of earshot of him, the stable-hand muttered, 'I beg your pardon for lying, Lady. The beast ails nothing.'

I stopped and stared at the shabby, loose-limbed figure. 'Why did you say it did?'

'I reckoned you wanted away from yon fellow,' he said simply.

His round face looked too honest and much too stupid for trickery. It also had an oddly familiar look to it. 'Do I know you?' I asked.

A great grin split the red cheeks. 'Aye you did, long ago. I'm Ban that used to work in your father's stables.'

'Ban!' I remembered him: his grin, his hot, sweating hands and his kisses. I stared down at the clean gravel in confusion. 'How came you here?'

'I came to work for the monks when your father's household broke up. But,' he added, 'I never thought to see you come south again – and so great as you've become.'

'It's good to see you, Ban. And . . .' I hesitated, 'thank you for your service just now. I'm afraid my husband's steward had become rather impertinent.'

'I'm glad to help you, Gru . . . my Lady,' he said and shambled off to the stables.

The next day, Macbeth sat on the black stone on the low man-made hill within the Abbey grounds and, before the assembled Thanage, took upon himself the Crown of Scots. And in the long ceremony (much of which was older than the abbey, older than the Christ God, as old as the green hill and the stone itself) the Lord of Fife was as active as the little pink, fringe-headed Abbot. For it seemed that Kingmaker was one of those titles he'd bought himself.

I watched his sallow, sunken face as he placed the crown on Macbeth's flowing black hair, and I thought: aye, if he'd had the choosing, it'd be a different head, even though it might not be his own. The look and the memory it brought with it of that meeting among the mint spoiled the moment which should have been so sweet. The moment when

Macbeth achieved everything he wanted. And later, when the feasting began, there was a worse moment.

The loud shouting of speeches through the hall was over. The cups had been raised and drained a dozen times to wish the new King well, and down in the body of the hall men turned their minds to their meat. On the dais I was growing weary and watching for the earliest possible chance of escape, when the fat Lord of Ross smiled blandly across the board at MacGirrick.

'We lack the company of the lady your wife. I hope she is not sick.'

'She's well enough,' growled MacGirrick. 'I sent her home directly from Moray. A man does well to keep his family away from gatherings such as this, I think.'

Beside me, I felt Macbeth stiffen and, looking up, I saw his brows drawn together in the deep furrows that'd got all too common of late. 'What do you mean, man?' he demanded.

Fife stared back and pushed away his cup with a quick fastidious gesture. 'There's too much drunk,' he said sourly. 'A deal too much, I think, when sottish servants knife their royal masters in their beds.'

Macbeth's own cup crashed down on the table, slopping liquor, and angry colour rose high on his cheeks.

'Aye,' said the Lord of Ross smoothly. 'Duncan Mac-Crinan's death was a terrible business. But there's no need to brood over that now, man. The fellows who did it are dead and we can all sleep quiet in our beds.'

'Can we?' MacGirrick looked from Ross to Macbeth, almost opposite him. 'You, Lord King, were so quick to kill them we never learned who else was party to their villainy.'

Macbeth slammed his hand down on the board, jolting knives and drinking horns. 'There was nothing to learn,' he said. Their eyes locked and I watched the long brown fingers tense on the table till the knuckles whitened and the nails clawed at the wood amid the grease pools and the bones and the spilled ale.

'As you please, my Lord,' said Fife quietly.

I looked up at Macbeth's face. His mind's on the crone's warning, I thought. He was scowling with a dark twisting bitterness that clouded the straight, clean openness of his face. I clutched at his arm in horror.

1996

'Things bad begun make strong themselves by ill.
So, prithee go with me.'

Footsteps across the stage. The sudden darkness of the wings.

'For God's sake, Abby, let go of me!' Greg's voice hissed warmly against my ear and, looking down, I saw my own fingers gripping convulsively at his arm through the heavy sleeve of his shirt.

We were out now into the gloomy space beyond the flats, moving back to make room for the people going on for the next scene, but staying close enough to make our own re-entrance soon.

'Abby, please. Let go.' With a warm, firm hand Greg unfurled my chilly fingers. 'Are you OK?' he asked nervously.

'Yes,' I said. But I felt pretty unsteady as I stood in what seemed almost complete darkness after the brilliance of the stage. Everything seemed so confused. We were so far on in the play and I hardly remembered any of it. It all seemed to be out of my control.

'You're fantastic, Abby,' whispered Greg. 'Just keep it up.'

'Thanks. I just feel a bit . . . tired.'

He leaned over me anxiously. 'What was that business with the knife Alan told me about?'

'Nothing. Just a mistake.'

'Abigail, can I have a word?'

Alan's hand fell on my shoulder and before I could resist he'd pulled me out into the corridor behind the stage where the stairs led down to the dressing rooms. The light was brighter here, ordinary. It hurt somehow. It forced me out of role; gave me no choice but to be Abby West and to feel her pain.

'Let go of me, Alan,' I said resentfully.

His beard twitched impatiently. 'Just a minute. For God's sake you can let me have a minute of your time, can't you?' He leaned over me, smelling of leather and the sweat the stage lights induced. I realized he was about to kiss me and felt quite ludicrously frightened.

'My scene. I've got to get back, Alan.'

He gripped my shoulders with both hands and suddenly seemed very large. 'I've had enough of this, Abigail. Stop playing around.'

'I don't know what you mean.'

'Yes you do.'

'Alan, please. People will see us.'

'You think anyone cares?' He was speaking louder, more wildly now. 'You think Gregory cares? Hardly in a position to act the wronged husband, is he?'

'Shut up!' In a reflex action my hand flew to his face. A clichéd dramatic gesture that made me feel silly as my fingers made contact with his beard.

'Bitch!' He jerked my shoulders painfully against the wall. 'You lead me on and then you treat me like dirt.'

'Leave me alone, Alan,' I hissed furiously. 'Go and take a cold shower. I've never . . .'

'No. You listen to me. I'm not putting up with your tricks any longer.'

Miss West, your entrance for the banquet scene. You're about to miss your entrance.

'I've got to go.'

'OK, but just remember this: I know things about you that you wouldn't want Gregory to hear. I think you'd better start being a bit nicer to me, Abigail.'

His hands slackened and I ran for the stage.

'I'll see you after,' he called in a hoarse whisper.

1057

Whenever men drink together there is always a time when they forget all their other concerns and care for nothing but the jugs and the drinking horns slopping on the board in front of them. Later, if the serving lads keep pouring, they will remember their differences drunkard-fashion, all magnified and distorted by the ale: like things seen through water. But for a while they are content just to drink.

When the coronation banquet had reached this oblivion I made my escape. But weary though I was, I was in no mood for sleep. My mind was pulled about with fears and doubts, some of them so dark I dared not name them.

The sneer on the face of Fife lingered with me like the sourness of tainted milk. Did he know what he should not? Did he wish us ill? These thoughts were painful enough, but they were as nothing to that deeper, more fearful question. Had he the power to harm us?

'Never defeated by any man of woman born.' That was the thought that the brooch had slipped into my brain when I'd sought Macbeth's weird. And the words – such as anyone might use to mark something sure and certain – had never troubled me till the wise woman had raved about her daughter's death. Now I was haunted by the thought of a man not born at all, but cut from the womb of his dying mother.

Did it mean, could it mean, that in the Lord of Fife lay my man's doom?

Macduff's sneer rose again into my head like bile.

Macbeth was near at hand, his mind not yet too distorted
with liquor to understand. I could turn back, go into the
crowded hall, draw him aside and say, 'My love, the old
power misled me and you are in danger. Beware the Thane
of Fife.'

What then? Feud between the houses of Fife and Moray?

No, that must not be.

Another face rose before my inward eye. Macbeth's face
as I had just seen it in the hall, dark and twisted with
bitterness. And, though I hated myself for it, I could not
but fear for Beatrice – and the bairns. I remembered too
how he'd spoken of little Kenneth's death all those years
ago. If feud began I dared not hope he'd spare the children
in Beatrice's house.

I could not tell him of this any more than I could tell him
of Seyton's threats. The silence was like a terrible wall
between us, parting us farther than all the miles Macbeth
had ever ridden on campaigns. I felt utterly alone and
desperately in need of help. Any kind of help.

I had come by now to the low mound where the
coronation had been performed. The ground around it,
churned by many feet, smelled fresh and damp from a
shower just passed. A dropped drinking horn and a couple
of broken shoe thongs littered the mud and the whole
natural grass arena had the jaded look of a place that has
lately been crowded. Enough daylight remained for me to
see the shape of the Stone of Destiny gleaming darkly at
the top of the little hill, backed by the outline of a few
young oak trees. Black and powerful it looked.

I picked my way through the mud, climbed the slope to
it and laid my hand on the polished hollow that formed a
kind of seat. I saw, now that I was close to it, that the Stone
of Destiny, traditional crowning place of the Kings of our
land, was not marble as some folk say, but seemed rather
to be of the same stuff as the black stone elf-bolts that the
ploughs sometimes turn up.

A strange thing indeed.

I could also see now that the stone was not altogether smooth but carved on the sides into ancient patterns worn beyond meaning. It is old, I thought, older than I expected. And as I stood there with my hand on the cold smoothness of it, I knew that it held the same ancient power that I felt in the brooch.

The priests, who wish to claim all ceremonies for their church and who would make us believe that there never was a time before the Christ God came to Alba, claim that the stone was the altar of the monk Columba. But I swear that if it was then he stole it from an older use. Not all their holy water can wash away its memories.

Now, in the mud-scented dusk, I felt my heart reaching out to that old power. I plucked the gold brooch from my breast and studied the calm staring faces. Then, knowing no other kind of invocation, I knelt Christian-fashion, laying my cupped hands on the stone. Through my fingers the round faces of the three sisters stared up at the last few shreds of daylight. The wet grass chilled my knees as my mind reached out searching in the Old Wisdom for answers to the tortured questions in my mind. For a moment the world around me faded.

'Don't move, my Lady,' muttered Seyton's hateful voice. 'And don't cry out or you'll be dead before anyone can reach you.'

I didn't move; I could feel his knife point pressing just below the bone of my shoulder. It was a mild night and I was wearing only the fine gown I'd feasted in. In the stillness I heard the blade tearing the thin stuff as he pressed. My hands clutched the brooch and I waited, scarcely breathing. 'Stand up.' His words were hot against my bare neck.

I stood slowly and turned to face him. As I did so the blade crept coldly round to my breast.

'I've come for my answer, Gruoch.' The knife pressed at

my bodice so slowly I seemed to feel the fine threads of the weave breaking one by one. 'What is it to be? Will you pay the price for my silence or shall I tell MacGirrick what I know?'

He drew the flat of the knife across my breast in hideous parody of a caress. He was facing into what remained of the light and I could see his face clearly as it hung over me, greasy and pale between beard and hair; his lips fat and red and wet.

Suddenly I had a ghastly vision of the payment he was demanding: the wet mouth devouring me, the single hand crawling on my shrinking flesh. Through the mild summer muddiness I seemed to smell the long-forgotten stench of Gillacomgain.

'Never,' I whispered.

The blade slid to my throat, nicking the skin. 'Then scream,' he said simply, 'and die.'

The silence stretched around us; on its very edge I could distinguish the mutter of the carousing men. The thin trickle of blood running from his knife's point tickled my neck and made it hard to keep still. Nothing stirred near us and I knew that this time there was no hope of rescue; the blade would be through my throat before anyone could reach us.

I did the only thing I could.

I spat in his face.

For one brief moment I watched the white froth run through the darkness of his beard. Then his great heavy hand moved quickly, bringing the hilt of the knife hard against my temple in a single, well-aimed blow. Darkness closed round me, painful and smothering as a fever.

As sense crept back into me, the first thing I knew was that the pin of the brooch had been driven into the palm of my hand by the force with which I'd clutched it. The next thing I knew was Seyton's sweating face inches away from my own, his breath, with a taint of onion, in my nose. His lips were parted.

Then the full horror hit me like a flood wave. He had dragged me over to the trees and I was lying on the ground. My skirts were round my waist, wet grass brushed my thighs and his knee had forced my legs apart. I could feel his hot groin pressing on the inside of my thigh: I could feel the hardness of his lust.

Unaware that my senses were returning, he had released his single-handed hold on me to fumble with his belt. I shifted the brooch in my bloody hand and aimed the long pin for his leering eyes.

It came so close it scraped his cheekbone but his huge hand trapped mine and I watched the thick fingers with their coarse black hairs try to take the brooch. I held on. He grunted a curse and struck me again. As brief, hot oblivion took hold of me the two things uppermost in my mind were the old brooch, warm in my bleeding hand, and the furious face of the man I hated: white greasy cheeks above black beard, thick open mouth.

That must have been why the charm worked.

I saw his weird.

It's hard to describe what I saw in that instant. But if you take one mirror and place it in front of another you will see whatever lies between the two, reflected again and again as if for ever. Now it seemed in my vision as if Seyton was trapped between two such mirrors. His likeness was repeated over and over again before my eyes. I looked along the stream of ugly faces and I knew it for the bloodline he would found. And sure enough it was as the old crone had foretold the night Gillacomgain died; there upon the ugly heads, diminished by the distance of time, was a royal crown.

But listen, that is not all I saw.

In that instant when I lay in his foul grasp I also saw something I longed for. I saw the fall of his line. It was far away along that line of time, faded and small. But this is what I saw: I saw two crowned heads bowing down, stooping to the bloody block and the blow of the common executioner's axe.

I have seen it and I know it will be.

His face gleamed horribly above me as the brief moment of vision faded, but his look had changed. The fleshy lips were drawn back from his teeth in a grimace of terror.

'In Christ's name!' he muttered. 'I believe it's true what they say of you. You are possessed by the devil.'

'Did you see too?'

'I saw the look that came on you, woman. And it was evil.' He seemed frozen, unable to move. His hand was gripping mine still but the power in it seemed to have drained away.

'I have seen your weird,' I whispered. 'I saw two of your line falling to the executioner's blow.'

His hold on my hand relaxed and he moved away from me, but not before I understood the cause of his confusion. His groin was still pressing against my thigh and I knew that what a few moments ago had been hard was hard no longer.

I pulled down my skirt and stood up to face him. 'It doesn't need my husband's sword to unman you, Seyton. A woman's look is enough to do it.'

His face burned with anger but I could tell he dared not touch me. His lust had turned to revulsion.

'This is not done with, you witch!'

'Strike me then,' I taunted. 'Strike the witch if you dare.'

'I'll strike, Lady Gruoch,' he said, looming over me and tainting the air with the stinking sweat of fear. 'I'll strike a blow you'll never recover from.'

Then he was gone and I sat down shaking under the trees and wept wildly till the banquet ended and Macbeth, sulky and suspicious, found me there in the darkness.

1996

Greg scowled suspiciously as I joined him, but there wasn't time for a word between us before Lady Macbeth swept on to the stage on the arm of her husband, King of Scotland.

No time to talk, but I could feel his anger through the taut muscles under my hand: anger and suspicion. The face that had been so cleanly cut and open scowled now, furrowed with suspicion. Now Macbeth suspected everybody. Torn by guilt over the killing of Duncan which had transgressed all his own ideas of honour, he was yet driven to shed more blood. Now he thought he saw the ghost of Banquo whom he'd just had murdered and yet he was already thinking of killing again as he became more and more suspicious of those around him.

> 'How sayst thou that Macduff denies his person
> At our great bidding?'

We were alone now the banquet was ended, and the face he turned on me was sulky, like a child in a temper. But this is no child, I thought with a terrible lurch of the insides. This is a powerful man, vindictive, full of resentment.

> 'Did you send to him sir?'

I said placatingly.

> 'I hear it by the way, but I will send.'

He was so hasty. He did jump to conclusions. Why did he look at me so suspiciously? Wasn't it obvious that I'd never wanted any man but him? But his suspicion of me was the least of the terrible changes in him. He was talking so wildly and angrily. Could this be the man I loved?

> 'I am in blood
> Stepped in so far that, should I wade no more,

> Returning were as tedious as go o'er.
> Strange things I have in head that will to hand,
> Which must be acted ere they may be scanned.'

Wearily I pressed my lips to his hand that was clenched into a tight fist.

> 'You lack the season of all natures, sleep.'

He seized my shoulders and pulled me hard against him.

> 'Come, we'll to sleep. My strange and self-abuse
> Is the initiate fear that wants hard use.
> We are yet but young in deed.'

1057

Macduff refused to come to help in the building of the royal stronghold at Dunsinane. You've probably heard about it, girl, for the story's still talked of, though it happened years before you were born. It was that refusal that brought Macbeth's anger to a head. Materials and workmen were sent from Fife, but the thane himself did not come and it was deemed a grievous insult. Men set great store by such trifles.

'It seems so much the worse that he lives not a day's journey off,' said Morag. 'And here there are thanes and mormaers travelled half the length of the land to honour the King and play their part in the building.'

That was true: the rounded hilltop of Dunsinane was crowded with men and ox-teams and piles of stone, timber and peat so that I began to wonder how any man knew what was to be done. And we, crowded into the new hall at the centre, were stoutly defended, not yet by ramparts but by a vast treacherous expanse of mud, that would, I reckoned, bring down the horse of any attacker more surely than a whole company of bowmen.

Macbeth had set about building the stronghold within

months of his coronation. He was determined to have Dunsinane stronger than any fort in Alba and to test the loyalty of his thanes by their readiness to join him in the enterprise. Indeed the ramparts of Dunsinane were to become a passion with Macbeth: he was to build and rebuild, strengthen and improve them through every year of his reign, as he desperately sought the security which, in truth, stone walls could never give him.

He was beginning to fear, if not his own shadow, then at least the shadows of everyone around him. And now, remembering the crone's warning, his thoughts had turned against Macduff.

'But surely he'll do no real harm to Macduff, a man that's kin to him,' I said.

Morag didn't reply. In her slow quiet way she was as loyal to him as I was. Morag always needs someone to be loyal to; now she's got no one else she's turned to the priests. Then it was Macbeth; but in spite of her loyalty, I saw doubt in the faded blue eyes. It was a doubt that gripped my own heart too. For sour-faced MacGirrick himself I cared nothing and I'd have seen him killed without a qualm. But there was Beatrice and the children to think of. If there was fighting they'd be in danger.

'Morag, I must send word to Beatrice: warn her to get away from the broch to one of Fife's other houses.'

She looked doubtingly at me. 'A messenger from Dunsinane would not be well received and besides, the King has taken the best men off to fight in Cumbria. There's scarce anyone to send.'

'Ban, the fellow who looks after my horse, will go for me,' I said. 'And I'll give him this to take as a token to Beatrice.' From the bottom of my jewel box, from under the hairpins and silver necklace where I kept it now, away from my husband's cold suspicious eyes, I drew the old brooch with the three brooding faces. 'She'll trust anyone who carries this.'

He was back within two days but he brought little comfort beyond a kind assurance that Beatrice and the bairns were all well. 'And the youngest growing into a fine healthy lad almost ready to be weaned.'

'But she will not move?' I spoke low not to be overheard by the other women spinning in the window's light.

'Nay, she reckons she's safer at the broch. If she goes, she says, it will look as if Macduff prepares for battle.' He scowled as he stood before the great hall fire, steaming slightly for it was a wet day and he was just come from his horse. 'The Lady Beatrice always had a way of understanding such things.'

'Better than me?'

His pale face glowed crimson. 'I meant no offence,' he muttered.

Maybe he was right. Maybe I didn't understand the business of battles and feuds and men's notions of honour too well. It'd never seemed much more interesting to me than the games the children played in the yard. But I had another kind of knowledge. Something darker, that seemed to come from inside me; perhaps from the Pictish blood of my mother – and that wisdom was telling me now that there was danger; deadly danger.

And the danger was of my own making. I had not understood that in urging Macbeth to strike against Duncan; by repeating to him the wise woman's words, I had set in motion events that would end in the loss of his love and the destruction of everything I cared for. That I had doomed myself to face a nightmare worse than anything I had ever imagined possible.

It was three days after Ban's return that more messengers came skidding through the windswept mud of Dunsinane. First came news that Macbeth and his party were almost home: just a day's march to the south. But then, later the same day, in an interval of ragged sunshine in the dreary storms, another messenger arrived. I saw him coming far below as Morag and I walked on the terrace of rubble that was to become the stronghold's rampart, and as soon as I saw him set his stumbling pony to the smooth slope of the hill, in the flying light and shadow, I knew he carried news of doom. I reached out and clutched at Morag's hand, my fingers clenching round it as I waited for the blow to fall.

'Macduff of Fife is fled to England, Lady,' cried out the messenger as soon as he was within hailing distance.

'Fled? Is he a coward as well as a traitor?'

'Aye, Lady!' said the fellow, pulling his mount to a standstill beyond the rubble foundations. He hung from the horse, damp-haired, breathless and exhilarated with speed and news. 'So says the King. His anger is high and he's taken his company westward to lay siege to the broch.'

Morag put out a sinewy arm to hold me as I swayed and spoke what I'd not strength to say. 'How so? Why go to the broch when MacGirrick is not there?'

'To take just vengeance, so he says.'

'In God's name,' whispered Morag. 'Not his wife? Not,' she glanced at me in dread, 'not the bairns?'

'But the place is well-defended, isn't it?' I cried in anguish before the fellow could reply. 'It won't be taken quickly?'

'Aye, it's well-defended.' He pushed back his sweat-sodden hair. 'And the King has promised a rich reward to any man that can break the siege and get inside the walls to . . .'

'Hold your tongue!' shouted Morag angrily. 'Can't you see the Lady is faint?'

Faint I was. The stone walls and the steaming horse, the ragged white and blue sky and its broken reflection in a thousand muddy puddles, all swept themselves into a blur before my eyes. But I must keep my wits about me and do something before it was too late.

'Morag, find Ban and tell him to get a horse ready. I'll meet him by the stables.'

She let go of me reluctantly; her chin was trembling and

she looked close to tears. 'Go on, Morag. I'll go to my chamber and get the brooch.'

Without waiting to see if she obeyed, I kilted up my skirts and went slopping and squelching back to the house. But I was scarcely half-way when I saw a huge, dark-haired man come out of the hall and turn towards the stables.

'That looks like the steward, Seyton!' I cried to the messenger who'd brought his horse over the rubble and was now a few paces behind me.

'Aye, likely it is,' he said. 'We rode together from the King's camp but he got ahead of me a little way back, as we left Birnam Forest.'

'What's he about?'

'No knowing with that one, Lady,' he answered cheerily.

Panic rose like bile inside me. I ran, stumbling and skidding, my heart struggling wildly in my chest and my breath roaring in my ears; I fell once, clawing on my knees in the mud, but was up and through the door of the house before the messenger could offer his help. Oblivious to the questioning eyes of the other women I staggered mud-spattered through the hall to the stairs and my own room that led off the narrow gallery above. Panic drummed in my head and shook my knees.

In my little chamber I could actually smell him – smell the rank sourness of his sweat through the scent of newly sawn wood. I knew he'd been there before I even saw that the jewel box was upturned and ransacked, my silver necklace snaking down on to the floor and the jewelled pins sticking in the wooden lid of the clothes chest. I knew, but stupidly I knelt down and searched; searched the scattered contents of the box, searched my clothes chest, searched the bed; searched wildly, wasting precious min-utes. And all the time I knew that the brooch wasn't there. All the time I knew that Seyton had taken it.

And I knew why.

When at last I could force myself to stop searching, I

stood for a moment and drew breath. In my head the messenger's words echoed. 'The King has promised a reward to any man that can break the siege.'

Whether he'd known how I'd used the brooch in the past I couldn't tell. Perhaps he'd just hit upon it as a token that Beatrice would be sure to recognize and trust. But that he'd taken it to gain entrance to Macduff's stronghold was certain.

'He rode westward,' said Ban when at last I dragged myself out to the yard. 'Not south to join the King.'

Almost calm now with the stillness that comes when the worst has happened and it's clear exactly what must be done, I told him to get ready two more horses.

'And will you have me go to the Lady Beatrice?' he asked.

But I shook my head. 'No, Ban. Morag and I will go to the broch. You must ride as fast as you can to the King. You must take a message that I can't trust with anyone else.'

1996

'The castle of Macduff I will surprise,
  Seize upon Fife, give to th' edge o' th' sword
  His wife, his babes, and all unfortunate souls
  That trace him in his line . . .'

Greg's voice, hollowed out by the speaker system, echoed round my dressing room and calmly and purposefully I got to my feet as if it had been a signal.

No, it wasn't really like sleepwalking because I was awake. I could see myself moving, but I wasn't in control. I know you don't believe me. I don't really expect you to. All I can do is tell you what happened – and what it all felt like to me. If you want an explanation, perhaps you'd better talk to a psychologist. Plenty of them have offered

explanations for what I did that night; most of them
without even bothering to meet me. I've read some amaz-
ing things about my own psyche in the newspapers!

But I'm not at all sure what really happened. All I can
remember is hearing Greg do that speech as I was sitting in
my dressing room wondering what on earth I was going to
do about Alan and his crazy threats . . .

Oh yes, Alan had made more threats. He had followed
me to my dressing room during the interval and his
behaviour had been . . . crazy, absolutely unbelievable. He
kept raving about how I'd 'led him on'; making out I'd
wanted . . . well, that I'd wanted more than a listening ear
from him. One minute he was insulting me and calling me
a bitch (or maybe it was 'witch' – or maybe it was both)
then the next minute he'd changed tack entirely and he
was all sort of wheedling.

'Come on, Abigail, we get on well together, don't we?
And you don't owe Gregory anything.'

'Get on well?' I was incredulous. I just wished the
wretched man would leave me alone. 'I thought I was an
evil-minded little bitch. And anyway, what was all that
about us being sworn enemies?'

He perched his huge frame on the edge of the bench in
front of me and leaned sweatily over me, putting a hand
on the back of my chair. 'Whatever you are, Abigail, I can't
get you out of my mind. I know you're just a troublemaker,
but I can't stop myself wanting you. And do you know,' he
went on slowly while, disgustedly, I watched his thick red
mouth, inches away from my face, 'I wonder whether that
wasn't the sort of trick your ancestor played on that poor
sod Gordon Stewart. They say she was a witch; well,
perhaps you've inherited her spells.'

'God! You are crazy, Alan. Get out of here,' I said
furiously. 'And stop blaming me. It's not my fault you got
the wrong idea. You can't expect me to act like a nun just
because you can't control yourself.'

The thick mouth snapped shut and colour filtered up through the forest of beard. Then he reached along the bench and picked up an evening paper that someone had left lying there for me to see. 'Is this why you don't want me?' he demanded.

Gazing out of the grey newsprint was my own face – with Greg and Luke. It was the picture taken that morning and the headline underneath it read: IT'S A FAMILY AFFAIR AT THE MAYPOLE.

'Breaking up the happy family, am I, by showing you the truth about Mr Happily Married Bloody Mortimer?'

'You sent me along there on purpose! You knew Chrissie was with him!'

'Christ! You had to face the truth sometime. He's been screwing around for years and you've been shutting your eyes to it.'

'You mean bastard!'

'Me? Just a minute, Abigail. I'm not the one with his trousers down. It's not me that's been making you look a fool in front of everyone.'

'Get out!' I screamed. 'Get out of here now!'

'Now you just keep calm. You don't want Gregory to think you're having another breakdown do you? In fact,' he threw aside the paper and leaned over me, 'there's probably quite a lot you don't want him to know about; like the ghost that's been haunting you: the spirits trying to possess you. Gregory would love all that, wouldn't he? Squeamish about that sort of thing, isn't he? He'd probably want you locked up if I told him some of the things we've talked about. He'd certainly not want you anywhere near the little lad, would he?'

'I trusted you!'

'Then trust me a bit further, Abigail.'

With a kind of fascinated horror, I watched his hands, blunt with black hair on the back of each finger, crawl like ugly creatures over the silk, taut across my breasts. I struggled to my feet, stumbling over the trailing hem of the white nightgown I was wearing ready for the sleepwalking scene.

'Don't ever touch me again. Don't come near me, or I'll have you out of the company.'

He swung his feet up on to the chair and crouched scowling on the bench. 'Shall I tell Gregory all about your strange experiences? Shall I tell him about how you don't even know what you're doing sometimes? Shall I tell him how you pick up dangerous knives and don't know why you've got them?'

'I don't care what you tell him,' I said wildly. I just wanted him out of that room. I couldn't bear being near him. 'I don't care if he thinks I'm mad.'

But of course I did care. After he'd slouched off I sat a long while by the mirror, staring at the grey photograph: Greg posing rather like a Victorian patriarch with his arm on my shoulder, Luke standing very straight and tense, but his little freckled face grinning proudly and me with one hand resting on Greg's hand and the other gripping Luke's fingers; even in the newsprint you could see how tight that grip was.

I kept remembering Alan's last words as he stormed off.

'You'll regret this, Abigail. No more bloody happy families, I warn you!'

I knew something terrible was about to happen; I told myself, the faces in the mirror warned me of it. Then I'd think: it's not too late. Greg's still on stage so Alan can't have spoken to him yet. I could go after the wretched man and try to placate him. No, I couldn't do that. I couldn't bear the thought of even being near him.

But he was right. If Greg started to seriously doubt my sanity, he would try to take Luke away from me.

I should never have had anything to do with Alan Stewart, I thought; everyone warned me not to trust him. But I'd been so determined to make Greg jealous.

I began to realize how stupid, how blind, I'd been. All through rehearsals I'd been behaving as if Greg was all that mattered to me. Everything I'd done had been designed either to please him or make him notice me.

But something else was more important to me: my child mattered more than anything – even Greg. No one, I thought, is going to take Luke away from me.

As I said at the beginning, Lady Macbeth taught me to be strong – to go all out for what I wanted. But I also learned from her mistakes. She too had wanted the attention and approval of the man she loved. And in the end she'd been destroyed by her infatuation. Well, I wasn't going to make that mistake any longer.

I turned up the speaker, as if to reassure myself that Greg was still safely on stage. The first scene after the interval was just drawing to a close with that speech of Macbeth's about the massacre of Macduff's family. And as I listened, everything changed. The worry and the guilt were switched off suddenly like an electric light and I felt a kind of determination. There was something I'd got to do. I didn't know what it was, but I knew I'd got to do something.

And then the dream took over. That's the only way I can explain it. It was just like the dream, but I knew now that I was awake. Out of the dressing room door I went and along the passage, like a ghost myself in that long white night-gown. People looked up – Jo still warty, drinking from a Coke can and reading a magazine; Duncan in regal cloak, a furtive cigarette between his fingers. But I couldn't speak to anyone. I tried; I tried to tell them something terrible was happening. But the words wouldn't come out. I just walked on past them.

Ahead of me were the stairs, seeming darker than they should be. Gloomy as they were in the dream, with a dark tunnel at the top and a hint of light beyond.

I watched myself begin to climb the stairs.

1057

I stood at the foot of the stairs that led to the private rooms of Macduff's family. Behind me the great oak door of the broch stood wide open, clearly unbolted from within, and bodies lay in the smoke-filled courtyard. Macbeth and his men had got there hours before us. As Morag and I approached we'd seen the lights of their camp in the thicket of trees beyond the ransacked stronghold. In the broch, even the fires had died down and the tower showed black as a broken tooth on the skyline.

'No sense in going on, Gruoch,' Morag had said.

'You turn back if you wish,' I'd said. 'But I've got to see for myself.'

So here I was on my own in the corpse-strewn yard with acrid smoke clutching at my throat and the stone stairs twisting up into darkness before me. The moonlight, fitful with flying clouds, came in through the open gate here and sliced across the first half-dozen stone treads. On the highest step that it lit lay the out-flung hand of a corpse, the rest of which was mercifully hidden. Into the hollow worn in the centre of the stair, blood had run to form a darkly glinting pool.

With my hand shaking against the rough stone of the wall, I began to climb to the hell that awaited me.

About half-way up the dark, twisting stairs my foot slipped on something wet and I stooped down to touch the stone. More blood: cooling and sticky on my fingers. I stood up and walked on. Ahead of me a narrow window dropped a block of moonlight across the stairs and beyond it I could make out a heavy door that stood ajar. Someone had set fire to it and it was charred across the bottom.

Just a few more steps and my hand touched the scorched wood. I felt sick: sick with fear and with the stink of death and fire around me. I was shivering with cold from the wind that jabbed through the gaping window. I felt desperately weak, but I'd got to go on. I had to see for myself. I had to know for sure.

I pushed the heavy door. It opened loudly and drunkenly on its broken hinges and I stepped into the cruelly bright moonlight of the room beyond.

1996

This was the third dream and the worst. Ahead of me, at the top of the shallow theatre steps, lay something worse than the stairs of wood or twisting stone had led me to. But I must go on. There was something I must do.

'Go on,' whispered the voice. 'Go on.'

Just a few more steps and I was in the passageway that backed the stage. Bare brick wall, benches cluttered with a jumble-sale array of props. Low voices off to my right from the prompt corner, a couple of figures in the wings. On stage the voices of Chrissie and Luke beginning the scene of mother and son in Macduff's castle.

I moved on stealthily along the passage as if I didn't want to be seen. Then by one of the props benches I stopped. I watched myself reach out and take up a knife, turning it carefully to check the hilt.

Sure enough, the red danger mark was on it.

As if satisfied, I tucked my hands into the loose sleeves of my nightgown, concealing the weapon. Then I turned back towards the dressing rooms.

1057

It was a small room with a double oblong of window drawn in moonlight across its wooden floor. And in that light lay Beatrice, a dropped spindle unravelled at her side. I think her throat was cut; there was a lot of blood but I couldn't see her wound and didn't try to.

Clinging to her skirts was a little girl, just toddling age, who lay half in light and half in shadow with her brother, a lad of six or seven. They had both been stabbed.

Dry-eyed and shaking, I stepped away from them and as I did so, my foot caught against something hard.

Looking down at the patch of moon-soaked boards, I saw the wooden baby that the little girl had been playing with when the murderers broke in upon this peaceful family. Beside it (the gold pale in the unearthly light) lay my brooch, with the three hooded figures staring blankly on the carnage around them. As I stooped to pick it up, I thought: he knew just where to find them and he came straight to Beatrice. This was done before Macbeth's main army broke through this far. She was still spinning, the child still playing. In God's name! He was determined to have it done before Macbeth could change his mind.

Shakily I clutched the cold gold to my breast and stared down at Beatrice: my childhood companion that I'd played with in the mud and muddle of my father's house.

'The Thane of Fife had a wife. Where is she now?'

Her blood was dark in the patchy light and, her face, twisted sideways, showed one horribly open eye stretched wide in terror.

But still I knew that this wasn't the worst. The shadows held a greater horror.

Trembling, I turned to the darkness beyond her. An outline blacker than the blackness of the room showed where the cradle stood. I could see nothing there, but I reached searching hands down into the depths of the little bed. It was empty and for one wild moment my heart soared upward in hope. But no sooner had my hands finished searching the empty, cold wool and linen, with its sweet smell of baby that mingled horribly with the stench of blood, than my eyes began to grow used to the kindly deception of the darkness, and I saw what at first seemed just a shape slumped on the floor – a bag or pillow thrown aside, perhaps.

But then the little huddled shape slowly resolved itself and took on the terrible, lifeless likeness of a baby. Shaking too much to stand, I crawled on my hands and knees across the floor to him and picked him up. Cold and limp in my arms. And then, because I had to know, I groped about the floor and the wall feeling for blood. I felt the cold slimy smear down the wall where the little head had been struck against the stone.

Crouching like an animal on the floor, I threw back my head and howled. And I clutched to my dry breast the body of my baby: the baby that I'd failed and betrayed; the baby that I'd given into the care of the only woman I could suffer to take my place.

1996

'No you don't.' Alan's voice was damp against my ear. 'I know what you're doing.'

He dragged me round to face him, pressing my back against the props table; his hands gripped hard at my shoulders. I knew such a grip ought to hurt, but it didn't. I seemed oblivious to everything but what I must do.

The oblivion must have shown in my eyes.

'God! I believe it's true,' whispered Alan. 'You really are possessed.'

He grabbed my wrist and twisted it (painlessly) upwards before forcing back my fingers. I tried to cry out but I couldn't. Like it always did in the dream, the cry just stopped in my mouth, choking me.

Once he'd got hold of the knife and put it carefully back on the table, he wound an arm around me and dragged me towards the stairs. As he did so two young men in black cloaks sprinted out into the passage. One of them was chewing gum. Their faces, greasy with make-up, looked surprised under their sinister black hoods.

'She's feeling a bit faint,' said Alan.

They were so close I could have touched them. I could smell the spearmint gum. But I couldn't speak to them. The cry continued to choke me.

Murderers of young Macduff. Your call.

The two young men shrugged to show they were unable to help and hurried off to collect their knives from the props bench.

1057

Peace, the charm's wound up.

I've found my way to peace now, child. It's been my study these long lonely years to find a way to peace. A way to escape the curse.

But this is how it is. Listen carefully, child.

There are three of us. They must share my suffering . . .

Where are they, these other two women? They are somewhere in the future, girl, and it has taken much hard work to find them. There were old things to be learned about the ways of seeing through time and I've searched for them through my dreams year after year. But now I have found them. They are joined with me. We share one fate, one weird. They, like me, have sought the power of the blind-worm.

Listen girl: it is the blind-worm you must remember. This is how you must remember the story I've told you. Remember the toad that is slow and quiet as I was in Gillacomgain's house. Remember the bat that dwells amid the dark places and the ruins of men's battles and ambitions, like the wise woman in the broch. Remember all things strange and ugly and other. Remember the dog behind whose servile tongue lurks the savage tooth, like Seyton waiting to be avenged on his master. But remember most of all the blind-worm: the blind-worm has no sting and yet it has the power to harm men because they believe it poisonous.

Remember too that it is in the name of these outcast creatures that I curse the line of Seyton who wronged me. The prophecy said that his line will prosper, even winning the crown of Scots. But I swear there will come a time when the curse of the blind-worm, the curse of the weak and the wronged, will be worked against them and even the crowned heads will bow before the executioner like common criminals.

Remember, girl. Remember the curse of the blind-worm. Remember the power of the weak: for that is what it is, child, the blind-worm's sting. It exists only in men's minds and yet it has the power to harm them because they fear it.

Though I never meant to harm him, I was the blind-worm to Macbeth. He feared what I might do and yet it was only his belief that gave me any power at all.

But it is a chancy thing, the blind-worm's sting, and likely in the end to hurt those that'd wield it. They'll learn that too: those other women. Like me they'll face a woman's worst nightmare: the guilt of her own child's death.

And by sharing my fate with them, I can break free of the curse.

Take the brooch and go now, girl. If I'd got anything good left in me, I'd bless you, but I've not; I'm hollowed out and empty of everything but my purpose. Remember though, I have claimed you as my kin and I've given you all I have left to give. Go now. Go north to the Highlands, but not to Moray.

Seyton is in Fife's pay now and Moray is the first place he will look for the one who carries the shameful secret of his weird. Go to Glenlagan. Ban has gone back there to his family. Show him the brooch for a token and tell him it is my will he weds you when you are of an age to wed.

To your eldest daughter you must tell everything I have
told you. The memories must be carried in our bloodline.

Go now, the draught is working; sleep – and the dream –
come upon me for the last time. One more time I must
dream the same dream. Once more. This must be the last
time. Tonight there must be release.

1606

My legs feel near to breaking with cold and weariness. The
jailer's song has slurred into silence now and even the rats
seem to be asleep. My senses stretch into the emptiness
but I can find nothing to hold off the sleep that I fear so
much. As I strain in the silence to catch some sign of
the waking world – the weeping or snoring or just the
stirring of my wretched fellows – I can hear nothing. But
somewhere beyond the silence there is the voice of the
spirit.

'Peace. The charm's wound up,' it whispers. 'We must all
dream one more time.'

I fear that dream!

And yet . . . And yet the spirit torments me now with a
kind of cruel hope. A hope that just once the dream might
be different. That just once the little cheek will be warm
against my breast and the soft mouth close on my teat.

It's a hope that makes the dirty straw and sleep seem
very sweet. And I know I have no choice.

I must dream once more before I go to the gallows.

1996

'Peace! The charm's wound up.'

The words echoed in my head as I struggled against
Alan's grip.

'One more time we must all dream the same dream.'

I knew that somehow I must get free and I felt, as if it were a loaded spring, quite beyond my control, my knee rising and making vengeful contact with the warmth of Alan's groin. From a distance where everything seemed to be showing in slow motion, I watched with pleasure as the shock and pain spread across his face. Then I was free and running back along the passage to the table.

Behind me the murderers were going on stage.

I began to search among the remaining knives on the bench, but the one with the red paint was missing. I kept searching stupidly for several seconds, as if unable to believe it wasn't there. Then finally my hand rested on an empty label: *Act 4 Scene 2 Young Macduff's Murderers.*

'That's right, Abigail. I put it there.' Alan was moving towards me, still doubled-up, but grinning madly. 'You shouldn't play around with knives, Abigail. What will Gregory say when he finds your crazy neurotic behaviour has got his son hurt?'

At last I understood what the nightmare was that waited for me at the top of the stairs. And I knew what I must do.

Yes, I understood!

But even as I thought that, I was running. Running as I'd never run before, out from among the props and along the bare brick passage behind the stage, under the green glow of the emergency exit sign, to the centre-back stage-entrance. But it was a long way and hard-going.

A long way because I seemed also to be running across a smoky courtyard and up a slippery, twisting stairway. And hard-going because all the time I was running I seemed to be crippled by labour pains. But I'd got to keep going because ahead of me a man with a sharp and dangerous knife was rushing upon my child. I'd got to reach him in time. This time I'd got to get there before it was too late. I had to dream the dream one more time. One more time for all of us. Because this time the ending must be different.

We must all go through it one more time.

Run for the entrance. Climb the stairs. Struggle against the pains and try to wake.

Run, climb, struggle.

Just one more time. The dream must run one more time. There was just one chance to change the dream: to end the nightmare.

Here's the entrance: run on to the stage; push open the door; wake up and see what's happening to the baby. Stage light spilled into my senses; moonlight patching a little room; the grey light of dawn, a wet bloody bed and a new-born baby in red cracked hands.

One more time.

'Young fry of treachery!'

The murderer on stage lunged towards Luke who stood with his head thrown back in innocent defiance, his big brown eyes gleaming and just the slightest hint of a tremble in his open lips. There were shouts from the audience. Pushing Chrissie's shocked fat face aside, I leapt across the stage like a demented thing.

The young murderer had all his weight behind the knife that he knew would fold harmlessly as it struck, and he was unable to stop as I threw myself between him and Luke. The knife struck my shoulder.

It didn't fold.

Pain seared through me, cutting me off from the stage, from the young lad with the damp, shocked face who was staring aghast at what he'd done, from Luke's trembling little hands clutching at my arm. I sank down into pain and darkness and felt their hands in mine again.

Who were they, these two other women caught with me in the endless dance? I looked into their faces and saw my own fear and suffering reflected there.

'It is done,' said the voice. 'Now we are all free. We have all dreamed for the last time.'

Then suddenly the scene changed.

As the heavy door swung open, there was warm firelight in the room as well as moonlight and the fair-haired woman was spinning by it. On the floor at her feet a little girl was rocking a wooden doll and a boy was listening with fire-brightened eyes to the tale his mother was telling.

I turned to the dark corner beside the fire where a deep wooden cradle stood in the shadows. Bending over it I picked up the sweetly sleeping baby, pressing my face hungrily to the soft, living smell of it.

'I've come to warn you,' I said. 'I've come to warn you.'

The peaceful, firelit scene faded into chaos: bright light and a voice shouting above the pandemonium. 'Curtain! Curtain for God's sake!'

'Are you hurt, Mum? Are you OK?'

I pulled Luke to me, squirming in his loose nightshirt, and buried my face in the sweet smell of his hair, careless of the blood flowing on to him. 'I'm fine my love, I'm fine.'

Jo, calm and practical, standing over me. 'It's not too deep, Abby. Keep still. I've called an ambulance.'

'Get the police too.'

'Why?'

But darkness was closing in again. Darkness, cold hands in mine and then a bare room with a low bulging ceiling.

The little wild-looking woman lay on the bed, her eyes were closed; her newborn child lay beside her on the filthy grey mattress. I moved across the uneven boards of the floor and looked closely at her hands. They were dirty and covered in blood. In places the blood had dried into little cracked cakes. The fingernails were black. Though the woman lay unconscious the hands were moving – slowly and clumsily, like the hands of a sleepwalker. They reached towards the baby, fumbling awkwardly for its neck. I peered closer in the dull, thin light.

And at last I saw what those hands were trying to do.

The baby lay still and silent and already its crumpled little face was tinged with blue. The umbilical cord had been wrapped so tightly round its neck that simply being born was strangling it. While its mother lay unconscious with pain, oblivious to the danger that her child was in, the spirit that animated her body was releasing the slippery cord; but the hands were clumsy. It was taking too long. In seconds the baby would be dead.

'Wake up!' I screamed. 'Wake up and see what's happening to your child!'

She woke, suddenly. Sitting up wild-eyed, hair streaming raggedly round her shoulders. She crouched on the filthy bed looking like a caricature of a witch.

'My baby!' she screamed and the raw red hands moved swiftly and consciously. She slipped off the cord. Breath rattled into the fragile new lungs and with a doting smile she put the fat, ugly little face to her breast.

They were all crowding round me on the stage. Chrissie was crying, the lad with the knife was stammering, 'I didn't know. I didn't know,' over and over again. Out in the darkness of the audience, several people were screaming. John was still shouting for the curtain, which was desperately slow in falling. I could feel blood, my own blood, flowing warmly over my hands from the pain in my shoulder as I clutched Luke's struggling form to me. I watched it spread its dark stain across the stage. Then, through all the meaningless faces and shapes gathering round, I could see Greg as, half-armoured for the last scenes, he stumbled, pale and aghast, on to the stage; anger, confusion and fear were muddled on his face. But the expressions of that face no longer mattered to me. Lady Macbeth had changed me.

I was free of the curse.

All that mattered now was that the dream had been dreamed for the last time. And, for me at least, the last ending was the real one.

EPILOGUE

1057

By dawn the shivering girl was well away from Dunsinane, though she had no idea where she was heading. She was carrying food for three days and wealth enough in jewels to last her all her life, besides the golden brooch that the Queen had said she must keep.

But surely the Queen had been mad.

She paused to rub life into her chilled fingers inside her cloak and sat down on a damp rock on a hillside a little to the west of Dunsinane. From here she could see the great rambling fortification silhouetted against the grey sky of the dawn. Shapes wheeling high over the towers reminded her of the Queen's words about the carrion birds that'd gather soon. It was the sort of saying that'd always frightened her; she'd never been comfortable near her mistress – none of the women had been. She'd feared her really, despite the favour she had always been shown.

Now she was free of Dunsinane and the Queen's service, with a tidy fortune in the leather purse she carried inside her cloak. There didn't seem much to fear now. The Lady Gruoch had not been wicked, or even clever, just mad. What nonsense she'd talked of curses and spells and people in the future. That strange story of two women in the future who'd share her suffering, 'Unless I can change their fate. If just one of us can escape the misery then the spirits of all will be free.' What had it all meant?

Well, she'd not mind it now. She'd go her own way and not trouble herself with remembering some old words that were supposed to be a curse. She was certainly not going back to the Highlands, to the remote poverty of Glenlagan and marriage to a man old enough to be her grandsire. And she wouldn't keep the brooch either, if she could get a good price for it.

She got to her feet with a smile and began to run through the scrubby heather and gorse towards the Tay seaport. But she'd scarcely gone a hundred yards when her eye turned southwards and she saw something that made her drop on her knees in the heather.

What she had seen in the strengthening light of the morning was a forest; a green blur across the neck of the valley between the brown hill on which she stood and the grey hill on which loomed the dark sprawl of Dunsinane. An ordinary forest.

But it was moving.

As the grey of dawn gave way on the highest hills to the gold of sunrise, and light and shadows sharpened round the towers and ramparts of the stronghold, a forest marched upon Dunsinane.

The girl stared. What was it Lady Gruoch had told her man? 'You'll never be defeated till the forest walks.' And today the Lord of Fife was to take Dunsinane.

So today the forest walked.

'I'm sorry, Lady,' the girl whispered, wretchedly fearful, into the cold air. She looked about her as if she expected to see her mistress come to chastise her for her disbelief. 'I promise I'll remember the curse. I'll go north as you said – and I'll keep the brooch.'

She took one last, terrified look at the marching forest, creeping inexorably towards the doomed walls of Dunsinane and then she went on her way chanting the old words over and over to make sure she'd not forget them.

1606

The man in the blue coat put his hand to his own throat as the rope jerked upward and the woman's body twitched spasmodically before it came to a merciful rest in the embrace of the noose. It didn't matter how many hangings he saw, it was always the same; it always felt for a moment as if the noose was round his own neck: as if it was him staring into the terror of oblivion. It seemed to be his fate to feel others' pains and griefs and joys as if they were his own. To feel so much he could never judge or condemn anyone.

Not that he wanted to condemn poor Jennet. He'd done his best to get her free, but the wench hadn't had the wit to help herself. Rambling so about evil spirits and spells. She'd been a strange one; almost seeming as if she wanted to die. Last night when he'd gone to the prison she had seemed almost content. 'Peace,' she had said. 'The charm's wound up. I've dreamed the dream for the last time and I am at peace. I know my hands are clean. I'm ready to die.'

It had almost seemed that he was suffering more than her.

He gazed ruefully across the village green where heads crowded below his horse's grey flank and he rubbed his aching throat as the slender corpse twisted gracefully on the gallows. This terrible sharing of others' misery was what had always prevented him from getting involved in politics like Kit and some of the others. To act the spy or politician a man had to believe that one set of ideas was definitely right and another wrong. But he saw right and wrong in everything and everybody, just as he saw grief and joy and beauty and humour in everything and everybody. He saw some good even in the things that others most despised. And the folk that other Christians made such a show of hating, like Jews and Turks, were to him just people, each with their faults and their virtues. Even animals he could not hate; so what if a toad or a bat or a creeping thing was ugly, there was no reason to suppose it evil. He saw so much and felt it so acutely that there was only one way of curing the pain.

And that was with his pen. He just wrote it all out and then it was gone.

Seeing so much and understanding so much doesn't make me any kinder, he thought; trapped by the horror of the moment into rare self-accusation.

Poor Jennet; he'd treated her badly. He'd seen the joy and the beauty in her. Maybe he'd even loved her in his way. And this was the end of it all for her.

'She told you the words of the spell, didn't she?' A harsh, nasal voice broke into his agonizing thoughts and he turned to see that another horse had made its way through the holidaying villagers. The skinny-faced inquisitor was now beside him, holding a scented handkerchief to his nose against the stench of crowding bodies.

'She told me a great many things,' he answered vaguely. The skinny man unnerved him. Who he was and what his business was in this rustic matter, he didn't know. But he suspected that he was the one who'd thwarted his attempts to save the poor wench. And he knew for certain he was a court man. He'd seen him in the King's presence several times.

'I warn you,' droned the inquisitor, 'it's not a safe thing to know. The King doesn't want it known.' His pious grey face twitched and he jerked a nod before pulling round his horse's head and riding carelessly through the crowd.

The man on the grey horse sat for a long time staring after the inquisitor as he got clear of the green and set his horse to a trot between the low thatched eves of the village houses. That was a threat, he thought. And I'm the one who's never cared for affairs of state! Now it seems that from a poor little country girl I've learned a secret that'll make the King put a price on my head.

The rabble began to meander home and left him alone
with the dead woman, who was swaying gently now in the
breeze, like a child on a swing. Would he end like this? he
wondered. No, it'd more likely be a dagger in the back in a
dark alley. Or maybe a sudden, squalid and apparently
accidental death in a tavern brawl. That's what happened
in London to men who knew things they shouldn't. But
what could he do? Words once known can't be unlearned.
And the only weapon he wielded with any skill was his
pen.

He smiled. Of course, it was obvious. As always, the
answer lay in his pen.

He couldn't stop himself knowing the spell; but he could
make sure that so many people heard it, it'd be impossible
to kill them all.

He pulled his horse round and set off for Oxford, working
on the words as he went. Some rhyme to make them more
memorable. Maybe a tune. One of those jingle-jangle tunes
that'll chain words into people's minds.

> 'For a charm of powerful trouble,
> Like a hell-broth boil and bubble.'

He liked it. But a bit more of the same kind of thing
would make it sound better. What else did self-righteous
Christian men fear and hate? What other scapegoats were
there besides the poor toad and bat and blind-worm? The
words formed beautifully in his head as he rode on through
the lengthening shadows of the afternoon. By the time he
got to Oxford his mind was busy with other things Jennet
had told him. Words and ideas were flowing so smoothly
that he didn't stop in the town.

He kept to his horse and his work, riding on through the
thin summer twilight to Stratford.

1996

A tall woman in elegant middle-age came through the
theatre's glass doors on to the street, slipping a small tape
recorder into her shoulder bag as she walked. She hesitated
on the pavement to belt her coat against the sharp bright
November air, then stepped towards the crowded street
where a taxi had stopped. But when her hand was almost
on the door, she drew it back.

It was a lovely day; she'd walk back across the park. She
could think about her interview on the way. She followed
the path along the blank brick side of the theatre and came
out on to a gravel path beside a small lake. The sun shone
crisply on a scene made rather harsh with winter and park-
keepers' orderliness. A few brown leaves seamed the gravel
and a handful of ducks drifted on the grey water.

It was here, she thought, pausing on a pretentious little
concrete bridge, it was here that Abigail West, so small and
fragile, had walked with that weird man. She remembered
Alan Stewart from the television pictures – a great lumber-
ing giant of a man with a look of obsession in his eyes. Yet
Abigail had trusted him.

In many ways, the famous and beautiful Abigail West
had been incredibly naive.

She felt obscurely disappointed. She had been granted a
rare interview with this very private woman; she had been
given a glimpse inside the marriage of the pair who had for
years been seen as the theatre's ideal couple – a chance to
understand the much publicized break-up of that marriage.
But what could she write now?

Nothing that could compete with the stories of violence
and betrayal that the less well-informed had already woven
around the events at the Maypole. Just a sad, ordinary
story of slow attrition; of Gregory Mortimer's powerful
personality gradually wearing down his wife's self-esteem;

of her depression, her nightmares and her desperate jealousy.

There was her claim to have been possessed, of course. But that was too far-fetched. Who would believe it? What evidence was there for it?

True, Abigail had seemed to know just in time that Stewart had devised a crazy plan to change the knives for the little boy's scene. And in his confession the man had admitted he meant Abigail and everyone else to believe that it had been her fault. There was certainly plenty of drama in her last-minute discovery and sudden appearance on the stage, running desperately to her child's rescue. But there had been enough written about that already and all the tapes in her bag could add to what had already been told was a highly implausible account of how Abigail had known about the swap.

But really it was much more likely that she'd guessed, or even seen him alter the knives.

The woman strode on along the gravel between hard black stubs of rose bushes. She thought of that frail little figure sitting cross-legged on the edge of the stage as she talked, long brown hair flowing down her back, one shoulder still held slightly stiffly from the knife wound.

There had been something impressive about her frankness, her readiness to admit her past mistakes; something impressive too about the new strength and determination she seemed to have gained from the business. It was impossible to deny that the experience had changed her; but no one was going to believe her far-fetched explanation for that change. No one would believe that she had been possessed by a spirit; what was the point of printing such a story?

The gravel walk ended in an iron gate that opened near the steps of an Underground station. Near the top of the steps was a scarfed and mittened man with a newspaper stand. As she passed, she caught sight of the headline on a tabloid paper.

'I WAS BEWITCHED' SAYS MAN
IN MACBETH CURSE CASE.

She rummaged in her bag for her purse, bought a copy of the paper and read it as she wove her way expertly along the crowded pavement:

> Alan Stewart, the man at the centre of the Maypole Theatre stabbing case, has denied attempting to murder young Luke Mortimer on the grounds of diminished responsibility. He says that he was so infatuated with the sexy Abigail West that he was not able to think rationally. After sexually provocative behaviour, that included cuddling and kissing with Stewart during secret rendez-vous in the park, Ms West rejected him and denied having any interest in him.
>
> 'I didn't mean to harm her son,' said a heart-broken Stewart. 'I just meant to teach her a lesson. I was so crazy about her I didn't know what I was doing. I was bewitched.'

The tall woman stopped suddenly and perilously, causing several other pedestrians to collide. With a gesture of disgust, she dropped the cheap newspaper into a rubbish bin.

If that sort of stuff could be printed, then Abigail had a right to have her own story told in her own way. It was as believable as Stewart's defence. Unconsciously gripping the bag that contained her tapes, the woman strode on through the November streets to her waiting keyboard.